(book one of the Flyday series)

by Laura E. Bradford

I would like to thank the following people for their support of this book: my family, especially James and Lynn, who saw it first; Jeff, for logistical support; Kathy, for everything; and the many others who gave encouragement and thoughtful critiquing.

Chapter One
June 15, 2507

A missile exploded into the *Halcyon*, sending it into a dive.

"No, no, no!" Zoë yelled, righting the ship. "No, you are *not* doing this to me."

One of the control panels blinked, and a voice crackled: "Pilot, explain your actions immediately. You are in violation of international law—"

Zoë shut off the radio com. "Jack, why is the communication system working on *their* end, but not mine?"

"I don't know, Miss Martínez." The robot plugged one of its arms into a port in the cockpit. "It was functional when we left."

Another blast sounded, knocking the ship off course again.

"Perhaps you should let them board," the robot suggested. "We can explain the discrepancy in person."

"Sure. If they don't decide to shoot me down completely." Her ship blasted forward, skirting past the fighters. Okay, she'd been selected for a random search; quite reasonable, as she was flying from Paris with no passengers. And with no way to contact the ship that was tagging her, she'd been labeled a threat. Also a natural progression of logic.

On the controls, she saw a wide Celestial ship attach itself to the *Halcyon*. "Celestials boarding," came the pleasant voice of the ship's computer. "Manual piloting locked."

Zoë sat back, defeated. "That's it." She heard loud knocks on the hatch door, then swung toward her co-pilot. "Jack," she said, "let me handle this one, okay?"

The hatch's lock twisted with several clicks, and the hatch burst open. Five soldiers, all carrying weapons, marched toward the pilot's cabin.

"Hi," said Zoë, putting up her hands. (Her robot, too, raised its wiry arms.) "I can explain everything—"

A Celestial officer, sharply dressed from his white beret to his black combat boots, pointed a blaster at her. "Pilot, give me one good reason why I shouldn't detain you immediately and take a blaster to your 'bot's processors."

Zoë looked down at the robot. "Maybe you should take this one."

2.

Thomas Huxley tapped his fingers on the desk, watching the seconds tick by on a wall clock.

"And what is your relation to Miss Martínez?" a stern clerk asked.

"I'm her *fiancé*," said Thomas. He glanced over at Zoë, who was sitting with her hands in her lap, dejected. They were in the security office of the Tenokte airport, and a police officer and a clerk were looking over Zoë's identification and running down a list of questions.

"Tsk, tsk," said the police officer, glancing over a written report. "Failing to obey a captain's orders, resisting a search, fleeing from a Celestial ship ... we've looked over your ship's systems, Miss Martínez, and while the communication system was indeed malfunctioning, that doesn't excuse your behavior."

"My *behavior*?" said Zoë, lifting her head. "You guys were shooting missiles at me. What was I supposed to think?"

"But the laws are quite clear on the matter. You were chosen at random for an inspection; there's a one in ten chance of that happening. You were supposed to slow down and allow the Celestial patrols to board. You did not."

"They didn't give me enough time. By the time I got their messages, they were right on my tail. I sped up because I thought they were going to crash into me."

The police officer ignored her, pretending to be immersed in his paperwork.

Thomas leaned over the counter. "Is she being charged with anything?"

"No. But her pilot's license will be suspended."

Zoë stood up. "My license? But I've never been in trouble before. There's usually just a fine—"

"I could pay it right now," Thomas offered. "What's the fine?"

"Five hundred credits," said the clerk.

"Uh … well, I could pay it in a month or two…"

"I'll pay it now," Zoë said. "Just run it through, and I'll authorize it."

But the police officer held up his hand. "It's not so simple. Reports have to be filed. You understand."

"I have a lot to do today," said Thomas; but he instantly realized it was the wrong thing to say.

The police officer looked at him, raising an eyebrow. "Oh, really? Where are you from?"

"Tenokte."

"Hah, not likely. What's your accent, British?"

"He lives in London," Zoë supplied, weary. "But he grew up here."

"Ah. So you've just come back home to visit family, I see." The police officer's eyes narrowed.

"Actually, I came for work."

"Really."

He tried to explain: his editor had sent him here to cover the king's speech and the annual summer celebrations, and his fiancée, a pilot, wanted to rediscover in a vacation the city she had known briefly as a teenager.

"But I'm usually a music journalist," he finished. "I interview bands, talk about new releases."

"Hm," said the police officer, looking at Zoë. "That's right. Didn't you run around with that band? What was it called ... no, now don't tell me; Bio—"

"Biological—"

"Bio ... bio something..."

"Biochemical Pathways," said Thomas, finally.

"Yes!" said the clerk. "That's it."

"Are you sure? That doesn't sound right at all."

"Oh, you know, Biochemical Pathways! With that crazy singer, Jamie Parsons."

"He's not crazy," Zoë replied, defensive. "He's just ... sensitive."

The police officer and the clerk looked at each other, not convinced, but they dropped the matter.

"What did you say your name was?" the police officer asked Thomas.

"Thomas Huxley."

They exchanged a glance, then the police officer coughed and quickly started shuffling through their paperwork.

"Uh, I'm sorry," said the clerk, "but what was that name again?"

"Huxley." Thomas pulled out his ID card and handed it over.

The clerk picked it up and studied it. Thomas Huxley was indeed born in Tenokte, MA; his last place of residence was London, England. The clerk handed the card back, and the police officer nervously flipped through the report.

"So what was that, a misdemeanor? Not responding to a Celestial cruiser?"

"Easy mistake," said the clerk.

"Exactly," said the police officer. "I'll let you off with a warning. Miss Martínez, you're free to go."

"Are you sure? What about the fine?"

"That won't be necessary." He pushed the perplexed couple toward the door. "Your ship's communications system malfunctioned, happens to everyone. Just make sure you get that fixed before you take off again, hm? Have a good day now."

And then they were back in the middle of the airport, with the door to the main security office slammed shut behind them.

Zoë looked at Thomas, amazed. "How did you do that?"

"Oh, you just have to argue with them for awhile." His hands were in his pockets as he walked. "They get really edgy in June. All the diplomats and politicians are flying in for their summer meetings; security's a nightmare."

"No, you just said your name and they backed off."

"Oh ... well, my dad's a cop."

"Really." She was smiling now. "I think you told me that ... hm, I'll have to keep that in mind." She kissed him. "I see you managed to survive the week without me."

"Just barely." He smiled. "How was Paris?"

"Amazing! As usual. I just wish Tenokte was as ... welcoming."

He took her hand. "Don't let it get to you," he said. "Come on. Let's go get some lunch."

3.

By destiny or bad luck, which are often the same thing, Jamie Parsons received a visit. The rock star—who was neither crazy nor sensitive, though he probably fell somewhere in between—was, at that moment, sifting through shelves in a music shop. Electric fans spun lazily overhead, but they were mostly for ambiance; an air conditioning system ensured that a cool breeze circulated throughout the store.

His adventures with Zoë and the band were not far from his mind as he flicked through the shelves. What he needed, though, was inspiration. And what better place than here? Posters and vinyl records filled the shelves, and instruments of every type sat on hooks on the walls: guitars, violins, flutes, clarinets, keyboards. A display in the front showed off the newest releases, but Jamie wasn't interested in those.

A group of teenage girls stood by the cash register, watching the rock star and sighing with admiration. A little silver robot wheeled through the store, tidying up the shelves. After a few minutes, Jamie picked out an album and walked up to the register. The girls shrieked with delight, but he seemed not to hear them.

"Working on some new songs?" said the cashier, as he scanned the record.

"Yes."

"When are they coming out?"

Jamie swiped his ID card, paying for his purchase. "Dunno. I haven't written a single note." He walked out, and six female eyes followed him.

"He's dreamy," said one girl.

"He's strange," said another.

The third checked her watch. "We have to get to class!" And they dashed out, smiling sweetly to the singer, who held the door open for them.

Jamie stood outside the store a moment, reading the track listing on the album. A year ago, he'd be signing autographs and chatting with his fans ... but now he wanted to distance himself from his rock-star image. He felt washed up, bored, depressed. But music always cheered him up.

"Oh, that's a good one," came a familiar voice beside him. "*Abbey Road*. Man, the Beatles knew how to make album covers."

Jamie looked up and saw a red-haired girl standing next to him. "Ariel," he said.

She grinned. "Hey. I've been off exploring Rome—you'd really like it. How've you been?"

His mouth was open, but he couldn't speak. "I..."

"I know, I know, stupid question. Have you started the band yet?"

"Uh ... the band's *done*. I started it years ago."

She seemed perplexed, then pulled out a copper pocket watch and checked the dials. "Oh, it's the year twenty-five-oh-*seven*. Well." She lifted the watch, a gesture he recognized instantly: she was getting ready to leave.

"Wait! Ariel, how much time has passed for you? I mean, you don't look any—"

"I'm a few days older," said the girl. "Two, to be exact. Sorry for the confusion. I'll be back soon."

Jamie blinked, and she was gone. He looked out into the street. Rain poured down, and the few people hurrying past under umbrellas took no notice of him—or of the fact that a girl had just vanished. He suddenly felt very alone.

Two days. How could it be possible? He'd long ago dismissed his recollections of her, thinking he'd imagined the entire incident. And why not, after he'd gone so long and heard nothing? But as he gripped the album, he had to wonder. A few days older? He had a feeling Ariel was telling the truth, but he hadn't seen her in six years.

4.

Meanwhile, Thomas Huxley stood with his fiancée on a lonely boulevard. Rain poured down endlessly, creating a shimmering mist under the gray skies. They were outside the steps of a restaurant.

"It used to have a different name," he said, hesitant.

"It's still a restaurant," said Zoë. She took his hand and pushed open the door, and they walked inside. Wide, bright, and quiet, the restaurant had lovely décor and inviting redwood paneling. The tables were filled with just the right mix of tourists eating extravagant dishes, college students clutching coffees, and well-dressed businesspeople discussing reports over their lunch break.

"I like it," said Zoë, as the waitress guided them over to their table. She sat down and took in the atmosphere as Thomas scrutinized the menu. "What did it used to be called?"

"I don't remember. But next door was a bakery."

"No, next door was always a law office."

"Fine. If you say so." He was drumming his fingers on the table.

Zoë decided not to press the matter. "So you need to be at the speech for…"

"Eight o'clock," he said, still immersed in the menu. "But we should leave early to get through security."

"Got it," she said, picking up her own menu. "You know, I've never seen one of the king's speeches before. Except on TV."

"Mm. I haven't either, but they always send reporters to cover it. And our Tenokte correspondent is out on maternity leave, so I … volunteered." A familiar song played in the background, and Thomas listened, trying to place it. "Is that Biochemical Pathways?" he asked.

She nodded. "From their first album."

It sounded vaguely familiar, but Zoë had heard the song a hundred times, no doubt: her brother Damien had been the drummer for the band, and she had been their pilot when they were on tour.

The song had a lovely melody. He listened:

I'm going down, down
To see the turning of the world
Leaves turn green and then to gold
To be trampled on a rainy day

"What's Jamie been up to lately?" he asked, referring to the band's singer.

"Hm, I don't know. I've been kind of worried about him. Their last album was banned, and they can't release it."

"Banned? Why?"

"Something about censorship. Anti-government messages, that sort of thing. You know how security is." She put down the menu. "I should have a salad, but I really want a milkshake and some crinkle-cut fries."

"Right," he said distantly. "They call them fries here."

"All right, *chips*," she said, faking his accent, and they both laughed.

A little robot appeared, its eyes flashing as it spoke. "May I take your order?"

"Yes. I'll have a salad and small plate of fries, with a vanilla milkshake." Zoë handed over the menu.

"And I'll have a steak, medium rare, with …" He would've said a soda or a glass of wine, but he was out of London now, and with his fiancée, whom he could trust with anything. "A Strawberry Jolama Heartache," he said, referring to a popular ice cream soda.

"Thank you, sir and madam. Your meal will be ready shortly," said the robot, and it wheeled away.

Thomas drummed his fingers on the table.

"Your accent's breaking," said Zoë, smiling.

"No, it's not," he said quickly.

"There! You're sliding back into your American one."

"Well, maybe I just want to be more like you."

Zoë rolled her eyes. "Of course." She had only ever known Thomas with a standard British newscaster's accent, so it amused her to hear his natural voice come out.

"That reminds me," he said. "I have some good news. Apparently one of the hosts of the morning news show is leaving when his contract's up, and in November they'll need a replacement."

"You're kidding! They asked you?"

He smiled.

"Thomas, that's fantastic!"

"Well, I haven't taken the offer yet. It's a tough job. I'd have to live in London for three more years, and be in the studio twelve hours a day, every day. I can't just film a segment or two in the morning and take off."

Zoë looked down. "Three years. Well, I could settle down, live with you."

"You won't want to travel to the stars in your dad's old ship? You've never even been off the planet."

Zoë touched the screen of her cell phone, and a tiny, translucent hologram of a golden starship appeared, revolving and hovering above the disk. She pondered it for a moment, then pressed the screen again, and the image flickered and disappeared.

"Right," she said. "Well, I promised Jamie I'd visit him while we were here. Do you want to come along? He only lives a few blocks away."

"Uh, sure."

"Ah!" said Zoë, when their food arrived. "I love these fries. Why did I ever leave Tenokte?"

Thomas looked outside. It had stopped raining.

As the couple walked to Jamie's house, the clouds cleared to a blue sky, and everything seemed drenched and clean. Sunlight shimmered in the air, making the world shine as if dipped in liquid gold.

The rock star could live anywhere, but chose to hide himself away in Tenokte. He'd originally built the mansion as a summer house, and paid for it with the money he made by captivating the world. But when Biochemical Pathways disbanded the previous summer, he never moved out, confusing his already nervous diplomat and politician neighbors.

A mob of photographers stood at the gates, but Zoë only had to give her name before the guards allowed her in with her guest. A white pergola arched over the cement walkway that led to the house. When they reached the door and knocked, there was no reply.

"That's odd," said Zoë. "He said he'd be here."

Thomas turned and looked to the street, and saw someone running up to the gates. The young man wore tinted sunglasses, had a five-o'-clock shadow, and carried a guitar on his back. Jamie Parsons moved past the flash of cameras as if they didn't exist, then slipped through the gates and dashed toward the porch.

"Zoë!" the musician called, tossing up his arms as if he'd scored a goal. He hugged her. "Zo, my dear, how have you been?"

"Oh, you know—same as always."

"And this is Huxley, right? We've met." Jamie shook Thomas's hand. "Saw you on the news the other day, by the way. Brilliant work, good sir, very nice." He turned to Zoë. "What brings you to Tenokte?"

"The king's speech tonight. Do you want to come with us? We don't know many celebrities."

He unlocked the door, considering. "Hm ... I'd love to, but I can't. I think I'm on the government watch list by now. And I'm waiting for someone." He opened the door wide, then glanced at Thomas and grinned. "But it looks like you have company."

Zoë smiled. She looked absolutely enamored with the charming musician, and Thomas suddenly changed his mind: he didn't like Jamie very much. The singer had known Zoë since she was seventeen, and Thomas had known her for a year.

Jamie stepped into the house. "How long has it been, now?" he said, sliding off his guitar case. "Six years since we started the band, do you think?"

"Six years," said Zoë, considering. "Wow."

"Can I get you two anything to drink?" He slipped into the kitchen.

"Just water for me," called Zoë.

"Something stronger for you, Huxley? Pinot noir?"

"You read my mind," said Thomas, astonished.

The rock star's living room was uncluttered and generally unexciting: gray carpet, framed black-and-white photos on the walls, a sofa and a coffee table. Zoë sat down.

Jamie reappeared a moment later with three glasses, one filled with water. He handed it to Zoë, and filled the others with red wine.

"You know," he said to Thomas, "Zoë's the only reason the group got started. She introduced me to Damien and Kyle, and wham, we had a band."

Zoë smiled politely. "Oh, they were looking for a singer all summer. They were going to find him eventually." Her cell phone started to ring. "Excuse me," she said, and slipped out of the room.

Jamie put his glass down and grabbed his guitar from its case. He clipped a capo to the fret board, then sat on the couch, strumming. "So, what's life like for you, Thomas Huxley?"

"Good. No complaints." He looked at the photos on the wall: close-ups of a keyboard, saxophones, and a page of sheet music. It was a wonder Jamie didn't try to *talk* in 4/4 time.

"So, you and Zoë are getting married this summer?" said Jamie, strumming the strings.

"Yeah. We're really excited."

"Hm." Jamie seemed absorbed by the notes. "Your accent's breaking."

Thomas's eyes narrowed.

Zoë walked back in the room a moment later, her phone in hand. "Damien's going to the king's speech, and we can meet him there. No one else can make it; they all have plans. Are you sure you don't want to come with us, Jamie?"

"Go on, have fun," said Jamie, who was still strumming. "I'll be fine."

They left at nearly three o'clock, and the sky's golden hue had faded into a clear day.

"Jamie Parsons, the greatest singer of the century," Thomas murmured, as they walked out of the gate.

"I know. He seems so normal, doesn't he?"

It took Thomas a few seconds to realize she wasn't joking.

Tenokte, pronounced "Teh-*nock*-tay," received its name from a 500-year-old license plate: TNOKTE.

The actual meaning behind the city's name had been lost to history. The plate, and the car it identified, belonged to the great leader Dimitri Reynolds. He founded the Celestial Federation, a world government dedicated to peace and security, in the middle of the twenty-first century.

The current leader, King Richard Montag II, traced his lineage back to Dimitri. His white-uniformed police, known as "Celestials," protected citizens in countries within the Federation, and waged war against those few still resisting.

The residents of the Federation enjoyed their prosperity, their safe neighborhoods, their ability to travel from New York to Paris to Sydney without ever needing a passport or a change of currency. They were citizens of the world, and they viewed their king as a symbol of their future. Which is why what happened came as such a surprise.

At nearly eight o'clock, Thomas and Zoë made their way to the Capitol Building, which housed many of the world leaders' offices. A wide crowd of people had gathered in the grassy field in front of the building's marble façade. The king's speech was a long-standing tradition, and would commemorate the second day of a week-long celebration before the summer solstice.

Cameras pointed toward the empty podium, waiting for the young man to appear. The speech would be televised all over the world.

Thomas flashed a press pass, and guards led the couple to the front, where he had a better view. Photographers from various networks and Internet news sites had already set up their cameras.

"Damien should be here by now," said Zoë. She glanced around at the crowd, looking for her brother. She pulled out her cell phone to check her text messages, and soon reported that he was on his way.

The sun slid toward the horizon, throwing the buildings into silhouette. Thomas put a hand up to shield his eyes, and they waited.

At eight-thirty, it was nearly dark. Fireworks shot up toward the sky, whistling, then exploded into sparks of blue and silver. The crowd oohed and aahed, watching the display for a few minutes.

"Look," Zoë whispered. "It's the princess."

Sixteen-year-old Emily Montag sat off to the side, flanked by her guards.

"Have you ever interviewed her?" Zoë asked her fiancé.

"No. She doesn't really talk to the press."

The fireworks ended to thunderous applause, and the doors to the Capitol Building opened. The young king walked up to the podium, smiling and waving at the crowd, which gave him a standing ovation. He waited for the applause to subside before he began.

"Welcome," he said. "I'd like to thank you all for coming here today. In a few nights, we will be celebrating the Flyday!"

The crowd cheered.

"Hundreds of years ago, Dimitri Reynolds united a group of warring countries and founded a new world order, dedicated to peace and prosperity. And today, we gather as one global force, to show—"

A loud *crack* sounded, then another. At first Thomas thought it was thunder or another ostentatious display, but the king had stopped speaking.

"To—to show—" the young king stammered. He put a hand to his chest; a red stain had appeared on his shirt.

Guards were rushing to the king's side, and the young man collapsed. As people realized what happened, they screamed and started to panic.

Thomas felt more confused and astounded than anything else. This couldn't be happening. How could the king be shot, and on such a lovely night, when people were supposed to be celebrating…?

Zoë gasped, clutching him tightly. "Thomas, is he going to die?"

"I don't know." Everything he knew was now up in the air.

Paramedics put the king on a stretcher and then into an ambulance, which whisked him into the sky. Before long, someone shouted that a shooter had been found.

Thomas saw everything before Zoë, but he couldn't react fast enough to block her view. Celestial police were pulling a handcuffed man out of the building to the left.

Zoë looked devastated. "No—it can't be—"

Thomas's heart sank. He recognized the young man instantly, but the image didn't fit in his mind with that of an assassin. The man was a drummer, not exactly known for revolutionary thoughts or a history of violence.

He was Damien Martínez, Zoë's brother.

Chapter Two
August, A.D. 79

Ariel Midori was no stranger to death. People seemed to be dying all the time, and for any reason: diseases, hurricanes and floods, boats sinking and cars crashing. She had first heard about the volcanic eruption of Mt. Vesuvius as a marginal note in a history class, and was fascinated by it. An entire town dead, smothered under ash, buried for thousands of years...

It wasn't the deaths that interested her, of course, but the life. As she strode through the open-air marketplace of Pompeii, the streets bustled with activity. Storekeepers stood alongside the road, hawking their wares, and shoppers stopped to inquire prices or haggle. When they spoke, Ariel was reminded of high school classes: vocabulary, declensions. Only now, a certain language was alive and well.

"*Salve!*" someone called to a friend, waving.

Ariel Midori smiled. *That's Latin*, she thought. *You're in ancient Rome, and people are speaking Latin.* She could understand most of the words, but didn't bother to start any conversations: she would only speak with an American accent.

People passed her by, and many of the men were wearing togas, but she saw other garments as well: of all shapes, colors, and cuts. This was a trading town, with a busy port and merchants from all over the Mediterranean. But she stuck to the classic look: a white dress and period-perfect jewelry, with her reddish hair loose. No one gave her a second glance. And if under the roar of the crowd, people close to her happened to hear a ticking noise, they didn't attribute it to a clock: such a device hadn't been invented yet.

Ariel was a time traveler.

Mt. Vesuvius loomed in the distance. It didn't yet have its trademark two-peak shape, but of course not: its famous eruption, which would bury Herculaneum and Pompeii, would not occur for five days. She stopped to look at the volcano a moment, marveling.

I wish Jamie could see this, Ariel thought. Then she stopped. How long had it been since he left? Two days, and she already missed him.

She'd intended to visit him in his own time, trying to give a few weeks' leeway since he last saw her, but she had messed up the date: the year 2507 instead of 2501. Ariel peered down at her copper watch. Whatever happened in 2501, besides the formation of a rock band? The other year was far more interesting, from a historical perspective. Someone had been shot, some sort of world leader...

She turned to look back at the street, and something caught her attention. She squinted. Not far behind her, a man wearing a sky-blue helmet and white uniform pushed his way through the crowd.

Gladiator? she thought. No, they didn't have riot gear. The man carried a clear plastic shield, emblazoned with the word POLICE. In English.

So definitely not Roman. Ariel might have been from another time, but at least she had the good sense to blend in.

The oddly-dressed invader, who was garnering a lot of strange looks, noticed Ariel and started running toward her. She took a quick breath and slipped through the crowd, saying an instinctive "Excuse me, excuse me," even though no one knew what the words meant.

She darted into a side street with two tall buildings on either side, then pressed herself against a wall, trying to think.

Someone had followed her through time. How? It didn't matter. She had seen that gear once before, but when?

Celestial, she thought suddenly. *He's called a Celestial.*

They were from her old partner's time, which she'd just left. She pulled out her copper pocket watch, her time machine. It let out some sort of signal; perhaps it could be tracked?

Heavy footfalls sounded nearby, and after a moment, the Celestial walked into sight.

"Ariel," he said.

She didn't move. She was eyeing his blaster, still in its holster at his belt. "How do you know that name?"

"We've been tracking you for awhile. You have a teleportation device."

"Oh, do you think?" she snapped. "We're only speaking English in first-century Pompeii. Why are you here?"

"My lieutenant wishes to speak with you."

"Uh-huh. Not gonna happen. How did you follow me?"

He held up a silver pocket watch.

Her eyes widened. "That's—" She shook her head. "Doesn't matter. You're *thousands* of years behind where you should be. Doesn't that scare you? That thing behind us isn't a mountain. It's a volcano, and in a week it's going to blow."

He seemed startled by that, and for the first time looked around, to the buildings on either side of the narrow street, to the gray volcano in the distance behind her. Then he pulled off his helmet, ran a hand through his light hair. He looked remarkably young. The uniform connected with the images of Celestials she'd seen, but the shoes didn't: Converse low-tops. Not much of a police officer.

"I'm Agent Six," he said. "I didn't mean to frighten you. We don't mean any harm; we're just really curious about you."

"Uh-huh. Why are you following me?"

"You have a time machine! My lieutenant thinks it's just a teleportation device, but this…" He shook his head at the volcano, smiling. "Always there in times of death and destruction, huh? You removed a prisoner from a cell four years ago."

"Four years … relative to your time." She squinted, looking up at the sun. She hadn't broken anyone out of prison, as far as she could recall. "Okay, listen. I'm a *time traveler*. If I'm going to do that, I haven't even done yet." She pulled out her pocket watch. "But I'm looking forward to it."

He fired his blaster, but she dodged it. The hologram showing her Roman clothing flickered and then vanished, revealing a black jacket, jeans, and green-tinted sunglasses. A sheathed sword was slung over her back. Was it her stress or some action of her timepiece that killed the hologram? She had no idea, but it didn't matter. She didn't need her disguise now.

He was momentarily confused by her change of form, and she took the opportunity to run. She darted around a corner as he fired again, sending off sparks.

She hid in the doorway of a building, listening for his footfalls.

"Ariel," he called. "My lieutenant just wants to meet with you. You could work for us."

Ariel glanced down at her watch. She had to get him out of Rome—but how? She suddenly had an idea.

He turned the corner and came into view, holding the blaster steady at her. "I only ever wondered one thing," he said. "Of everyone on the ship, why did you go to Thomas Huxley?"

Ariel, perplexed, didn't answer.

The agent pressed the fob of his pocket watch, intending to take her back to his own time. The silver cover, etched with an image of crescent moon, popped open—but nothing happened.

Ariel grinned at the agent's confusion. "You don't know how to set it, do you?"

He didn't reply, just held the blaster steady.

"Agent Six, huh? What are you … special ops? Secret police?" She stepped closer, pulling out her own watch. "Here's a hint: they're telepathic."

She pressed the fob, opening her watch's face; it let out a golden glow. He yelled and reached out to stop her, but too late; her watch's cover closed with a click. The light cleared, and he was gone.

Ariel took a step back, and her hologram flickered back on. A warm breeze swept through the street, then drifted away.

"Wow. I've always thought the watches could communicate with each other, but I've never actually tried it. Don't you think that's…"

She turned her head, and realized she was alone.

People walked by the narrow opening of the alley, unaware of the brief stand-off under the shadow of a volcano. In a matter of days, everyone who had seen the oddly-dressed invader would be dead, their knowledge erased from history.

The sky darkened to a deep blue, with the sun a gold disk lowering in the sky. Ariel held up her watch: on the cover, it had a raised image of either a sunrise or a sunset.

A voice buzzed in her ear. "Ariel, report. I'm getting a strange reading. What just happened?"

She tapped her earpiece. "You will not believe this, Bailey. I'll be right there."

The hands of her clock moved to show the correct time for what she needed. The inner dials showing the day, week, and month spun quickly, and she closed her eyes.

After a moment, anyone walking past saw only an empty street.

2.

Bailey Tyler was the leader of the Saturnine Order, a pretentious name for a tiny group of time travelers. Now that Ariel's partner had left, it had only three members.

Ariel didn't know much about the Order, beyond that the base was hidden underground somewhere in the future. Its founders had lived after the thirtieth century, and started the group secretly to continue travels in time. How long the group had existed, Ariel had no idea. The founders started choosing partners from earlier times, and then left or died long before she arrived.

Bailey wore a white lab coat, and sat at a desk in her laboratory. A clock ticked overhead as Bailey looked through a microscope.

"Studying ancient microbes?" Ariel asked, leaning against the door frame with her arms crossed. "I wouldn't be any help. I got a B- in biology. A+ in history, but—"

Bailey pushed away the microscope. "Did you see anything unusual?"

"You ... could say that, yeah."

"I traced a signal." Bailey slid off the stool and walked over to a computer. "It originated in June of 2507, and went straight to A.D. 79. It was another time machine."

"I gathered that, thank you. He had a silver watch."

"Who?"

"Some sort of police officer. I think they call them Celestials." Ariel explained the encounter.

Bailey listened intently. "If someone from the twenty-sixth century is following you, we need to go there. They've stumbled upon a timepiece I haven't accounted for, and we need to find out how."

"By 'we' ... you mean me, right?"

"You won't be alone. I found a new partner for you." She picked up a folder off the desk and handed it to Ariel. "You need a guide, someone who knows this time, someone who will be sympathetic to your cause. He's perfect."

Ariel opened the folder. "Thomas Huxley, journalist. Ah, born in the same city as me. Wait!" She snapped her fingers. "The Celestial mentioned him. Said I've gone to him before."

"It's possible you bumped into him before, without realizing it. And he's not as well-known as your last partner, but you still need to be careful."

"Got it. Will they track me again?"

"The other signal is dead; no activity. The watch is probably malfunctioning, but that doesn't mean it can't start up again. I don't think they're done. If it happens again, don't try to reason with them. Run."

"Uh-huh. I'll try to remember that."

"Good. Find Huxley right away. All the information you need is in that file." Bailey walked over to a safe in one corner and unlocked it. "Oh, and Ariel?" She pulled out a pistol, checked the magazine for bullets, then handed it to her.

"A *gun*? Bailey, I'm not twenty-one or anything, and I wouldn't know how to use it—"

"They're illegal in the Federation, for a civilian anyway, so your age doesn't matter. That flimsy sword isn't going to do you much good. If you need this, take the safety off and shoot. I take it that's easy enough for you to understand?"

Ariel took the pistol, hesitant. "Bailey, that Celestial knew what I looked like, knew my name and everything. I've apparently done something in their past to draw their attention. What if every police officer on the globe is on the lookout for me?"

"Ariel? Trust me. They'll have something bigger to worry about."

3.

June 15, 2507, 8:30 p.m.

Lt. Kira Watson stood over Agent Six, who was leaning against the glossy wall of a laboratory.

"All right there, Six?" Kira asked.

The agent blinked, amazed. "I saw her, Captain! The girl … she was right in front of me."

Kira grabbed him by the shoulders and slammed him against the wall. "And you didn't think to *bring her back*?"

The agent shoved her off him. "*She* sent me back. If it wasn't for her, I'd still be stuck there. You sent me in without knowing how this works." He handed her the watch, then stormed toward the exit.

Two technicians sat in one corner of the room, monitoring the readings on computers. They kept their eyes firmly on their computers to avoid the lieutenant's stormy glare. Kira looked down at the pocket watch.

"Where was she?" she asked, quietly.

The agent turned. "Pompeii. She said there was a volcanic eruption coming."

"Pompeii?" Kira raised an eyebrow. "Last volcanic eruption there was in A.D. 79."

"I swear, it was something out of a history book. Ancient Romans and everything. Remember a few years ago, when she broke out a prisoner? She said it hasn't happened to her yet. She really is a time traveler. Maybe we're starting a causal loop, a predestination paradox—"

"She's lying."

The agent blinked. "I'm just saying."

Kira walked out the door, shaking her head.

A man in his forties stood in the hallway. He was tall, with frizzy, sand-colored hair. "Lieutenant?"

"Not now," said Kira, waving her hand and passing him by.

"Did you see him, Melo?" the visitor asked the agent.

"That's classified," said Agent Six.

"Oh, please." The visitor followed Kira, lagging a few steps behind her. "I see you're having trouble with your latest project, *Captain*."

She turned. "Who sent you?"

"Commander Delacroix. I'm your new personal assistant." He held up a silver card. "I volunteered to be transferred back to your squad. I left a few years ago when I moved to the covert ops in New York. Agent Five, John Caxton, at your service."

Kira sighed. "I remember you." She kept walking. "I really don't need any more agents, though. And this project is none of your concern."

"Since the Commander sent me here, I think it is. You only have fifteen agents, by the way, when you should have more than twice that. And since one of those agents has been out of service for several years, that makes fourteen. You could use the help."

"Fine. Why are you interested in this project?"

"Curiosity," he said. "Not every city is investigating time travel."

Kira slid a card through a slot by the door, and it opened. "We're not, either. I'm closing the file. This is getting a bit bizarre."

"What? There's been a new development. The servants saw your red-haired girl in the palace just this afternoon.

They said she was wandering the hall leading to the king's chambers. They haven't seen her since the epidemic a few years ago, and she always comes before someone dies."

"Really? Hm. I'm glad I have someone to report servants' ghost stories for me."

"She's a time traveler, Captain. I believe it, your agents believe it, Delacroix believes it. Why can't you?"

She pressed a button for the elevator, then turned to Caxton. "I'm not really a fan of chasing legends. Report back to Commander Delacroix: the device finally worked, but the target was not apprehended."

"So you'll be trying again?"

"I don't know. We'll have to wait for the clock to light up. That's how we sent Six through—it lit up this morning. In the meantime, I want every agent in the city to be watching out for Thomas Huxley. If she reappears, she might go to him."

"Why?"

The elevator doors opened, and she stepped inside. "This girl represents a threat to the Celestial Federation's security. The Commander appointed me to investigate it, and I'm following every lead."

"You never did find that escaped prisoner, did you?"

"No," she said.

"Do you even care if you find this girl?"

Kira didn't reply. She heard a crackle in her earpiece, and paused to listen to the message. Her eyes widened.

"What is it?"

She looked up at him. "Palace ghost, you said? Only shows up right before people die?"

"Yeah?"

She put a hand to her ear. "It's the king."

Thomas Huxley could think of better things to do at 11 p.m. than write a statement for the police. Sleep, that would be nice. But here he was, watching the clock tick away the minutes, writing everything he knew about Damien.

Thomas had already made a call to the news studio in London, excusing himself from the story. He couldn't really give unbiased reporting about an attempted assassination if his future brother-in-law was the shooter. His editor recommended he write a commentary piece instead, but he couldn't even think until he saw Zoë.

He walked over to the window, watching the rain drizzle outside. The king was lying in a hospital bed, his condition critical. He was alive, but no one knew how long that could last.

How could this have happened? The greatest leader in decades, gunned down by a musician? It didn't seem possible. He heard the police discussing the story over and over again: Damien was found running down the hall, away from the only elevator that led up to the balcony. No one else had been seen entering or leaving.

They were talking about the death penalty.

"I wondered when you'd come back," came a voice behind him.

Thomas turned. A brunette in full officer's dress stood before him. He smiled. "Hello, Kira."

Lt. Kira Watson strolled up to him, amused. "Four years in London, huh? Have you been avoiding me?"

"No, just … avoiding the city."

"I can understand that." A pause. "I heard you were engaged. Congratulations. Your parents mentioned how happy they were."

"Thank you," he said, his voice flat.

"I'm sorry," she said quickly. "Things must be hard for your fiancée right now. I could hardly believe it when they told me."

He really didn't want to hear her speaking about Zoë. Kira had ties to Commander Edward Delacroix, who would most likely assume control of the Federation until the king recovered, and to the World Council, which would decide Damien's fate.

"Is the king going to be all right?" he asked.

"It could go either way," Kira murmured.

He stared out the window. Raindrops clung to the cold glass, sparkling in the night. In the starless sky, he could only see the dark outlines of buildings.

"I've lived in this city for two decades, and I feel like I've never been here before," he said finally.

"How much do you remember?"

"Nothing. Very little." He listened to the rain patter outside. "Some days more than others."

"It's good to see you, just the same. I like your new accent."

He smiled a bit, inwardly.

"I'm actually looking for someone, and I was wondering if you could help me. It's a girl with red hair, and she might wear green sunglasses. Missing person. Calls herself Ariel. If you see her, can you let me know?"

"What?"

"Just promise me. We were friends once, even if we've changed since then."

He wavered for a moment. "Kira, I've been meaning to ask you. The day I was shot—"

A door behind them opened. Thomas and Kira both turned and saw Zoë shuffling in, wiping her eyes. "Hey," she said, when she saw Thomas. Her eyes moved to Kira for a moment, and then back to her fiancé.

"Oh," said Thomas. "Zoë, this is…"

"Lt. Kira Watson," said the woman, walking over and shaking Zoë's hand. "Thomas and I grew up together. I'm terribly sorry for what happened. I can't even imagine what you're going through."

"Thank you," said Zoë. "I … appreciate it."

"Thomas, were you about to ask me something?" Kira asked.

Zoë looked at him expectantly, and Thomas stared at the lieutenant for a moment.

"No," he said. "No, it was nothing."

The couple walked to their hotel a few minutes later. When they arrived, Zoë tossed her purse onto a desk. "I guess I'll have to get my stuff in the morning," she said, yawning.

A flash of lightning streaked the sky outside their window, followed by a peal of thunder. Thomas's suitcase was already in the hotel room; he'd dropped it off that morning, but Zoë's belongings were still in her ship.

She didn't fall asleep until almost midnight, since there were so many people calling, and so many calls to make. All of her friends had questions about Damien's place in the tragedy. It wasn't necessary to call any members of her family, however. Besides her brother, she had none.

Finally the exhausted young woman fell asleep sitting in the recliner, her phone still in her hand. She left it on in case someone called during the night, seeking illumination. For now, it didn't ring.

Thomas put a blanket over Zoë, took his contact lenses out of his eyes, then sat awake for a long time.

When he finally drifted off, it was only after replaying the scene of the king's attack in his mind over and over again. The room was damp from the day's rain, too damp for summer, and he tossed and turned, restless. He kept waking up and reaching for an alarm clock that was thousands of miles away, back in his flat in London.

When morning neared, the sound of a gunshot jerked him from his sleep. He sat up in bed, startled, looking for the source of the noise. But Zoë still slumbered in the chair, the world around her undisturbed: he had only heard it in a dream.

Chapter Three
June 16, 2507

The day dawned bright and hazy, and a pale mist clung to the ground, throwing the colors into sharp relief. Everything seemed soft and dreamlike, and at last Thomas knew he was in Tenokte.

He scanned the skyline from his hotel window, lost in his thoughts. At eight o'clock the flat TV screen flickered on, showing footage of the assassination attempt, as well as snippets of interviews detailing people's shock. And then came the news he wanted to hear even less: Damien Martínez had confessed to the attempted murder.

Thomas walked into the bathroom and called his seventeen-year-old sister, Audrey.

"Hey, kiddo," he said, when she answered.

"Thomas! Did you see what happened last night?"

"Yes."

"They're saying the king could die. But he won't, right?"

"I don't know."

"What will happen if he dies? Who's going to rule?"

"Kiddo, I don't know."

A pause. "Right. Um, Tuesday's my last day of school. Mom and Dad said I can stay with you this summer, if it's okay with you."

His heart nearly did a somersault in his chest, and he wanted to scream out, "Yes!" Instead, he glanced out from the crack in the door to make sure Zoë was still asleep. "That's great, kiddo. But you'll have to go back home during the honeymoon."

"But I can stay with you until then?"

"Yes."

"Awesome. Love you, Thomas. Come over!" A click.

His cell phone showed over a dozen texts and missed calls from work and friends. The messages varied: his editor dogged him to investigate the story; friends wanted to know what he wanted out of the coming trial. He decided to call them all later, since he felt completely overwhelmed. Just yesterday he had been a reporter who investigated tragedies, not a man trapped on the wrong side of them.

He sent a text to Zoë's phone and slipped out of the room. His fiancée stirred when he opened the door; he hesitated a moment, but she didn't awaken. He walked out, closing the door gently behind him.

Tenokte hadn't changed, but he had, so he decided to explore it again. He wandered through the city's parks, admiring the stone fountains and lush rose gardens where he and his family spent many happy afternoons in his youth. His memories were starting to come back. He walked through the downtown shops, all linked by aboveground tunnels, and saw vintage clothing stores, diners, cafés, and bookstores. He passed an electronics shop before realizing he'd walked down this street the day before, with Zoë.

The road ended by the canals, and he stopped for a moment and leaned over the edge of the bridge's railing. He gazed out at the water. The canals seemed calm: flawed, yes, and not as lovely as a natural body of water, but interesting all the same. They powered most of the electricity for the retail district of the city, and had been built centuries before.

After a moment he became conscious of someone watching him, and turned. A young woman stood across the street, her head turned to read a sign. After a moment she looked at him and then crossed the road, glancing both ways—for what, he had no idea, since almost all traffic was air-based.

"Hi," she said, smiling. "Are you Thomas Huxley?"

"Yes." It wasn't unusual for people to recognize him from his TV segments, but he still hadn't adjusted to it.

"Perfect. Can you tell me what year it is?"

"What?"

"The year," she repeated, patiently.

He stared at her.

"Hm," she said, glancing up at the sky, then the street. "Flying cars of this style puts me after the twenty-third century. From your clothes I can see I'm closer to the twenty-fifth or twenty-sixth. It wouldn't be completely out of place for me to guess that this could be 2507."

"You're not from around here, are you?"

"Believe it or not, I was born in this city."

"Uh-huh. Well, it's 2507. June sixteenth, to be exact."

"Perfect," she said.

He stared at the girl; she seemed vaguely familiar. Her reddish hair fell past her shoulders, and she wore sunglasses tinted a lime-green. Though it was at least seventy-five degrees and humid, she wore a black jacket, zipped up and closed at the throat. A pocket watch with a cover lay clasped to her belt, its copper chain dangling like an afterthought.

"Someone's looking for you," he said suddenly.

"Who?"

"But I've seen you before," he said, circling around her. "Years ago. You looked exactly the same."

"Really? What did I do?"

He stopped. "I ... don't really remember. It's a long story."

"Oh. Right. I don't remember it either, which means it hasn't happened to me yet. In any case, my name's Ariel Midori. I'm a time traveler."

He smiled. "You know, no one's ever said that to me, but now that I think about it, you really look it. Lost in time or something?"

"Do you want me to show you?" she asked, completely serious.

"Listen, you saw me on the news; that's nice. I'm not really in the mood for this."

"You spent a year working for the secret police when you were in college," she replied.

He blinked. "What?"

"Do you want me to show you how this works?" She held up the pocket watch.

The girl knew he'd say yes before he could even open his mouth. He felt only a sensation of movement, as if the world had shifted around him: as if he stood in an elevator that moved in every direction. When he turned around, he stood on the same bridge, but a blazing red sunset filled the horizon.

He turned to her, shocked. "How did you—?"

"Time travel. And distance travel, but that's not so revolutionary, is it? Watch this."

An instant later they stood under an inky, moonlit sky. Snow covered the bridge, and the canals were frozen. He shivered. When he spoke, his breath came out in a mist.

"You're not joking," he said.

She made a snowball. "No. Afraid not."

In a moment they stood on a similar bridge, but it was old and rusting, and the buildings weren't sleek skyscrapers, but crumbling, abandoned brick factories. The roads were made of cracked asphalt, with painted yellow and white lines. The constant buzzing of flying cars had disappeared, but he heard something else in their place. A blue machine on four wheels zoomed by, roaring and clunking as it passed them.

"Automobiles," said Ariel, at his puzzled expression. "Cars. Non-flying, obviously." She tossed the snowball into the canals, where it sank and melted.

He had never seen a land-moving automobile of that sort before, save for museums and old photographs. "Where are we?"

"Where I lived. From your perspective, it's about five hundred years ago."

He turned to look at her again, and found she'd changed. The cut of her clothing looked different; it seemed older, more outdated.

"How—?"

"Hologram," she said. "What you see me wearing now is only an image projected into your mind. In your day you have a similar technology, but it'll be awhile before people perfect the little details."

Thomas took a sharp breath, then let it out. "Okay, I'm officially impressed. Confused, yeah, but impressed. I'm dreaming, right? How can you travel in time?"

She held up the pocket watch. "This is my time machine. It takes me anywhere I want to go."

"Right." That didn't quite answer his question, but he let it slide. "So why come to me? Why not pick winning lottery numbers, or stop murders, or—"

"Lottery winners attract attention. And we could stop murders, in theory, but it's not recommended."

"Why not? This is incredible. You could change the future."

"That's what I need to explain. You can't, at least not easily. Things are set one way, and it's not a good idea to change them. If you try, bad things happen."

"How bad? End of existence bad?"

"No. But bad. I need to ask you something. You understand that I'm from another time?"

"Uh—" He glanced around at the cars, the buildings, at her clothes. "Sure, I believe you."

"I need your help. The people of your time tracked my signal, which means they know I exist."

"Your signal?"

Ariel held up the pocket watch. "This lets out a very faint signal when it jumps from time to time. I'm not sure how it works, but the Celestials figured out how to track it. You were one of them once, and the agent who caught up with me mentioned a lieutenant. Do you know someone who would work on secret projects like that?"

He did. But his head was buzzing, and he couldn't think. Suddenly he felt a migraine coming on.

"This is a trick," he said. "Did she set this up?"

"Who?"

He looked around, feeling lost. He felt as if he were staring at an old photograph—only his surroundings were real, tangible. But it didn't make sense. His mind told him he should be seeing a skyline of elegant silver buildings, not rectangular brick ones.

Another booming automobile passed, and panic suddenly took over.

"Take me back," he said.

"Thomas—"

"Take me back!"

He blinked, and a white light washed out the world.

Like a painting in progress, everything reappeared in pieces: the skyscrapers, the streets, the early morning sky with a touch of mist, now burning away from the summer heat. Then the flying cars emerged, crisscrossing underneath the clouds. He was back in Tenokte, back home.

He still felt dizzy, and the world seemed upside-down. Left became right, and he stood on the bridge but had the sensation of falling and spinning.

"Ariel—" he said.

He saw the girl's lips move, forming words that he couldn't hear. A golden glow blinded him, and he fell backward in time.

2.

"He's awake."

"No, can't be."

"Look."

Thomas's eyes opened, and he blinked, seeing the bright lights of a hospital room. A dozen faces surrounded him, and his head throbbed with a pain that he couldn't quite identify.

"Thomas," someone in blue-green scrubs said, "we're going to do a quick surgery to fix you up. Stay with me..."

Someone slid a clear plastic mask over his face. Sure, he thought. He could stay with them...

Thomas sat up, awake. He'd been lying on a cot in a wide, windowless room. The red-haired girl sat by his bedside, reading a book. Only, it wasn't a file on an e-reader: it was a paperback book, a rare thing in his time.

"Hey," she said, and put down the book. "You were out for a few minutes. How do you feel?"

He put a hand to his head; he had a migraine. "Ow. Dizzy. What year is it?"

She smiled. "No idea, but I just took you from 2507." She paused. "The disorientation is a side effect of the rapid travel. The world moves around you about a thousand times a second, and your body stands still. Freaks out your brain for a minute or two. There are no long-lasting effects, and it goes away after you travel a few times. But I've never seen anyone pass out..."

He grabbed her arm. "I had a brain injury a few years ago. You could've killed me."

She pried his fingers from her sleeve. "Then maybe you should rest a bit longer." She brushed herself off. "You know, I never felt anything, but my old partner did. Dizzy spells, that sort of thing. Used to drive him mad."

"Uh-huh," he said tonelessly.

"He was also into hallucinogenic drugs, though ... time travel probably seemed normal for him."

That didn't make Thomas feel much better.

"Anyway, you're in the headquarters of the Saturnine Order. We're a small band of time travelers."

He looked shocked. "Saturnine? We're not on—"

"No, still Earth. Named after the planet Saturn, though, and right now we're a few centuries in your future, give or take. Can I get you anything? Coffee? Tea?"

He slid out of the bed. "This doesn't make any sense."

"No?"

"How are you doing this? Drugs? Mind simulations?"

"What are mind simulations?"

"You know, virtual reality games. The Celestials use them to train police."

"Did they use them to train you?"

He stared at her.

"Yes, I know about your time with them. And that could really help me right now."

"I can't help you," he said, backing away.

"I didn't mean to freak you out. This is all really hard to explain. My friend Jude had this amazing way of describing it…"

Thomas had to get out, if only to prove her wrong, prove that none of what she said was true. He stumbled out the door and looked for an exit, but he couldn't find it, and soon he lost the way back.

He heard her in the halls, calling his name, but he ignored her. Eventually he came to an open door leading into an office, and he slipped inside. A golden clock and several paintings adorned the walls, and shelves of books lined one side of the room.

A plastic tank sat on a desk. The cover had tiny holes in it, and inside, several brown beetles were flying around or crawling on leaves and grass.

"Fireflies," came a voice.

Thomas looked up and saw a woman standing on the far side of the room. She had dark hair pulled back into a ponytail, and wore a white lab coat. "Here." She flicked off the light, and Thomas looked at the tank. The insects glowed with a green light, flashing in a pattern. There was a sort of indifferent elegance to them.

"Bioluminescence," said the woman. "I've been studying it." She looked at the test tubes, the vials, the equipment. "Among ... other things."

"Who are you?"

"Bailey Tyler, the leader here. If you do well, you'll probably never see me again."

"And if I don't do well?"

"Well, let's not get ahead of ourselves." She winked, then picked up a microscope and put it on a shelf.

"Is any of this real?" he asked.

"Yes, of course. It's just outside your reality. A long time ago, people didn't understand how fireflies glow. But it's simple science."

"What I mean," he said, "is that I could still be asleep, dreaming about this."

"But you're not. I'm pretty sure someone your age knows the difference between dreaming and real life."

Obviously Bailey had never been in a coma. She had never woken from what seemed like a long night's sleep to find that weeks had passed and that many of the people she knew were dead. If she had, she would be more careful about these things.

"Thomas?" said Ariel. She stood in the doorway. "I can take you back, if you'd like."

He turned to Bailey. He wanted to ask her to divulge everything about what was going on, to start at the beginning and keep going to the end, but he could see from her pleasant smile that she wouldn't. She was the leader here: that's all he knew, and that's all she would ever let him know. So he glanced down at the fireflies, watched them shine.

"Thomas?" Ariel repeated.

"I can stay a little longer," he said.

She took him to the Saturnine Order's tiny museum. All of the artifacts the group had collected, representing ancient history to the far future, lay on shelves in a dusty room. Everything fascinated Thomas. He observed a stone figurine from Sumeria, a bronze arrowhead from the Stone Age, and gold jewelry from ancient Egypt.

"I am, at heart, just an explorer," said Ariel. "I can take you anywhere in the world, at any time, and get you back before anyone knows you've gone."

"So you just .... wander around and study everything?"

"Wouldn't you do it if you could?"

He had never been much of a traveler, but he thought of the possibilities.

A dark-haired young man walked past the doorway, but stopped when he saw them. "Hey, Ariel."

"Hey. Oh, Jude, this is Thomas. Thomas, this is Jude Fawkes, Bailey's partner."

"Nice to meet you," said Jude. "You're the newest member, huh?"

"Possibly," said Thomas, eyeing Ariel.

"Well, welcome to the team. Oh, and Ariel, I'm still trying to track down the signal for you."

"Thanks," she said.

Jude nodded and walked out.

Thomas turned to Ariel. "I have a feeling you don't just need me for one problem."

"Sort of. My partner left a few days ago. If you'd like, you can take his place."

"You can't travel alone?"

"It's more conspicuous that way. People don't look twice at a couple walking down the street, do they?"

He could see her point. "Let's just take one thing at a time. You can go to the future, right? Does the king survive?"

"Who?"

"King Richard Montag II."

"I'm not exactly an expert in your century's history ... is he the one who gets assassinated?"

Thomas gaped.

"Oh, I mean, the one who *might* get assassinated. Perhaps." She glanced down at the watch. "We left on June 16, 2507, right? Let's go see."

Before he could stop her, Thomas found that their surroundings had shifted. Instead of the dark museum, they stood in the bright hallway of a hospital. A doctor wearing a white coat passed by without looking at them.

Thomas put a hand against the wall, feeling overwhelmed. He thought of his last major trip to a hospital.

"You okay?" she asked.

He nodded, his eyes closed. "Just a headache. Can they see us?"

"In a second. There's a filter involved. We come gradually into their field of vision."

He glanced up at a clock: 8:45 a.m.

"I figured that would give you enough time to get here, in case someone saw you at the canals, or noticed you left the hotel," she said.

"Right." He still didn't fully understand the implications of time travel. "How did you know where I'd be this morning, anyway?"

She only smiled and walked on.

They passed several rooms, and came to one with two guards standing outside it. A group of workers wearing scrubs wheeled a gurney down the hall.

A white sheet lay over the gurney.

"Is that—?" Thomas whispered. But those were the king's personal security guards. "That can't be the king. Can't be—"

"Come on." Ariel walked around a corner, to the other end of the hall. Thomas spared one more glance at the stretcher, then followed her.

Near the front of the hospital, a Celestial officer was speaking to a group of reporters. Other people had also gathered, most of them stunned or in tears.

The travelers couldn't hear what was being said, but Thomas immediately ducked into a side hallway once he saw the scene.

"What's wrong?" said Ariel.

"See that officer down the hall? He's my father."

She peered at the man. Full officer's uniform, with a white beret. "What is he, some sort of captain?"

"Police commissioner," said Thomas.

She whistled.

"Yeah. I want to avoid him, if at all possible."

"Then we will. Come on." She took his hand, and he reluctantly allowed himself to be pulled out. They walked to the back of the crowd and listened.

"The time of death was 2 a.m.," Commissioner John Huxley said. "Cause of death is believed to be trauma. An autopsy will be performed. No further questions."

Thomas and Ariel stood in the lobby, expressionless, as the reporters filed out.

"He just died in the middle of the night?" Thomas said, stunned. "They couldn't save him?"

"I guess so. How old was he?"

"Twenty-six."

"Wow. What did he do to get murdered? Make any enemies, bad policies, something like that?"

"Nothing. Everyone loved him."

"Someone didn't."

"They think my fiancée's brother killed him."

"Yikes."

"Yeah … that pretty much sums it up."

"Where did you get kings, anyway? Rulers of the world, I mean—when did that all start up?"

"Oh, the royal family's descended from Dimitri Reynolds. He started the Federation in the middle of the twenty-first—"

"Wait, who?"

"Dimitri Reynolds," he repeated patiently. "He'd be alive in your time, I think. Did you ever hear of him?"

She hesitated for a moment. "We've met."

Thomas barely registered her response. "The king just died, and his sister's too young to replace him. And—aren't you interfering with time by being here? What if you do something that changes history?"

"I won't change history. I'll explain later." She turned around, and they walked back the way they came.

"Tom!" someone shouted.

Thomas cringed, then turned around. Ariel stopped, too. The police commissioner walked up to them, smiling.

"It's been a long time," said Commissioner John Huxley. "Audrey said she talked to you this morning."

"Yeah…"

"You should stop by with Zoë tonight. I don't think we've met her. And…" He looked at Ariel. "Who is this?"

"Oh, I'm just a reporter," said Ariel. "Investigating … you know. This is all terrible, don't you think?"

"Yes, a tragedy."

"Yes. So … sorry, silly question, but if any suspect is charged and convicted, how long will he have to wait before execution?"

"It depends. It might take less than a week to assemble a trial."

"Wow," said Ariel. "That's … not very long."

"It's actually quite standard for regicide. Are you a local reporter? I don't think I've seen you before."

"Oh, Ariel's just visiting the city," said Thomas. "So, tonight! Maybe dinner? I'll bring Zoë."

"Good. I can't wait to see her. Pleasure to meet you, Ariel." He gave a nod, and walked down the hall.

Thomas and Ariel watched him go.

"Not very close?" she asked.

"No."

"Did you move to London to get away from your parents?"

"Not them. The whole city."

"What do you mean?"

"Kiddo, it's a long story."

"I've got all the time in the world."

He turned to her. "When I was twenty-one, someone shot me in the head and left me to die. I was found alone on a street, unconscious, with a broken leg and wrist. When I woke up, I found out that I'd been in a coma for eight weeks, and I'd lost most of my memories. Wouldn't you want to run away if that happened to you?"

She paused. "Did they ever find out who did it?"

"No."

"Maybe I can help you with that. But…" She looked up at a security camera above a door. The lens had been shattered, and shards of glass lay on the ground beneath it.

"That's just vandalism," said Thomas. "People break cameras all the time."

"How many are there in this city?"

"I don't know. Thousands? They're to deter crime."

She looked up at it. "I need to be careful. The police are already looking for me."

"Great. So my future brother-in-law's an assassin, and I'm walking around with a fugitive."

"I'm not a fugitive. I just need to find out why they tracked me and get out of here. But I really do want you to consider coming with me."

"Hm, travel through space and time? Sounds nice, but I have to worry about Zoë right now."

"Then I'll investigate her brother's case for you, if you'll consider being my partner."

"Fine."

She stepped in front of him, blocking the door. "A Celestial followed me and mentioned a lieutenant. You know which one he was talking about, don't you? One who works on secret projects. You said someone was searching for me."

He sighed, then waited until a group of visitors passed before giving his answer. "You're looking for Lt. Kira Watson."

She brightened. "Thank you. That's all I need."

3.

Commander Edward Delacroix managed most of the military and internal security matters in the Celestial Federation. He had a silver beard and faded blue eyes, and looked a bit older than his age—sixty-one. He had been only at his current post for a few years, and he enjoyed it immensely.

Well, most of it.

The World Council had issued a state of emergency after the king's death, and at the moment, there was no ruler. The government was in absolute chaos. He sat in his Tenokte office, on the phone with the Council to try to set up a meeting, when he heard the door close. He looked up, but no one was there.

"*Bonjour*," came a voice.

He turned. A girl wearing lime-green sunglasses stood next to him.

"No." He dropped the phone, then pulled out a blaster from its holster on his belt.

Ariel was ready for this. She held her pocket watch in one hand, her finger poised on the fob at the top. "Try to shoot me and I'm gone. Which one of us is faster, do you think?"

The Commander stared at her, then started to laugh. At Ariel's incredulous look, he said, "Déjà vu, Madame Time Traveler. We've done this before."

"When?"

"The *Lunitron*, four years ago. I was only a military captain then. A small, elegant ship was moving through space, and then you appeared, out of nowhere."

"Where's Lt. Watson? This is her office, isn't it?"

"Sometimes. She's out at the moment."

"Why is she tracking me?"

"Because I wanted to find you. Why else would a person be tracked? Ah, and here you are. What a marvel."

"Listen," she said, "I don't know if you can comprehend this, but whatever I did to attract your attention, I haven't done it yet. I don't know what you know about me, but I want you to forget it. Stop sending agents after me."

"Agents?"

"One caught up with me in ancient Rome. He's alive, but the next one won't be."

He gazed at her, impressed. "My, all those years, and you still look exactly the same. The lieutenant has temporarily suspended her project due to the tragedy. If you'd like, I can tell her you came."

"Just tell her not to follow me again."

Delacroix blinked, and the girl was gone. He picked up his phone, and heard a voice on the other end: "Sir? Commander, are you there?"

He would have to tell the lieutenant about this new development, but things had become a bit more frantic than he expected. "I'm here," he said. "Now, about that meeting…"

4.

Zoë was less than pleased when Thomas walked into the hotel room at nearly 10 a.m.

"Where were you?" she asked. Her eyes were red, and her hair was messy from sleep.

He closed the door. "I just went out for a walk. I sent you a message, didn't I?"

"I was worried. I turned on the news, and there it was. Over and over again. They're saying that the king died."

Thomas didn't reply.

"They want to kill Damien as well. They said he confessed."

"I'm sorry."

"No, you're not. You see this every day. Death, disaster, news at eleven."

"Zoë—"

"He's innocent," she said. "I know he is. Did you see him shoot the king? Were there cameras pointed in that direction?"

"I—" He faltered. No, he hadn't seen Damien fire a shot. No one had. But that didn't mean anything.

"I know Damien better than anyone else does, and I know he didn't do that."

He grabbed the remote and turned on the news.

"*—police speculate that Martínez killed the king in anger over a ruling that his band's album could not be released. The ruling was made just two weeks ago by the king's censorship panel.*"

Thomas looked back at Zoë. "They haven't decided anything yet."

"Yes, they have. They haven't said it, but they have."

He realized she was probably right. Still, it seemed odd. Damien had confessed, but it didn't seem like the quiet drummer to pick up a weapon over banned music. There had to be more to the motive, if Damien even was the killer.

Thomas decided he'd call his studio and say that yes, he would investigate the story after all. If he could prove the police wrong, well, that could placate Zoë and very well save Damien's life.

He walked over to the bed and sat down. "I ran into my dad this morning, and he invited us to dinner. My parents really want to meet you."

She didn't reply.

"I was thinking—"

"I felt sick this morning," Zoë said. "You weren't here."

That surprised him: his fiancée had always been healthy. Then again, no one could take news of a loved one's upcoming death without feeling totally bewildered and upset. "It's just stress," he said.

"Maybe." She looked down. "I, uh, called a lawyer. You know, for the trial and everything. This guy was one of my dad's. He's really good."

"That's great, Zo."

She grabbed her jacket. "Come on. They gave me a visitor's pass; I can see Damien."

Chapter Four
June 16, 2507, 1 p.m.

Biochemical Pathways, comprised of Jamie Parsons, Damien Martínez, and Kyle Jones, was the most famous rock band in almost a century.

Formed in 2501, the group released three albums, won two Grammys, and played at sold-out shows for several years. Jamie performed vocals and guitar, Kyle played bass, and Damien rocked out on the drums. (Zoë, the band's pilot, sometimes filled in live as a guest synth player.) But when Kyle died in a car accident—shortly before the band finished their fourth record—Jamie and Damien decided not to replace him.

After the band broke up, Damien renewed his EMT training and started to work out of a hospital. Could he be capable of murder after having his life and music career destroyed so abruptly? With the album (which included Kyle's last recordings) struck down, it was certainly possible.

As Thomas and Zoë received ID tags and a prison guard escorted them to the elevator, the journalist pondered the implications. The king's death had thrown the government into panic: there was no ruler ready to replace him. Damien would almost certainly get the death penalty, which would devastate Zoë and Jamie, and break the hearts of an entire generation of fans. All over an album the government's censorship panels found unsuitable for the public.

Thomas stepped into the elevator, and the doors closed. He looked over at Zoë, but her eyes were cast down. The elevator jolted upward.

"Assassination," said the guard. "That's a pretty big deal."

Zoë glanced at her fiancé, but didn't speak.

"So, he's your, what—brother?"

"Yes," said Zoë.

"Must be tough, with the execution and all."

"There won't be an execution," she said coolly.

The elevator stopped, and Thomas grabbed the rail.

"I liked their music," said the guard. "Especially that song with the French lyrics." He turned to Thomas, then seemed puzzled. "Have I seen you before?"

As the doors opened, Thomas thought of his TV broadcasting. "Most likely," he replied, stepping out.

The hallways of the prison had been painted sea-green, and the dim fluorescent lighting on the ceiling cast strange shadows over the halls. The guard walked cheerfully along, swinging his nightstick as he passed barred and empty cells.

According to legend, Dimitri Reynolds designed the prison himself, though his followers hadn't finished it until after long his death. It was certainly secure: in four hundred years of use, no one had ever escaped.

The guard unlocked a gate, and held it open for the two visitors. Thomas walked in, but Zoë hesitated a minute.

"If I don't see him, then it hasn't happened," she said, staring ahead.

Thomas held out his hand. "I'll be right here."

She took it, and stepped inside. The gates clicked shut behind them, and they walked on.

"After the last door," he whispered to Zoë, "there'll be a keypad activated by a numeric code, a fingerprint reading, then a retina scan."

She looked at him, surprised. "How do you know?"

"I did an interview here once," he said. At least, he thought he did. Why else would the inside of a prison seem so familiar?

When the codes had been entered and the door swung open, they walked inside, led by the guard. Zoë smiled: Thomas had been right about the security system.

After a moment, the guard said, "Here we go. Cell 45, Damien Martínez." He turned to Zoë. "You have fifteen minutes."

Zoë walked toward the bars, her heels clicking on the floor, and peered inside.

From where he stood, Thomas could see part of the tiny cell's shadowy interior: a chair, a cot. A man inside the room looked up. He was twenty-four, one year older than Zoë, with dark hair and rugged good looks.

"Hey," said Zoë.

Damien stood, walking toward the bars. "Hey yourself," he said. "It's been awhile."

"Not that long. They told me—"

"That I'm going to die."

"No, no, that's not decided yet." Her eyes grew watery, and she blinked back tears. Then she turned away and motioned toward Thomas. "This is my fiancé, Thomas Huxley. You've met."

The prisoner squinted at Thomas. "They let a reporter in?"

"Lt. Watson gave us special permission," said Thomas, quietly. He thought he saw a flash of copper to his right, blinked, and it was gone. How strange. It looked just like—

"Do you think I did it?" Damien asked his sister.

"You confessed."

"But do you think I killed him?"

She looked down. "No. I don't."

"You're probably the only one," Damien replied. "If I die—"

"Don't say that!"

"But if I do, I'm going to go down in history. So don't worry about me."

Thomas hadn't thought of that possibility. Damien Martínez, once a drummer in a well-known band, suddenly finds himself a no-name paramedic, and wants his name in the history books…

Zoë bit her lip, her eyes watering. "I called one of dad's old lawyers. Milton Apollo—remember him?"

A pause. "Zo, I didn't get arrested for—"

"He's done murders before," she interrupted. "He's gotten people off."

"Uh-huh. Well, I'm pleading guilty."

"Damien!" She clenched her fists, then composed herself. "Will you talk to him?"

"Sure."

She relaxed. "All right, then."

For a few minutes they talked about things they had done when they were young, their parents, their memories of the band. Thomas felt uncomfortable listening, and he walked over to the guard.

"I have seen you before!" said the guard. "You're that reporter."

"Yeah."

"I saw that bit you did with—" The guard suddenly stopped.

Thomas looked up. The overhead lights flickered, then went out, darkening the hallway. Zoë and Damien's conversation had stopped.

"Zoë?" he called.

No response.

"What happened?" came Damien's voice. "What's going on?"

Ariel appeared next to Thomas, making him jump. Her eyes were partially obscured by the colored glasses, making her irises appear blank. She held a flashlight, and flicked it on.

"I'll tell you if he's innocent," she said.

Before Thomas could react, Ariel strode forward, vanishing for a second and then reappearing on the other side of the bars of Damien's cell. The prisoner jumped back, shocked.

As the light flickered slightly, Thomas looked around. The guard to his left had frozen in place, his eyes open, and Zoë stood immobile in front of the bars, one arm outstretched.

Thomas's heart pounded. He let out a breath, and it came out a mist.

"Ariel, what did you do?" he yelled. He knew that she could move in time, but not stop it entirely. Or stop it for some people, and not others.

"Is this some sort of trick?" Damien yelled. "Interrogation technique, or—?"

Ariel ignored the prisoner. "Did you try to kill the king?"

"Yes."

She threw the flashlight down. It hit the concrete floor with a clatter, casting bright patches of light and then shadows as it spun. Then it stopped, illuminating Damien. He stared at her, his eyes wide.

"You're lying," she said.

"Ariel!" Thomas yelled. The prisoner and the time traveler ignored him.

Damien looked at the frozen figures. "I see," he said to Ariel. "You've drugged me."

She leaned in close. "Damien, if you tell them you did this, they're going to kill you. Whatever they've threatened to do, they're not going to try it. Help me out. Give me something to look for, anything, so I can find the killer."

"I'm the killer."

"You're a terrible liar."

Damien didn't respond, and Ariel tilted her head. "I see." She turned to Thomas, who stared back at her.

"Sorry," she said. "Just an idea."

And she vanished. The lights turned back on, washing the hallway with light. Thomas stepped back, blinking.

"—the Flyday celebrations," said the guard, nonchalant. "It was really good. I—" He looked around, then saw Thomas standing ten feet away. He seemed confused. "Mr. Huxley?"

"Damien? Are you all right?" Zoë asked.

"Yeah," the prisoner replied. He looked stunned, but blinked and regained his composure. "I'll be okay, sis."

Zoë glanced at her fiancé, who had turned pale. "Thomas?"

Thomas tried to say something, but nothing came out. His whole body went cold. Sitting ten inches away from Damien's foot was a flashlight.

He felt dizzy again, and the last thing he saw was Zoë rushing over toward him.

2.

Emily Montag sat at the head of a long table, with the six members of the World Council at the sides. Commander Delacroix sat at the other end. Emily slouched in the chair, one hand to her mouth, and looked off to the side.

"Princess, I know this is hard for you," said a councilwoman, "but we need to start thinking about your future. Your brother wasn't just a king. He was your guardian. With his absence, we need to find someone to look after you."

She moved her eyes to the council. "Oh, you're joking, right? I've been taking care of myself for years. I've been sitting at most of Richard's meetings for his entire reign. I know I'm still young, but I know how to run the government."

"With all due respect, Princess," said Commander Delacroix, "we can't leave the world in the hands of a sixteen-year-old girl."

Emily sat back. "It just doesn't seem real. I was speaking to him last night. How can he be dead?"

"All of us are grieving," said another council member. "We've found the assassin, princess, and we will deal with him swiftly."

"No," she said. "I saw what happened. Damien Martínez wasn't the killer."

"He confessed to the crime."

"I know he confessed, but I saw the man who shot him. He…" She balled her hands into fists, then relaxed. "It wasn't Martínez. I'm sure of it."

"Princess," said the councilwoman, gently, "can you really trust your memory in a situation like that?"

She didn't reply.

"We know that you have suffered a terrible loss, and you need time to recover. According to the law, no one under the age of eighteen can assume the throne. We will find a guardian for you. In the meantime, since you live in Tenokte, your case will be referred to the lieutenant here. She will assign someone to take care of you."

"No. I refuse."

"We don't require your consent."

Emily sat back. "So who's going to rule?"

"We have assigned Commander Edward Delacroix temporary leadership status. He will be taking on the king's role for now. And, Princess? We are truly sorry for your loss."

The Council members stood and filed out, leaving Emily with the Commander. This was the main meeting room of the palace, and she'd listened to countless discussions here. No one had paid any real attention to her until now, and only to sweep her out of sight.

Commander Delacroix walked over to her. "Things will get better, Princess."

Emily glared at him and walked out. She headed to her room, then waited until she could close the door behind her before she allowed herself to cry.

3.

Thomas felt a sharp white light over him and heard voices around him, as if from a dream.

"Nerves," said someone.

"Maybe it's the falling-sickness?"

"Nah, they haven't had a case of that in years."

"Has he ever had a concussion, something like that?"

Then Zoë's voice: "He had a brain injury a few years ago."

His eyes snapped open. They were in one of the offices of the jail, and half a dozen people were staring at him. He sat up.

"He's alive!" one of the cops said.

"Thanks," said Thomas, dryly. He put a hand to his head, then turned to Zoë. "What happened?"

"You just sort of passed out," she said. "We called for an ambulance, but considering that half the people here have medical training, they recommended that we wait and see how you felt when you woke up." She peered at him. "How do you feel?"

His head was clouded, and he felt uncomfortable with everyone staring at him. He took Zoë's hand and led her out of the room, then closed the door.

"Did I ruin your visit?" he asked.

"No, of course not. I mean, I got to talk to Damien, and I'm just happy you're all right." She paused. "*Are* you all right?"

"Yeah, of course. I'm just … tired, maybe. Stressed out."

Zoë searched him with her eyes, then nodded. "All right, then. I'll go let them know." She slipped back into the room, and he heard her speaking to the police.

He turned and saw Lt. Kira Watson standing on the other side of the hall, talking with another officer. But before he could go and speak to her, Zoë walked back into the hallway.

"Well," she said. "That's settled. Want to get some lunch before we meet with the attorney? We can stop by the ship later, too."

"Uh, sure. But—you didn't see anyone else come in, did you? When you were talking to Damien?"

"No, why?"

"I'm just wondering."

She stared at him. "Maybe we should stop by the hospital, just in case."

"I'm fine," he said. "Honestly. I was just a bit stressed out." *And I'm being stalked by a time traveler*, he thought, but decided not to say.

4.

The lawyer's office was on a corner on 14th Street, behind a huge sign that read JONES, DELANEY, & ASSOCIATES.

"What *did* your dad need lawyers for?" Thomas asked.

"Oh, you know. He was a diplomat."

Thomas didn't know, but he sighed and didn't press the matter. Financial issues, probably; when Zoë was only a baby, her parents had gone through a messy divorce.

Zoë greeted the receptionist warmly, and they walked through a set of double doors to a long hallway. The lawyer's office was behind an oak door with a frosted glass window. The brass nameplate read *Milton Apollo, Attorney at Law.* Before she could knock, the door opened.

"Miss Martínez!" The lawyer stood in the door frame, looking jubilant. He was short, probably in his fifties, and wore a gray suit and black tie. A pair of tiny half-moon glasses were perched on his nose; he looked more like a professor than a lawyer. "Come in, come in!"

He escorted them inside, and Zoë and Thomas sat down.

"You're early," he said. He sat down on a leather chair behind his desk. "And ... who's this?" The man riveted his eyes on Thomas.

"This is my fiancé, Thomas Huxley," said Zoë.

Apollo whistled, then smiled. "You poor girl."

The journalist swiveled in his chair, puzzled. Maybe it was his suit? Bright cerulean, of a tight cut, with a white tie—maybe it was a bit too British for the lawyer? Maybe the lawyer just didn't like his news show? Or what?

"Out," said the lawyer.

"Milton, Thomas can hear what you have to—"

"Out."

Thomas reluctantly jumped up. "I'm gone," he said, and closed the door behind him.

The lawyer turned to his client (or, perhaps more accurately: his client's sister) and raised an eyebrow.

"What?" she asked.

He sighed. "Zo, my dear, you have a lot to learn."

She smiled, not really surprised. "You don't like him?"

"*Love* him," said the lawyer, letting his hand hang limply.

Zoë rolled her eyes. "I'm not paying you four hundred credits an hour to call my future husband gay."

"Then I'll subtract fifteen minutes from the bill. Or, better yet, not charge you at all. I can't take this case."

"Why not?"

"I don't do murder cases anymore. Haven't done those in years."

"But my father always trusted you. This is my brother we're talking about."

"Yes, I was your father's attorney. But this isn't a case of—"

"Just hear me out," said Zoë. "They intimidated Damien, forced him to confess. It's obvious. Can't you convince a judge of that?"

"I suppose."

"But?"

He leaned back in his chair. "They've already demonized Damien in the media. This is the king's murder we're talking about. If I take this case, my career is over."

She blinked. "You're a lawyer, and you're worried about your reputation?"

"Zoë—" He sighed, then shook it off. He looked at her, beaming. "I didn't know you were getting married."

She smiled faintly. "We haven't sent out the invitations yet."

"You've really grown up, you know."

"Have I?" She grinned.

There was a reason Zoë grew up to be a responsible, well-functioning adult after her mother's death: someone stepped in to help her out. Apollo was in and out of her father's house during her teen years. He drove her to school when her father forgot, he checked up on her and Damien when her father was out late; he made sure she did her homework and that she ate salads instead of hamburgers.

And, looking at her, the lawyer knew he couldn't forsake his former client's son.

"Milton—" she said.

"Please, call me Apollo. I like Apollo better."

"Fine. Apollo. Will you argue for him?"

"My dear," he said, sighing, "to be honest? I was expecting you to call."

She smiled, then stood.

"I'll go by and talk to Damien this afternoon, then talk to the prosecution tonight. No promises, but ... I'll let you know how things go."

"Thanks." Zoë grabbed her jacket, then turned to leave.

"Oh, and Zoë?" He winked. "Cute boyfriend. I'm jealous."

She only shook her head, still smiling, and opened the door. She heard a shuffling of footsteps as she stepped into hallway and closed the door. When her eyes adjusted, she saw Thomas standing on the other side of the hallway, leaning against the wall.

"Were you listening?" she asked, surprised.

"No. Maybe." He paused. "Four hundred credits an *hour*? That's what I used to make in a week."

"He's one of the best."

Thomas glanced at the door, thinking of the rock band. "In Greek mythology, isn't Apollo the god of music?"

"I think so. Huh, that's neat."

He looked at her. "Do you believe him that I'm…?"

"Are you?"

He stepped forward, then kissed her. "What do you think?"

With her eyes closed, she smiled. "Nope."

Chapter Five

Thomas and Zoë reached the takeoff fields an hour later. Zoë's magnificent fighter ship, the *Halcyon*, gleamed in the sunlight. Primed and ready for a voyage, it was nearly a hundred feet long, and its armor held the luster and appearance of pure gold. Thomas circled around it, dazzled and feeling tiny by comparison.

"It's incredible," he said.

"My dad piloted it in the last war. Armor's strong enough to withstand most missile attacks. You could sit inside and watch the world crumble around you." Zoë walked over and pressed a button on the side of the ship, and a hatch folded down. She bounded up the steps, but Thomas hesitated, walking in with more caution.

"And you fly this?" he asked, peering into the ship.

"With a little help."

A robot rolled into place beside Zoë. It was fashioned mostly of tin, with wiry arms and oversized red eyes.

Thomas stepped back, alarmed.

"Thomas, this is Jack. He's a Proteus-5000 model."

"It is a pleasure to serve you, Mr. Huxley," the 'bot chirped. "I serve as co-pilot to Miss Martínez, perform maintenance, and make any necessary repairs. Miss Martínez, the communications system is now functional."

"Thank you," said Zoë.

The robot's eyes lit up when it spoke, and their shape and color reminded Thomas of a photo he had one seen of bicycle reflectors. The voice seemed human enough, if a bit choppy, but it lacked something Thomas couldn't quite identify, something that made it almost physically painful for him to hear.

"Come on." Zoë took Thomas's hand and pulled him inside the main hallway. "Right here is a storage closet for equipment. To your left is a small kitchen, and if you keep walking, you'll find four bedrooms. Here's the lounge."

He peeked inside and saw a red sofa (nailed to the floor, of course) and a paper-thin TV screen on the opposite wall. "Nice. A bit old-fashioned, but nice. But I thought this was a military ship?"

"It's been refitted for civilian voyages. Aha. Here we go." Zoë slipped into the pilot's cabin. It contained rows of dials and levers, all under three wide screens, which showed a glimpse of the outside world: the sunny sky of mid-day. She pressed a button, and a hologram popped up. "Let's see. Communication system fixed and operational. Takeoff controls, shields, missiles—"

"Missiles?"

She only grinned and sat down. "Kidding. We can fly it back to London later this week, but I need to stay here as long as possible. Are you sure you don't need to go back to work right away?"

"Positive," he said. "I've taken the whole week off."

She sat back in the chair, thinking. "The ship's got everything we need. Tonight we can move our stuff in here."

The idea came when they left the hotel earlier that afternoon and a group of reporters and photographers swarmed them, bombarding Zoë with questions about her brother. But Thomas still had concerns. "Uh, I'm not sure I'm comfortable sleeping in a place that could move."

"Don't go to California," she said dryly.

He walked out to explore the kitchen. It was tiny: two counters and a table. His kitchenette in his London flat had more square feet. But the cabinets unlatched easily, and the fridge had hooks to secure food in place. He pulled out a bottled Strawberry Jolama Heartache and went into the lounge to watch the news.

"The Council has appointed Commander Edward Delacroix as temporary leader of the Celestial Federation, as Princess Emily is two years too young to be crowned. They have scheduled an emergency trial for accused assassin Damien Martinez.

"Also, London reporter Thomas Huxley—"

"Hey, it's me."

"—is maintaining the innocence of his fiancée's brother."

They played a clip of him from that morning. As he watched, Thomas put a hand to his mouth, thinking of his words, expressions, movements. "Wow, you're right. I am slipping into my American accent."

"When did you do that interview?" Zoë asked, sitting down.

"This morning, when I was walking back to the hotel. They kind of cornered me." When he glanced back at the screen, the anchor was speaking again.

"Do you really think he's innocent?" Zoë asked.

"No. But they haven't convinced me he's guilty."

Zoë crossed her arms. "A man who has never shown any hint of disliking the king suddenly attacks him? They don't think that's suspicious?"

Thomas looked away. "What did you say about that album? Censored … for anti-government messages?"

Zoë stood up and grabbed her jacket.

"Wait, where are you going?"

She glanced at him over her shoulder. "To see Jamie."

2.

The singer sat in his lush, winding garden, strumming an electric guitar that wasn't plugged into an amp. Zoë followed sound of the tinny notes to the center of the yard, pushed past a sunflower and sat down on a bench across from him.

Jamie looked up at her, his silver sunglasses catching the light, then glanced down to focus on the solo.

"You didn't answer my calls," said Zoë.

Still strumming, he said, "I've been in police custody all night. They had lots of questions."

"Everyone does."

He slipped off the strap and put his guitar down. "We were mad about the album, Zo, but not mad enough to kill anyone."

"So you don't think he did it?"

"I honestly don't know. They're going to make an example of him, though. Death penalty ... that's a given."

She leaned back. "Are you going to be okay?"

"Sure. Perfectly. All my friends are dying around me. Peachy-keen, Zo."

"I mean," she said, "I don't want to lose you too."

Jamie grabbed the guitar and started playing again. She recognized the opening chords from "Dame de la Pluie," the band's first hit. The steady plunk of the tune echoed in her mind, and she felt perturbed. He had composed that song shortly before his first suicide attempt, at the age of nineteen.

"Jamie."

He looked up. "Yes?"

"Promise me you won't try anything. That you'll call me if anything happens."

"I promise."

"I can't lose you. Tell me you'll go stay with someone. Your parents, maybe. Or come with me and Thomas. We're staying in the city until things get straightened out."

"Can't, love," he said. "I'm a solitary creature."

She looked out at the garden: a tessellated patio of stones, then a jungle of sunflowers.

"Please."

"Don't worry about me. I have plans. I still have a visitor coming. Don't know when she'll be around, though."

"What do you mean?"

"Long story. But I'm working on a new album." He finished the last chord of the intro, and let it ring out. "You and I will get through this together."

Zoë sighed and nodded. She wasn't entirely reassured, but from Jamie, this was the best she would ever get.

3.

Thomas unpacked his clothes in Zoë's bedroom on the ship. When he turned to hook a jacket on the back of the door, he saw Ariel standing in front of it.

"Whoa!" he said, stepping back. "Don't scare me like that."

"I need to talk."

"Yes, let's. What were you doing at the prison?"

"Standard temporal time-slowing. It's an easy way to appear to freeze time—"

"No, with Damien! You could've scared him to death."

"Would've saved him a lot of trouble. But I think he's innocent."

"Right. But he told you, with no ambiguity, that he did it. He told the police that he did it, too."

"When he was arrested, he fought and at first claimed he didn't have anything to do with it. My guess is he changed his story when he knew the facts were against him. It's possible he'd be tortured if he didn't confess, and he would definitely be told as much."

"Uh-huh. Your temporal shift or whatever was messing with my head again, kiddo. I passed out after you left."

Ariel opened her copper watch. "You were fine this morning. The device shouldn't be causing any more problems, beyond momentary vertigo."

"Well, it did."

She closed the cover. "Then I'll go easy from now on. Anyway, I'm really interested in Damien's case now. Doesn't sound like he killed the king at all."

"So break him out, then. You've got that pocket watch."

"Hm. I could, but the world's seen his face. They've been running 24/7 coverage on him in every Federation-run country, and I'm sure they've declared it news in countries that are not. He could never go back to a normal life. You've been on TV a little bit, and you've seen how much people recognize you."

"So take him to another time."

"Maybe. But it's incredibly hard to integrate fully. He couldn't accept that. The only way is to clear his name. If his name deserves clearing." Ariel sat down on the bed.

"Kiddo, this really isn't the time for me to be thinking about this."

"Right! You seem like a morning person. How's tomorrow, then?"

Before he could answer, Zoë's voice sounded from the hall: "Thomas, is that you?"

He turned, and Ariel was gone. He blinked. "Uh ... yeah. I'm just unpacking my things," he called.

Zoë walked into the room a moment later. "Hm. That's weird. I thought I heard someone's voice."

"Nope. Just me."

"Oh. So, we're having dinner with your parents at seven? I'd better get ready."

"But it's only four o'clock," he said, confused.

She smiled and walked back into the hallway.

Two hours later, Thomas paced in front of the bathroom door.

"Zo, are you ready yet? We need to leave soon."

The door opened, and Zoë stepped out, looking radiant. Her naturally wavy hair was straightened and pinned up. She wore a yellow sundress and high heels, and clutched a matching handbag. Her blue eyes shone behind eyeliner and mascara.

"You look beautiful," he said, amazed.

She smiled. "Shall we go, then?"

"Right. I know the way."

They walked out through the takeoff fields, into the south of the city. Zoë flagged down a flying taxi, and it stopped, opening one of its eagle-wing doors. She slipped inside.

Thomas stared at the car, frozen in place.

"What's wrong?" she said, leaning out of the car.

"I ... don't do flying cars."

"It's the fastest way to get to your house."

How had he dated her for a year without ever telling her he didn't ride in flying cars? But he'd asked her to come, and he couldn't expect her to walk the whole way in heels. He slipped inside and closed his door.

Zoë gave the address to the driver, and the car took off before Thomas could get his seat belt on. The force slammed him back in his seat, and then into the window as the car took a sharp turn. He clicked the belt on and took a breath, trying not to look as the car blasted above the streets and soared into the sky.

"This really is a beautiful city," said Zoë, glancing down through her window. "Especially from here."

Thomas felt dizzy. "Yeah."

"Are you all right?"

"I just … haven't flown in years. These cars crash too much."

"You just flew from London on a plane."

"Planes are different," he said, looking out the window. "I can't explain it."

Flying cars were nearly unheard of in London: luxuries for the very rich, toys for the very daring. Tenokte had been designed to have roads in the sky, and the medium-sized city could handle the traffic. London, despite a bit of modernization, hadn't changed that much over the years. Perhaps that's why Thomas liked it so much.

The car soared through the cloudless blue sky, and it touched down on Thomas's old street, Rosewater Drive, in a little over four minutes. The journalist was grateful to step onto solid ground, and smiled faintly when he saw the house he grew up in.

"I can't wait to meet your parents," said Zoë, closing her door. "So you're father's a police officer, and your mother is..."

"A pharmacist."

"Brilliant. Why haven't we visited them earlier?"

He didn't answer.

They walked up the cobblestone pathway, and he rang the doorbell. In a few seconds a teenage girl opened the door. "Hey!" she said, hugging Thomas. She smiled. "You must be Zoë. It's nice to meet you."

Thomas glanced at his fiancée. "Zoë, this is my sister, Audrey."

Zoë held out her hand, beaming. "It's a pleasure."

Audrey nodded and shook her hand. Her dark hair had been pulled back, and she wore jeans and a brown hoodie, which on her looked like they came off a fashion runway. "Come in," she said.

They walked inside, and Thomas introduced her to his parents: his mother, Dr. (or Mrs.) Lily Huxley, pretty, light-skinned, with pale blond hair; and his father, Police Commissioner John Huxley, tall and handsome, with a dark complexion and steady gaze.

After a few minutes, Audrey pulled the dinner out of the oven and placed chicken, peas, mashed sweet potatoes, rice, and corn on the table. The family and the young couple sat down in the dining room to enjoy the meal.

"Have you lived in Tenokte your whole life?" Mrs. Huxley asked Zoë, passing a bowl of peas.

"No. I lived in Boston until I was thirteen, then I moved around a lot with my dad. I mostly lived here during high school."

"That sounds really interesting," said Mr. Huxley. "Where did you go to college?"

Zoë hesitated, and Thomas broke in: "Zoë went traveling with the band right after school."

"But I want to go to Stanford," she added.

That surprised Thomas. Zoë had only briefly mentioned a desire to continue her education, and not with a name in mind. She had dropped out of school at seventeen, when she would have been salutatorian of her class, and never looked back. Or so he thought.

"We chose a date for the wedding," said Thomas. "July 30th."

"Next month? Doesn't that seem a bit soon?" his mother asked.

Audrey looked at her. "What do you mean?"

"You only met a year ago, didn't you?"

Thomas glanced at Zoë. "We're both very sure, Mom. We're definitely ready."

"I just thought a little more time would be better. Perhaps next May? We could have the reception here. The apple blossoms look lovely then."

"My birthday's in May, too," said Zoë, "but we've already made plans ... it would be hard to change now."

"Mom, let it go," said Audrey. "They want to get married. Let them do the plans."

"So, Thomas, who was with you at the hospital earlier today?" Mr. Huxley asked.

Zoë paused, her spoon halfway to her mouth. "You were at the hospital?" she asked her fiancé.

"Yes, well—I heard about the king, so I decided to stop in. Just to see what had happened."

"You were talking to a girl there," said Mr. Huxley. "Ariel, I think her name was."

"Was it? I don't even remember. She was some sort of investigator."

"Oh. I thought you knew her. The way she spoke just made it seem like she was familiar with you."

Zoë was looking at him.

"I only met her today. And I only wanted to know what had happened to the king."

"Oh. So Zoë, isn't it your brother who assassinated the king?" Mr. Huxley asked.

No one said a word.

Finally, Zoë said quietly, "He was accused, yes."

"But he did confess, didn't he?"

"Zoë didn't even grow up with her brother," said Thomas. "And like she said, he—"

"I just think that's horrible. To kill a young man, in cold blood, and for what? For fame, probably. Aggression is a genetic tendency. It's carried through families. So is insanity."

Thomas stood up abruptly. "We're not listening to this."

"No," said Zoë, looking away. "It's fine."

"This is ridiculous," said Audrey. "Zoë is a completely different person from her brother. You can't judge her based on what he's accused of."

"Thank you," said Thomas. "But—"

"We're just saying," said his mother, "there's a media uproar. Thomas, do you really want to marry someone who's involved in that?"

Zoë stood up. "You know, Thomas is right. We really should get going." She rushed out of the room, and Thomas started after her, calling her name.

Audrey was drumming her fingers on the table, not looking at her parents.

"Mom, Dad, if I get married, you're going to find out by postcard a year later," she said. "And I'll be hiding somewhere in Mexico."

4.

Zoë silently cried as they walked to the subway. The last of the light began to fade under the horizon, and stars appeared on the still-blue sky.

"I don't talk to them very much," Thomas explained. "I got out of the country as soon as I could."

Zoë kicked at a piece of gravel. "My parents would have never spoken to you like that."

"I know. Don't listen to them; they really like you. When my mom heard about the engagement, she called and asked when she could meet you, and when she could expect grandkids."

For a moment, Zoë didn't reply. "They look young," she said finally.

"They are. Married when they were eighteen; I was born a year later." He looked up at the sky. "My mom and I used to study together when she was in college. I knew most of the periodic table before I could read. Can't remember much of it now, though…"

Zoë wiped her eyes. "It's because of the assassination, isn't it? They hate me because of Damien."

"No. It doesn't even matter. By the Flyday, everyone will know he's innocent."

Zoë smiled, consoled, but Thomas himself wondered if it were true.

Chapter Six

Zoë Martínez's parents never had the opportunity to do much more than daydream about their daughter's marriage: they died six years apart, during two separate outbreaks of the falling-sickness, when Zoë was entering her teenage years and then leaving them.

Due to advanced medical technology and routine vaccinations, serious illnesses were rare in the twenty-sixth century. Diabetes and most cancers had long ago been wiped out, and no one in recent memory had even suffered from the common cold. But there were exceptions: a rare disease strikes, an injury weakens the body.

Zoë had been thirteen, living in Boston with her mother, when the first falling-sickness epidemic struck. The virus, a mutation from a rare influenza strain, came with no warning. It manifested at first as dizziness, confusion, and a high fever. But no one understood what was happening until people started to die.

Her memories of the incidents could easily be confused with dreams. One afternoon she walked through the house, an autumn sunset blazing in every window, and saw her mother working on a painting. Two days later, she attended her mother's funeral.

The young teen packed a suitcase, leaving behind her school and all her friends, and boarded a plane to see the father and brother she barely knew. The disease burned out by the end of winter, taking only a few hundred victims: a scary news story that year, a footnote for the history books. But Zoë could never quite reconcile the loss of her mother and the sudden change in her life.

Then, at nineteen, she found herself sitting by a hospital bed. Her father lay dying of a rare disease whose name she never learned. His blood turned septic, poisoning him, and the infection wasn't responding to medication. The doctors couldn't do anything. Esteban Martínez, the famed diplomat who had once served as a fighter pilot, would die slowly in his sleep.

Zoë stayed in the hospital day and night. One afternoon she drifted asleep with her cell phone in her hand, waiting for a call from her brother, when the phone slipped from her grasp and hit the floor. The clatter made her sit upright, awake, and she went still. She could hear, in the distance, something like the flutter of wings.

When she pushed the door open, she saw doctors and nurses running through the hallway: their hurried footsteps had made the noise. Zoë stood there for a moment, confused, then grabbed someone's sleeve and asked what had happened.

"It's the falling-sickness," said a wide-eyed intern. "The hospital's under quarantine."

By the time a crowd gathered, a hospital official came and asked that everyone on the floor stay put unless they absolutely needed assistance. No one was allowed to leave the hospital, under any circumstances. Zoë called her brother in Sydney for the second time that week, asking for his advice.

"Stay put," he suggested.

So she sat in her father's room, stunned, and watched the news as the disease spread.

Biochemical Pathways had been on tour in Australia during the outbreak, and continued their tour even as the world death count reached the hundreds. The fans who showed up were enraged at the band's total disregard for the pandemic. One night, someone yelled out at Jamie, "You're playing music at the end of the world?"

"Hey, hey," said Jamie. "What did the band on the *Titanic* do as it sank?"

Fans started booing them. Kyle walked off the stage, and Damien shrugged and kept performing without the bass player for fifteen minutes. Eventually they were forced to stop the show. "This is how the world ends," said Jamie, and he trudged out of sight.

They had to call off the tour, and Jamie called Zoë later that night. "How's it looking in your lovely Massachusetts morning?" he asked.

"Oh, fantastic," she replied, from the other end of the earth. "I'm just waiting for the four horsemen to come."

The hospital's quarantine was lifted a few days later, as nothing could stop the spread of the virus. That morning, Zoë walked into her father's room and heard a strange buzzer go off.

It was an alarm signifying that the patient's heart rate had stopped.

Doctors and nurses swarmed into the room, and one escorted the shocked young woman to the door. She was waiting outside, in one of the hospital gardens, when a doctor came to deliver the news.

Damien flew back that night to help prepare for the funeral, officially halting Pathways' tour. On the morning of the burial, the two of them put daffodils on their father's coffin, and a priest gave a reading at the cemetery. Numerous businessmen, politicians, and former soldiers filed past, giving the children their condolences.

But Zoë and Damien weren't the only people who lost a loved one: the death toll from the falling-sickness was climbing, and people were panicking. King Richard II and the World Council met daily to work on a solution. They used military resources to distribute food and water to hard-hit areas, and sent police to quell rioting. Within a few weeks, the death toll fell sharply. The early quarantine efforts had made some impact after all.

Then scientists finished a vaccine for the virus, using research from the previous outbreak. Lines stretched for miles as people waited to get the injection.

"It was a futile, but polite, gesture," historian Pelé Zapata would later note. "Anyone who could have died from it already had."

But the king's swift response restored the people's confidence in their government. Early predictions of chaos and destruction would not be realized: the disease killed only a few thousand people across the world. Soon after the release of the vaccine, the king announced that the threat was over. But for people who had buried loved ones, the end hadn't come soon enough.

For his part, Thomas Huxley had no memory of the pandemic. He had been shot on the day it was announced, and woke from a coma eight days after it ended.

On what should have been June 17, 2507, Thomas drowsily opened his eyes, and had the same feeling: the world had changed completely while he was asleep.

Instead of waking up in a tiny bedroom in Zoë's ship, he found himself sitting inside an odd-shaped box with glass windows. The box moved over a flat gray ribbon that had white dashed lines painted on it. A strange roaring noise filled his ears, and he saw shining, colorful machines moving around him.

Was he still dreaming?

He looked to his left and saw Ariel holding a wheel. At least, he thought it was Ariel: he recognized her only by her dark red hair, since everything close to him was blurred.

"Hey," she said, without looking away from the road. (*Highway*, his mind told him. In London he would say *motorway*.) He realized it was filled with old-fashioned cars, and looked down and saw a seat belt over him.

"Where am I?" he asked.

"We're right by Tenokte. Except, it's not Tenokte yet. Right now it's autumn of 2007."

"I was asleep—"

"I know. Dreaming about the falling-sickness."

He paused. "Okay, I know you can travel in time, but how do you know what I was *dreaming* about?"

She turned and looked at him. "You talk in your sleep."

"Uh-huh," he said. "So how did I get here?"

"You were asleep in Zoë's ship. I thought it would be better that way: The brain doesn't register time travel when it's not fully conscious."

Tell me about it, he thought.

So he'd traveled exactly five hundred years to ... well, where was here, exactly? Outside Tenokte? It looked like another planet.

He looked out onto the highway, which he could see clearly enough. It was a picture-perfect day, with a cloudless blue sky stretching over them. The road curved and slid under an overpass, and cars moved past them on an identical road to the left.

Tree-covered hills sat to his right and, further back, he glimpsed a scattered assortment of houses. A faint purple mountain ridge jutted up above the tree line. Green signs overhead showed—

"Maps!" he said, amused. Of course: computer navigation hadn't been perfected yet, so people needed maps all over the roads to find their way.

"Sort of. They do give directions."

Thomas sat back. "You got me out of Zoë's ship, and into a car in your time?"

"Yep."

"Did she see you?"

"No. And when I get you back, she won't notice you were gone."

He frowned. "I have to tell her about you."

"So tell her."

He turned away. "Except ... I can't."

"How to explain a time traveler," said Ariel. "Maybe I can introduce myself. In any case, enjoy the 21st century sunshine. For your frame of reference, Dimitri Reynolds is twenty-three years old."

He was astonished. "Can I meet him?"

"Well, not without attracting attention. He's stationed in Iraq right now."

"Oh. That's right," he said, still looking out the window. "Dimitri was a soldier when he was young."

Ariel moved her hand and Thomas heard a distinct plunking sound, like a metronome. She turned her head, waited a moment, and then guided the car into the next path between white dashed lines.

"Isn't this dangerous?" he asked. "Car accidents are a huge cause of death in this century, aren't they?"

"Not as much as in yours. Flying presents some ... additional dangers. And don't worry, I checked ahead. There aren't any problems on this stretch of road today."

"But can't time change?"

She turned to him, her eyes hidden by a blur of green lenses. "I'm a careful driver."

That didn't do much to help his nerves. "Is this your car?"

"Sort of. I'm keeping it for someone." She pressed a button on the center console, and music started playing softly: faint vocals, backed by a mandolin.

"This song all right?" she asked.

He listened for a minute. "Sure. I kinda like it."

"Ha! I knew you'd be an R.E.M. fan."

He didn't recognize the name, beyond the fact that it had something to do with sleep. He really had no idea where she was from, beyond the turn of the 21st century. "Do you live here?" he asked.

"Yep."

"When were you born?"

"December 31, 1989, right before midnight."

Nineteen eighty-nine! He could hardly believe it. "So you're … how old?"

"Eighteen, if you count the time I spent traveling."

"Hm. That's a good age, eighteen…" He felt a little better for knowing, as if it suddenly made her more human to have an age. "Where are we going?"

"Nowhere in particular. I just thought I'd take you for a drive."

"Uh … Zoë's brother is scheduled to be executed any day now, and you woke me up to 'take me for a drive' in an entirely different century?"

"Yep."

"What if I don't want to go?"

"What are you going to do, open the door and jump out into traffic?"

He sighed. "I thought you just needed the lieutenant's name. Why are you still so attached to me?"

Ariel stared at the road ahead. "I need to know why they were tracking me, in case it starts again."

"Then go ask Kira."

"I tried. She wasn't in her office."

"You're a time traveler! You can go to any place, any time! What's stopping you?"

"I ruined my element of surprise. They know I'm coming. They'll have armed guards, traps, everything."

"So I'll go with you."

"What will that do?"

He didn't reply.

"I was just thinking about Damien," she said. "When I asked him if he shot the king, he said *yes*. But in my head, I heard *no*. What does that mean?"

"It means you have an overactive imagination."

"Possibly, but I'm going to stop by the police's forensic science labs today. I want to see the evidence against him."

"You took me out of the twenty-sixth century and put me in your car just to talk about Damien?"

"If you haven't noticed, there aren't any police officers with blue helmets and riot gear here. And I think better when I'm driving. Just listen for a moment. Listen. King Richard Montag died. Who gains from that situation?"

"Well … they said Damien was angry over the album. Jamie wouldn't re-record it to get around censorship laws, since he'd have to re-do some of Kyle's parts. Delacroix might release it now."

"Who?"

"Delacroix." He pronounced it *del-a-crah*.

"Who?" Her tone was patient. She knew who the Commander was.

He rolled his eyes. "All right, Commander Edward Delacroix is taking on the king's duties. But he can only rule for two years."

"Unless something happens to Emily."

"You're saying that this is an inside job? That he's responsible?"

She stared ahead. "I don't think Damien killed the king. I think he was framed."

"You don't have any proof. And why do you even care? I thought you time travelers tried not to meddle with history."

"There's something I'm missing," she said. "Something I don't know."

"Well, you know the future, don't you? Does Damien live, or does he die?"

She didn't reply.

"Kiddo, I have to get back to Zoë, and we need to get through this together. Then I'm going back to London, because I'm already behind on my work. I have enough problems as it is."

Ariel looked at him. "When's the Flyday?"

"What?"

"The date Damien's going to be killed. When is it?"

"June twenty-first," he said. "It's usually the summer solstice, but we just celebrate it on its own now. It's a holiday."

"Well, I'll work with you until then, and you can make your choice. If you want to come with me and travel, you can. If not, then by all means stay. But I'm telling you right now, you'll want to come with me."

"And why is that?"

She changed the subject. "You said I looked familiar, so I have a question for you. Have you actually met me, or have you just heard of me?"

"Why would I have heard of you?"

Ariel stared straight ahead. "Just tell me what you think. You have more memories than you know; you've just blocked it all out of your mind."

He stared at her. "I don't know. I think I met you."

"Hm."

"But if you know everything, what happened the day I was shot? Can't we find out?"

"Thomas ... a sprained wrist, a broken leg, a bullet through the head? You were a member of the secret police. What do you *think* happened?"

He noticed they'd left the highway. He closed his eyes, thinking.

"My partner's name was Madison," he said suddenly. "She had a young son, only a baby ... but after I recovered, I looked for them everywhere, and couldn't find them."

Ariel stared ahead. "That does sound strange."

"So it's true? I was in the secret police? Who is she? Is she safe?"

"I don't know." She glanced over to Thomas. "Just consider being my partner. We'll work out the rest."

2.

June 17, 2507

Milton Apollo strode into the police's questioning room. It was wide and bright, with a long table in the center. Sitting in the center, his hands cuffed behind his back, was the prisoner.

"Damien, Damien, Damien." The lawyer tapped his fingers on the table as he walked. "Last time I saw you, you were on a stage."

"Weird, huh?"

Apollo pulled out a chair and sat down, staring at the prisoner. "You *confessed*? How? Why?"

Damien cracked a faint smile. "I asked a question, and they took it as a confession."

"Huh." The lawyer sat back. "Where would you even get the gun? Or the training to properly fire it? It's a military weapon. An ancient military weapon. You'd need to be in the military decades ago to receive the training for it."

"Or know someone who was in the military decades ago."

"Please, your father was a lousy shot. And what'd they say the motive was …? Anger because some *songs* couldn't come out? Sounds pretty shaky."

"They were written by my friend. He's dead now. Kind of an insult to his memory. Apollo, I know my sister asked you to help me, but I don't really need anything."

"Nonsense. I've argued people out of far, far, worse. Why, back in '99, the Jolama Beverage Corp was about to file for bankruptcy…"

"Apollo—"

"And back in '86, there was that—"

"Apollo," he said, clearly, "I don't want a trial."

A few seconds passed before the words sank in; the lawyer turned, surprised. "No trial?"

"Nope. Nothing. They want to kill me? Good. I don't want any public spectacle. I don't want to spend the rest of my life in some secret prison. I killed him. End of story."

The attorney wasn't entirely prepared for this. "I can get your name cleared," he insisted. "They're not going to give me any time, I get that, and they probably think they've already made up their minds, but they haven't."

"Uh-huh."

Apollo headed for the door. "But if I can't get the confession thrown out, ask for a life sentence. Better than finding your neck in a noose. Life sentences can be overturned."

3.

Ariel stopped at a restaurant just off the highway. While they waited for a server, she tried to explain a few concepts of her time: the Internet, the simplicity of which astounded Thomas; transportation; money. The journalist's eyes lit up when Ariel reached into her pocket and pulled out a few round pieces of metal and crumpled rectangles of green paper, so she let him examine the different types.

"What are these called?" he asked, holding up the largest silver coin.

"Quarters," she replied.

He looked at the engraving, but found he couldn't make it out. He put it down.

"What is it?" she asked.

"Nothing."

Ariel picked up the coin, then moved her eyes to him.

"I'm farsighted, okay? I take my contact lenses out to sleep. Only thing is, I woke up in the wrong century this morning, and never got a chance to put them back in."

She sat back, astonished. "I'm sorry. I didn't know. I thought by the twenty-sixth century, they'd—well, you know."

"What?"

"Genetic engineering! People who don't need glasses, people who are smarter, faster. We had movies about it. Did it ever happen?"

"Yep. Well, sort of. Most children have modified DNA. Zoë does."

"Not you?"

"There are ... accidental conceptions."

She sat back, her eyes widening. "The movies predicted this too! So does anyone know? Is it a big deal?"

"Not really. Most people are descended from a 'preferred' individual—that's what they call them when their genes are modified. So it doesn't matter." He looked around.

The diner was mostly empty, but a few people sat at another table, chatting and wearing clothes of a style not too dissimilar to that of his own time. He saw the day's specials written in colorful chalk on boards above the—

"What is that?" he asked, pointing.

Ariel looked. "Cash register."

"What's it for?"

"It holds money."

He considered. There was no slot on the table to swipe his ID card and pay for the meal, but of course: Ariel would exchange those coins and papers as payment.

A waitress approached and asked for their orders.

"I'll have pancakes, and a Strawberry Jolama Heartache," said Thomas.

"A what?"

The time traveler smiled. "He means a Pepsi. And I'll just have a glass of water." The waitress was still a bit puzzled, but wrote it down and left.

"What did you order?" Ariel asked Thomas.

Thomas realized his anachronism. A Jolama, he explained, was basically a flavored soda. It had been named after its creator, Henry Jolama, a famed beverage-maker of the twenty-third century. Alcohol could be mixed with it, making a "Jolama soda on the ice." ("With ice" meant that frozen cubes of water had been added.)

Strawberry flavor would make a creamy pink "Strawberry Jolama Heartache"; chocolate, a "Chocolate Jolama Dream." ("Names," Henry Jolama once remarked, "are two-thirds of marketing.") Vanilla, cherry, and lime were also available, as well as a "plain Jolama," which Ariel knew as regular soda.

She was glad that the music drowned out their conversation.

"I'm still trying to wrap my mind around this time-travel thing," Thomas admitted. "Travel over distance is one thing, but *time...*"

"Well, you're better than I was. The first time I found out about time travel, I was floored. Just absolutely in disbelief. You seem to be taking it well."

"After what's happened to me, I'll believe anything."

Ariel lined up the salt and pepper shakers. "Hm. This is the last place I went with Jamie. For him that was years ago. For me, just a handful of days." She looked out the window.

"Jamie..."

"Parsons," she said. "He's a singer."

Thomas sat back, stunned. "Your last partner was *Jamie Parsons*? Why didn't you tell me?"

"I didn't think it mattered. He was about nineteen."

"Why did he leave?"

"It's complicated. You must know—every explanation for what he does is complicated."

That was true. Thomas tapped the table absentmindedly. In his interviews, he often pressed people for answers, but some only divulged information bit by bit. "So one day someone just approached you, asked you to be a time traveler, and you said yes?"

She smiled. "I was always dreaming about somewhere else I could go. Didn't you ever do that?"

He did: one of his dreams had been to be a reporter in London. Then he fell in love with a girl who didn't like big cities.

"Sort of," he said. "I did always think the idea of time travel was neat. If I were late for work, I could zap back and be on time."

"Mm. That type of travel gets confusing after awhile, though. Being in two places at once..."

The server returned with their drinks and Thomas's plate. He took the knife and fork, holding them in a way Ariel had never seen, and started to cut the pancakes.

"Syrup?" said Ariel.

"What do you mean?"

"I mean, don't you use syrup in your time?"

"No." He put a piece in his mouth.

She sighed.

Thomas looked at the glass of Pepsi, hesitant to try it. "When we go back to my time, you'll have to try the sodas there," he said. "How do you keep track of language, by the way? English has changed a lot in the past five centuries."

"I'm pretty adept at learning accents, and Jamie helped me with your time's lingo. Entire languages are a bit trickier, but I get along. I spoke French and a little Spanish before I left, so that helped."

"*Je suis impressionné,*" said Thomas: I'm impressed.

"*Oui.* That's right; you know French, don't you? You spent a semester in Montréal."

He thought about that for a moment, and realized he had. Wide streets, signs in another language ... it all seemed murky in his mind, like flashes of films he'd seen as a child, but it was there.

"You can go anywhere, in any time, can't you?" Thomas asked.

"Yep."

"Could we go back in time and see dinosaurs?"

"Ahh! Can you imagine me getting chomped on by a *T. rex*? No. No way."

"Aw, you've never gone that far?"

"Thomas, five hundred years, or even a few thousand, is nothing. But 70, or even 100 million years? This thing might short-circuit." She looked at her pocket watch, now ticking away the seconds on a sunny day in 2007.

"Come on, we could try it."

She pocketed the device. "Fine. For you, dinosaurs. But if it goes *Jurassic Park*, I'm outta there."

"*Jurassic Park*?"

"Never mind," said Ariel. "But what if we accidentally kill an insect or something and totally destroy the evolutionary tree?"

The waitress returned with their check, gave them an odd look, then walked away.

"I thought we couldn't change anything. Can we change anything?"

"I'm just postulating."

"Oh, what am I thinking? I can't do this. I mean, leave Zoë, travel?"

"She leaves you all the time to fly around the world."

"But that's her job. And she lets me know. And she doesn't encounter dinosaurs."

She watched him for a moment, then glanced out the window. "You don't have to do this. But if you do ... I think there's something you should know."

Thomas was struggling with the wrapper on his straw, and finally he tore it open. He plopped the straw in his drink, feeling victorious. "Oh?"

"My full name isn't Ariel Midori. It's Ariel Midori Reynolds. Dimitri ... is my brother."

Thomas followed her eyes out the window as he took a sip of the soft drink. When he saw the license plate, he spat the liquid all over the table.

Ariel stood in the parking lot with her hands in her pockets. Her '76 Camaro had black racing stripes and a fresh coat of yellow paint. When Thomas squinted, the license plate came into focus: TNOKTE.

"This plate is in a museum," he said.

"Really? Why?"

He tried to explain one legend of how the city was named: that Dimitri had heard the word in his youth and loved it, had emblazoned it on his vehicle, and eventually used it to title the city he built.

"It's meaningless," she said. "The person who sold the car to my mom chose it. It was the three states the guy lived in, I think: Tennessee, Oklahoma, Texas. Except TNOKTX was taken, so he put an E at the end."

"Ohh," he said, as if he were in pain. He stared, wide-eyed, at the automobile. "Why didn't I see it? Of course you looked familiar! Ariel Reynolds, red hair, born in 1989. Dimitri's deployed overseas, so you drive his car!" He paused. "You're related to the most famous man in history, you know."

"Come on. Is he more famous than George Washington? Alexander the Great?"

"Who?"

Ariel put a hand to her forehead, as Thomas circled around the car, smiling. "No wonder you care about the king! He's your nephew."

"Uh, my nephew, five centuries removed."

"Your nephew in spirit. Your brother goes on to become famous, and you ..." He brightened. "Your father was a famous epidemiologist, then. Studied diseases, patterns of death. That sounds a lot like you."

"There," she said, sharply. "You know more about him than I do." She slid into the passenger seat and slammed the door shut.

Thomas walked over and leaned in the driver's side window. "I'm sorry," he said quickly. "I shouldn't have mentioned it."

She didn't reply. If she was Ariel Reynolds, then her father would have died when she was four years old.

"It's just … I was named for him. Dr. Thomas James Reynolds … Thomas James Huxley."

"That's nice."

He slid into the driver's seat, then closed the door. He wouldn't see her as clearly, but he wanted to be close to her.

"We were meant to meet," he told her.

"It's possible."

"I studied you in history class," he added, as if it mattered.

"Keep it to yourself, then. I don't want to know when I die."

"No one knows. That's the thing. One day you just … go missing."

Ariel stared straight ahead. "Someone knows. Somewhere along the time line, I've already died. Isn't that wonderful to know? Don't tell me any more. I don't want to be like Jamie."

"Why? What happened to him?"

"He's … very famous. You know. In the future, they'll put up memorials for him—statues and everything. We were walking along one day, and he tripped over one of them. Inscribed on it was his name and the date of his death."

A pause. "Was this before or after he attempted suicide?"

"After, oddly enough. When he found out how successful he'd be, he wanted to go back. He had this theory…" She shook her head. "It was bound to happen, anyway, and I should've known not to take someone so well-known. But it's so much easier to *find* the famous people, isn't it?"

"Hey, wait a minute. I'm not famous?"

"Who are you again?"

He rolled his eyes. "Well, is that how they found you?"

She nodded. "Jude Fawkes is our leader's partner, but before that, he needed someone from the early twenty-first century. He read somewhere that Dimitri Reynolds's little sister could pick up languages well, and so he went to me."

"Uh-huh."

"He had a fantastic way of explaining time travel, too. Right now, he's out researching why the Celestials are tracking me. Which is what I should be doing." She looked at him for a moment, realizing he was in the driver's seat. "We need to switch places."

He was daydreaming, not really paying attention. "You don't know how many times someone's said that to me."

She stared at him. Something popped into her head, from the file she read or otherwise, about Thomas Huxley.

He leaned back and closed his eyes. "Give me a minute. I'm sitting in the driver's seat of Dimitri Reynolds's car. With his sister. This is too cool." He sighed. "Okay."

They each opened their door, walked out, and moved to the opposite side of the car.

"You know, I don't really mind old-fashioned automobiles," he said, slamming his door. "Flying cars kind of get on my nerves, though."

"Why's that? Fear of heights?"

"Fear of falling."

"Ah. Fair enough." She sat back, then adjusted her mirror, thinking about his file again. "So you ... swing both ways?"

Thomas looked out the window. "If that's what you want to call it."

"I think that's neat."

He turned. "No one knows. Not even Zoë—especially Zoe. I mean, it doesn't really matter anymore, but still."

"Hm. We should visit ancient Greece," she said. "You'd blend in perfectly. I read somewhere that bisexuality was really common there."

"I don't speak ancient Greek."

"I do. Well, a little. Jamie picked it up quickly. He once had a conversation with Socrates about the nature of music. I wanted to ask questions too, but he wouldn't speak to me. Something about women being inferior."

Historical figure or not, Thomas would punch out anyone who insulted Ariel Midori Reynolds.

"You can't win," he said, finally.

"No, I guess not. Well, I promised to explain how time travel works, didn't I? And you wanted to go home." She put the keys in the ignition, and the car roared to life.

Chapter Seven
June 17, 2507

"Time," said Ariel, "is not a straight line."

They were standing by the Tenokte canals at around eight in the morning. Flying cars darted among a few wispy clouds in an otherwise clear sky, and Thomas had his contacts back in his eyes.

"The long-standing opinion is that time is a circle or a wheel. That is completely inaccurate. The closest simile I've found is that time is like a DVD."

"A what?"

"Uh, imagine a little silvery disk that holds a movie. You pop it into a player, and a menu appears on the screen. You can either watch the movie from start to finish, or you can play with the controls. Fast forward, jump ahead, fall back and watch the same scene twice. *Comprende?* Time is like a DVD, and my little pocket watch is the remote."

He considered this for a moment. "But this isn't just watching an outside event. You're fundamentally changing that movie by being present, aren't you?"

"People will argue with you on that point, and there are two schools of thought: One is that everything that happens has already been decided. That our being here today is part of one long smooth sequence, and nothing can change it. So we were always meant to be in the movie."

"And the second..."

"Is that I'm an intruder, breaking apart events and changing them. Editing the movie. Bailey, and the rest of the Saturnine Order, believe in the first theory. But there have been dissenters. For example, Jamie believed in the second one."

"You believe you can't change anything? That whatever happens, happens?"

She paused. "I think some little things can be overwritten, but I've never been able to prove it. Most things cannot be undone. Think about it: you can't go back in time and murder your grandparents before they had children, because the fact that you exist means they weren't killed. You'd arrive there and you won't be able to find them, or you'd have a change of heart."

"That doesn't mean I can't go back and disrupt events that would have never affected me. Or change the future."

"No. It doesn't prove that, exactly. But I don't think it's possible."

"Okay, so where did you get your time machine?"

She clasped her pocket watch in one hand, its copper chain wrapped around her fingers. "In the long run, I don't know, exactly. It was invented some time after the year three thousand."

"How can you not know?"

"The Saturnine Order didn't start with Bailey. There have been dozens of travelers to come before us, and they didn't leave records about their founding. We do know that the inventors of time travel will ban its use and try to destroy all traces of it."

"What? Why would they want to destroy it?"

"They feared what time travelers can do. Think about it, Thomas. I can use this to travel anywhere, at any time. That's a dangerous device for your enemy to have."

"Maybe the Celestials think so, too."

"Exactly. In any case, a few pocket watches were stolen, and a few people founded the Saturnine Order in secret, since they wanted to travel. We do know that at one time there were almost a dozen members. Now there are only three. Four, if you join."

"So what do you do?"

"Travel, explore. Research historical events."

"That's it?"

"Yep."

"And you've never been tracked before?"

"No, which is what worried me. If people keep tracking me, I'll have to go home and destroy my device. And I don't want to do that."

"Yet you're talking to me and not investigating that."

"I spoke to Delacroix, Thomas. He said he's seen me in the past. I haven't really gone into your time at all, except to pick up Jamie, and I made sure not to attract attention then. So I'm thinking that whatever I did to cause attention, I'm going to do sometime in my future. And it's somehow connected to you."

He pressed his lips together, thinking.

"In any case," said Ariel, "I—"

She was cut off by a sudden voice shouting, "Thomas!" Both of them turned and saw Zoë standing about twenty paces away. She jogged over, smiling. "I can't believe I found you," she said. She looked at Ariel. "Hi. I don't believe we've met."

"Ah. This is Ariel Midori," said Thomas, sweeping his hand toward the girl. "She's investigating the case against Damien. Ariel, this is my fiancée, Zoë."

Ariel smiled at his description of herself: not quite a lie, but an obstruction of the truth. "It's a pleasure to meet you, Zoë."

"And you. How is the case going?"

"It's difficult, but I feel a breakthrough coming."

"I see." Zoë turned to Thomas. "I've been looking everywhere for you. Where were you?"

As Ariel dug out her pocket watch and read the dials, Thomas said, "Just out here, looking at the water. We also had a quick breakfast."

"Hm," said his fiancée.

"I'd better get going," said Ariel. "I have to meet with a forensic scientist in about an hour. Maybe I can catch up with you both later."

"Sure. You know where the ship is, right?"

She nodded. "Thomas told me. I'll drop in later, and we can talk more."

"I'd like that," said Zoë. "It was nice to meet you, Ariel."

Thomas said a quick goodbye, and the time traveler watched as they left, cutting a path through the city gardens. Fountains spurted water at every corner, and roses twisted like hearts among leaves and thorns.

For a moment the image of the couple seemed perfect: their smiles, their easy stroll. Then, just as quickly, they disappeared around a corner.

Ariel remembered what would become of them, and sighed. It didn't matter. The world still turned, no matter what she or they or anyone else wanted. Hopes were just colorful balloons that often floated away, getting lost somewhere in that wide expanse of blue sky.

2.

Dr. Charles Taber heard a sharp rapping at the door, and looked up. A young woman with copper-red hair stood inside the doorway. She wore a white lab coat over her aqua shirt and black slacks, and held a clipboard with both hands.

"Can I help you?" he asked.

"Lt. Watson sent me," she said, walking over and handing him her authorization card. "She wants to know how the evidence turned out in the Martínez case."

He scrutinized the ID, then looked up at her. "You look a little young to be a cop."

"I work in the lab. And if you really want to know, I'm just an intern."

"Ah," he said. "Don't they usually send you out for coffee?"

She put down the clipboard, revealing a latte, and took a sip. "Sometimes. So, Doctor, what are we looking at?" She peered over at the microscope.

Dr. Taber sighed. He had forty years' experience in his line of work, as well as a Ph.D. in criminology, and was tired of having to explain details to students. He worked in high-profile crimes, and had been called in especially for this one.

"There isn't much to see, Miss Midori. The Council has already examined the witness statements. The only evidence is the rifle used to commit the crime and the bullets extracted from the young king, as well as the autopsy report."

"Did you do the autopsy yourself?"

"No. I'm not a medical doctor. But all my questions have been answered. The bullets this rifle fires match the one that killed the king." The scientist wore nitrile gloves, and walked over and picked up the black M-16. "This model is ancient. Last manufactured 397 years ago, and could very well be much older."

"And it still shoots?"

"Yes. It's been well-maintained, to say the least. While possession of a rifle or ammunition for a non-military purpose is a serious crime—"

"As I work in the lab, I'm a little hazy on laws, but when did this happen?"

He raised his eyebrows. "Anyway, it's unknown how Mr. Martínez obtained this weapon. A few still exist on the black market. His prints were not found on it, however.

There's one fragment of a print, but I haven't been able to get a match. It could be an old print from a previous owner."

"Was Damien wearing gloves?" the girl pondered aloud.

"That's our working assumption, but he didn't have gloves on when he was arrested."

"Wait—you don't have prints, and they only saw him running through the building, but they're issuing the death penalty?"

"I don't choose what happens to him, Miss Midori; I just submit my information. But there's also the matter of his confession." He turned away. "Tell your lieutenant that I don't have conclusive evidence, from a physical point of view, to link the suspect to the crime. I'll write up my report and send it to her in the morning."

"One question," said Ariel. "If you find a match on that print, can you let me know?"

"I'll send word to Lt. Watson, and let her know you asked. Whether she summons you or not is her decision."

"No. Let *me* know." Ariel reached into her pocket, pulled out a slip of paper, and handed it to him.

"What's this?" he asked.

"A phone number. Call me. I'm easy to reach, and my cell phone works no matter where I am." She took a sip of her latte.

"Very funny, miss. But I'll send the message through the proper channels."

Ariel nodded, and walked toward the door. "Do that. Just don't mention me."

"Why not?"

"They're not really supposed to send interns; I'm covering for someone who can't make it. Submit your report. But if you find a match, can you tell me?"

Dr. Taber looked at her for a moment. "I'll consider it."

"A thousand thanks." She took another sip and walked out.

What a strange young woman, the scientist thought, and continued on with his work.

3.

"If you won't write an article," said Thomas's editor in London, through a voice mail on the reporter's phone, "just post a video blog. I don't care what it's about, but your fiancée's brother killed the king! Just put up anything."

Thomas opened his laptop and set up the camera while Zoë was out. He didn't even *do* much political reporting—his specialty was music—but one of his co-workers was on maternity leave, and he'd promised to fill in for awhile. If his editor wanted his opinion, he'd get it.

He turned on the camera and sat back.

"Hello, my name is Thomas Huxley. You might have seen some of the stories I've filmed for the morning news broadcast. In any case, I am a reporter, and this isn't a normal story. It's just an update as to how I'm doing.

"You probably know that my fiancée's brother, Damien Martínez, has been accused of murdering the king. Zoë and I have been holding up well, considering the circumstances. My heart goes out to Princess Emily during this time. June 15, 2507, will always be known as a terrible day.

"The tragedy seems to have lengthened my stay in Tenokte, and I will be returning to work after the Flyday. In the meantime, I ask—not as a journalist, but as a citizen of the Federation—that the Council re-examine the evidence against Damien. I feel his confession may have been forced.

"The sudden death of anyone is horrific, and the death of King Richard has caused the entire world to grieve. But I hope that the execution will be at least postponed until the Council can look at the facts, and not be caught up in the emotions of the times. A handful of days is not long enough to look at a case and decide someone must die, no matter what the crime.

"Thank you for listening. I know the Council will do whatever they feel is right, and Zoë and I will move on as best we can. I hope everyone else can do the same."

He turned off the camera and sat back. It all sounded inadequate to him now, and it would probably stir up controversy, but they had asked for something. Photographers and reporters would probably follow him and his fiancée around more than they already did, but that didn't bother him—though it was starting to upset Zoë.

Still, he hadn't insulted the Federation, which made it safe to put up. He clicked Enter, typed his security code, and posted it to the web site for every citizen of the Federation to see.

4.

The wake for King Richard Montag lasted all night, and the line to see the coffin stretched beyond the funeral home and for several blocks outside it.

The princess wanted to stand by the body and accept the visitors, but soon realized she could not handle it without tears. A member of the World Council, Marietta Jones, instead took that position, and filled it with dignity and respect. Emily watched from off to the side, trying not to look at the coffin, and at six o'clock asked a guard to take her home.

It still didn't seem real. When he came off the ambulance, Richard was clearly in pain, but still lucid. In his bed in the ER, he tried to laugh and joke, even as the gaping wound in his chest bled faster than the doctors could give him transfusions. Then shock started to set in.

When the young king started calling for his long-dead mother, the doctors ushered Emily to the waiting room. At 2 a.m., he went silent. A doctor came out to deliver the news.

They wanted to keep the princess away from the body, but she asked to go in, so a physician accompanied her. She walked in, trembling, and looked at her brother's corpse. Without thinking, she reached out and touched his hand. It felt as cold as stone, no warmth to it at all, but the texture was all soft skin and veins. She pulled back her fingers, startled, and looked up at the doctor.

"I'm so sorry, your Majesty," he said.

Her mother's words echoed in her head: "I hope nothing ever happens to Richard, Emmy, but always know that'd you'd make a magnificent queen." The princess had nothing to say.

She had left the hospital before they whisked her brother's body away, before two time travelers came out of curiosity, and before the world learned of their leader's death. She waited at home, confused and gripped by grief. She had not been born to be queen; she was supposed to be the advocate of the people, appear at charity events, and champion environmental causes.

And her brother was supposed to be king, but she would never see him again. And now, after she couldn't bear the wake, she sat alone and turned on her music box, which played Pachelbel's *Canon in D major*. A little ballerina spun above a mirror of glass, moving by magnetism, dancing to the tinkling tune.

She heard a noise behind her, and turned. Lt. Kira Watson stood in the doorway of her boudoir.

Emily stood up. "Come to ship me off to my guardian, lieutenant?"

"No. I'm still thinking about my choice."

"And...?"

"In the meantime, you can stay at the palace. I'll need to be informed if you wish to leave."

"So I'm a prisoner? My brother hasn't even been buried yet. Can't you give me some peace?"

Kira looked straight at her. "I'm sorry for your loss. I've lost loved ones, but to lose a brother, and so soon after your parents ... I can't even imagine what you're going through."

"Thank you," Emily said stiffly. "I'm glad the captain of Tenokte's secret police has some compassion."

The lieutenant smiled. "You know a lot more than you let on to. I'll find you a family to stay with, somewhere far from here. For two years you can have a normal life, then you can be queen."

"I'm not a child, lieutenant."

"Your Highness, this isn't because of your age. Even if you were 18, we still wouldn't rush a coronation. We'd send you away under protection until we could be sure of your safety. Your brother was just gunned down. Think of the implications."

Emily looked down. "Lieutenant, have you ever seen anyone die?"

"Oh, yes. Do you mean anyone I felt sorry to lose?"

The princess nodded.

"Many. I lost a lot of friends and family members in the epidemic, too many to count. Saw a lot of people nearly die, and that was almost as bad."

"Do you believe we have souls? That death is just another part of life?"

Kira shook her head. "No."

Emily's eyes filled with tears, and she took a sharp breath. "I *do*. How can you go on, thinking that's the end?"

"I don't know. I just think about everyone who needs protecting, and the problem just resolves itself. From now on, you're under my protection. I won't let anyone hurt you. You'll be safe here for now. Expect a decision in the next few days." Lt. Kira Watson headed for the door. Emily tried to look defiant, but silently she was crying.

"And your Majesty?" said Kira. "I really am sorry."

That twilight, Princess Emily Montag walked through the cold halls of the empty palace, sobbing. Both her parents had died when she was young, but that, oddly enough, had been easier to handle. Her brother had stepped in to take care of her, shielding her from the worst of the disaster. He'd guided the entire world as well; her parents died during the falling-sickness epidemic, and everyone had been as frightened as her. Now she felt utterly alone.

Very few things were ever known for sure, but she knew one thing now: she could never speak to her brother again, never hear his laughter, never see him smiling in the sun. No one could protect her.

London Bridge is falling down, my fair lady, she thought.

She was the last of Dimitri Reynolds's descendants, and she had met more than enough politicians to know which ones were deceiving her and which ones could be trusted a little. Lt. Kira Watson meant well, but her promises meant nothing.

All at once, she was the easiest and most desirable target from anyone who wanted the throne. Who could protect her from an attack on her life, when no one had seen her brother's assassination coming?

She walked past the portraits of her forefathers for a long time, but had only the silence of the long hallway for her companion.

5.

Ariel returned to the ship early that evening, while Zoë was out. When Thomas saw her walk in, he brightened and dropped the book he'd been perusing on his e-reader.

"I thought of another question for you," he said. "If time travel exists, how come we never see time travelers all over the place?"

She pulled off her sunglasses and sat down on the sofa. "We stay hidden, only reveal ourselves if necessary. If people recognize someone who's out of their time, they're much more likely to think he's a ghost than a time traveler."

"Okay, so how does your machine really work? I mean, time travel—that's not on the same level as moving a few gears."

She pulled out her pocket watch, then handed it to him. "I'm not sure. I've never broken one open to check. The large clock sets the second, minute and hour; the other dials are for day, month and year."

He examined it. The "day" dial inset was numbered from 1 to 31; it also had a sun and moon on it, with the moon faded and the sun shining. The year read 002507; the month, of course, was JUNE. The copper casing looked a bit tarnished, and the watch's face seemed faded and yellowed, as if it were centuries old. But perhaps that was part of the disguise.

"I can set it instantly by touch," she explained. "It's mildly telepathic. Jude was born in Florence, and he swears he can only see the months in Italian."

"Uh-huh. How do you go over distances?"

"Like I said, traveling through time is, by definition, traveling over a distance. It just lets me appear in the right place." She looked at his e-reader. "What are you reading?"

"*Cat's Cradle*, by Kurt Vonnegut."

"Really? I've been wanting to meet him."

"Most people just plan vacations," he said dryly.

She shrugged. "I'll be right back." She got up and walked over into the kitchen.

Thomas glanced over at the tinted sunglasses she'd left on a table. What were those for, anyway? Probably just a fashion in her time.

He walked over and picked up the glasses, turning them over in the light. Partially reflective. Completely flat lenses. Feeling curious, he slipped them on.

He blinked and saw the room around him filtered in a lime green. Then with a click, he felt like a storm rushed into his head through his eyes.

The room evaporated into shades of blue and red lines, with information feeding into his brain. Temperature and the contents of the air. He could see his hands in front of him, and then the bones and veins and muscles under the skin; he could see under objects and behind them.

And the sound! He heard voices and music so loud that a concert might as well be blasting in his ears. He closed his eyes; darkness and silence. Then he opened them, and he could see individual electric charges and feel the turn of the earth and the pull of the sun. Then he started to see things he knew he could not have experienced; he saw flashes of beaches, of buildings destroyed by his time, and of a young Dimitri Reynolds—

A moment later he was lying on the floor, staring at the metal framework of the ceiling. Ariel stood over him, the glasses in her hand.

"Green isn't your color," she said dryly.

He sat up, gasping, his mind still reeling from the information overload. "What happened?"

"You were screaming. What did you see?"

"Ariel, I could see everything. Images. I could see through walls, through objects. Oh my God, I can't even describe it. I think I could even see your memories."

Ariel sat down, perplexed.

"That was it, all along! You knew what I was dreaming, you 'heard' information you couldn't have—because you were reading minds. And Damien!" His eyes lit up. "He told you he killed the king, but you heard his mind saying 'no'! Ariel, where on earth did you get those?"

She closed her eyes, then leaned her head back. "The year three thousand … where people are telepathic."

"Oh my God," he said. "Tell me Jamie doesn't have those sunglasses."

Ariel averted her eyes.

He ran a hand through his hair. "He could know everything about me."

"Maybe not. Thomas, you have to understand, I never knew those could do that."

"Then why wear them?"

"Good luck charm? I don't know. They look cool. I never got lost while wearing them. But I never saw what you were describing. You really looked through walls? Read my thoughts?"

"Ariel, you were born in 1989. I was born in 2481. Think of how much the human brain has changed in that span of time. Maybe you can get a wisp of it, but I can get the full effect. I can tell if people are lying—"

"No. You can't use them."

"Why not?"

"It's not just because you're a journalist. They're not meant to be here, Thomas. It was overflowing your mind, overloading your nervous system. People in five hundred years will know how to use them. You don't."

"Jamie wears them."

"He didn't have a brain injury."

He stared at her, exasperated. "Ariel, the things I could do! I could read Kira's mind and find out what really happened to me—"

"—and then you'd short-circuit your brain. No. No way."

He glared at her.

They heard a ringing, and Ariel pulled a cell phone out of her pocket. At least, he thought it was a phone: he had never seen anything like it. "Will you excuse me for a moment?" she said, and slipped out to answer it.

Thomas sat back, hearing the murmur of a one-sided conversation in the next room. He was still reeling from the full impact of the glasses when she returned a moment later, her face ashen.

"What is it?" he asked.

"Jude. He … he went missing. Signal's gone dark. I told you the Celestials had started tracking me? Bailey thinks they arrested him."

"So let's go."

"No. Not you." She pulled out her pocket watch. "He was investigating the Celestials four years ago. I can't risk you crossing your time line."

"So what are you going to do? Break him out of prison?"

She slipped on the lime-colored glasses. "You used to work for them. What would they do to a prisoner with information they want, one reluctant to give it up?"

He faltered. "Ariel—"

"He's the reason I'm a time traveler. But Thomas, if I never come back…" She looked at him. "Then I think you'll know what happened."

If she was reading his mind then, she didn't show it. Thomas opened his mouth to tell her to stop, but she was already gone.

Chapter Eight
June 12, 2503

The *Lunitron*, an elegant white ship, completed an orbit around the Earth.

The vessel served as a docking and refueling station for many Celestial ships and probes throughout the solar system. About a hundred soldiers lived on board, monitoring flights or working behind closed doors on projects unknown to civilians.

The ship, under the control of Captain Delacroix, wound down for the night. By midnight, only a skeleton crew worked, most of them monitoring the security systems. The halls lay empty.

Ariel passed through a corridor, her boots clinking on the grated metal floor. The vents hissed as steam appeared, replenishing the area with oxygen, and a blue light glowed by each door.

She slid on an earpiece. "I'm in."

"The prisoners' cells should be right up ahead," came Bailey's voice through the radio com. Ariel couldn't see her, but she imagined Bailey sitting in front of a computer, tense, watching the screen. "They're very well-guarded. Are you sure you want to do this?"

"Absolutely," Ariel whispered. "Nothing's going to stop me."

She crept down the hall, then froze when she heard a sound.

A Proteus repair-bot wheeled through the hall, making a whirring sound as it went. It scanned for life, then moved on.

Ariel slid out of a closet, brushed herself off, then turned to step into the dim hallway.

She found herself face-to-face with a Celestial officer with pale blue eyes. He held a blaster in his left hand.

"Ah, you're very quiet," she said, taking a step back. "Captain Delacroix, is it? Now I see where you got your déjà vu."

The captain raised his blaster.

"One more shot and I'm gone," she warned. "And I think you'd want to hear what I have to say."

Delacroix took a step. "We thought someone would come for him. Who are you? Obviously you have some form of teleporting device."

"Yes, I do. Why did you arrest Jude?"

"Is that your friend's name? He was accessing confidential files about our global security agencies. Tsk, tsk. That's a serious crime."

"Let me talk to him."

"Oh, you'll have a chance to do that."

Two guards slipped into the hall, both armed. Ariel eyed them warily.

"Captain," she said, "you run this starship. The pride of the Federation, yes, but a ship. In one year out of thousands. Do you know how utterly insignificant that makes you? How tiny you are to me? This isn't a war, this isn't an attack, and this isn't a game. He doesn't belong here, and he'll never come back. Let him go."

"Arrest her," said Delacroix.

Ariel pressed the top of the watch and vanished.

Delacroix pulled the ship's main alarm, alerting all guards, and pressed a button on a hallway control panel. "There's an intruder headed for the security cells. Red hair, young. Couldn't have been more than eighteen. I want her found."

He put a hand to his forehead, as if he had a headache, then pressed the button again. "And guard that cell!"

2.

Last-second teleporting, especially when she didn't know where she'd end up, was the worst. Ariel opened her eyes and found herself lying on a grated iron walkway just above the ship's engines. She breathed heavily a moment, dizzy. Now she knew how Thomas felt.

She stood up and looked over the edge of the railing and saw the underbelly of the ship, its engines glowing orange from the oppressive heat.

Her time machine must have been confused, since it didn't have the Earth's magnetism to guide it. She pressed the button at the top of the clock, and in a flash of light, her surroundings morphed until she stood in an empty hallway.

She checked her watch, but its glow was fading, and its ticking had slowed. "No, no," she whispered. A faint alarm blared overhead, and she could hear the clamor of guards running in halls above her.

One door in the hallway was open, and she quickly slipped inside, then closed the door, catching her breath. The copper watch ticked once, then went silent. Ariel put her head against the wall, her eyes scrunched shut. If it didn't start working, she had no way back.

After a moment she looked around. The room contained a wide window, and in the distance she could see a blue-green planet partially covered by white clouds. She walked up to the window and put her hand against the cold glass.

In all her travels, she'd never left that planet. Her watch didn't just take direction from the Earth; it was powered by it. No wonder Jude had been arrested: his watch must have stopped. There was nowhere for him to go.

Ariel tried her radio com. "Bailey, can you hear me?"

No reply; only static.

If only her glasses worked like they did for Thomas, she could get an idea of how to get out of here ... if only she had *brought* Thomas, he would have thought of something by now. She sighed.

The beauty of the planet before her dazzled her, and she didn't hear a set of footfalls behind her.

She tried to think. The device had an auto-recharge, but she didn't know if it would work. If it did, it would recharge in twenty minutes, and after that she had to get planetside quickly, because she didn't know how long it could last.

So she had two options: hide away for twenty minutes, or try to rescue Jude. With her knowledge of the security systems and the general layout of the ship, the second option would be nothing short of suicide.

She glanced down at her watch, which was glowing pitifully. She couldn't leave him.

Ariel turned, but someone grabbed her and put a hand over her mouth before she could scream.

"Don't move," the man urged. Eyes wide, she complied.

"Are you the one they're looking for?" He slid his hand down, freeing her to answer.

"Uh ... yeah, I think I am."

He let her go. When she turned and caught a glimpse of his face, she took a step back, slamming into the glass. Moderately dark complexion, dark hair swept up. But his eyes, brown with flecks of green, hit her with enough force to nearly knock her to her feet.

"Thomas!" she said.

He was twenty-one, still very young, but completely recognizable. He blinked. "How do you know my name?"

"Oh my God, I have to tell you. Get out of the secret police, whatever you do. In a few weeks—" She stopped. "Say something again. Your voice is different."

He put a finger to his lips, and turned. The door was open by a crack, which threw a sharp angle of white light into the room. A Celestial walked by in the hallway outside, his footsteps clinking against the metal floor, but didn't seem to notice the open door.

"Come on," said Thomas. "And don't call me by my name. I'm Agent Nineteen."

She exhaled. "Wow. American accent. Wait—if you're in the secret police, aren't you going to arrest me?"

"The captain's orders are that any invaders on board be arrested, but—"

"But?"

"Someone's authority overrules his." He walked toward the door, and she followed, hesitant. "The prisoner's cells are about ten minutes' walk from here, in Area C. You can use your teleporter to get in, right?"

"It's not working, and how do I know this isn't a trap?"

"You don't. So what's it going to be?"

She squinted. "Are you wearing eyeliner?"

He rolled his eyes, and she jogged up to him.

"Come on." He stepped out into the hall, where four guards stood waiting.

"Good work," said one. "Arrest her."

Thomas's eyes moved to Ariel, but she already knew what to do. She unsheathed her sword and yelled, "Stay back! I'm a dangerous criminal and I've taken this young man hostage! Let me through!"

They still advanced.

"They don't like you very much, huh?" She grabbed Thomas's blaster with her left hand, pushed him aside, then fired four times, before any of them could draw. They all crumpled to the floor.

"You are insane," said Thomas.

"Thank you," Ariel replied. "I've played a lot of video games." She slid her sword into its sheath at her back.

"Don't kill me. Please."

Ariel paused, confused, and then moved her eyes up to the ceiling. A security camera was pointed at them. Of course: she'd taken him hostage, and he was acting the part.

She pulled him into another hallway, out of sight of the cameras. "You're twenty-one, right? What month is it?"

"June."

"June! Always. Thomas, we were meant to meet."

"Sure. Kid, when you get your friend, get out of here. The government wants the technology you have. They'll kill for it."

Ariel thought back. "In your future, agents are trying to arrest me."

"Agents? Really? Huh. Maybe someone corrupts the squad."

"What do you mean?"

"You're Ariel, yes? Our primary goal as the secret police is to protect the people and the monarch," he said. "But one of our duties is also to protect *you.* Long ago, when he founded the first squad, Dimitri Reynolds's son asked us to."

Ariel's eyes widened. "You don't say."

3.

Two guards opened the door to the cell, and Captain Delacroix strode inside. He tossed a file onto the desk and walked up to the prisoner, a young man in his twenties— handsome, dark-haired, and athletic, with gray eyes that glinted like dimes.

The prisoner's hands were bound behind his back and his arms were pulled up, tied to a rope attached to a ceiling. He averted his eyes when he saw the captain approach.

"Name?" said Captain Delacroix, turning his head to a guard, who sat at the table with a computer. The guard shook his head.

"The girl called him 'Jude,'" said Delacroix, thinking. He turned to the prisoner. "You were found with no identification. As a citizen of the Celestial Federation, you are required to give your name to an officer who requests it. Tell me your full name."

The young man simply looked at him.

"I thought you'd be difficult." He made a quick motion to a guard, who pulled a lever. A pulley on the ceiling moved to pull up the rope, until the prisoner was pulled a foot off the ground, screaming.

"Name?"

"No!" the prisoner yelled.

"This doesn't just cause excruciating pain," said Delacroix. "Give it a minute and it'll dislocate your arms."

The prisoner wouldn't speak. Delacroix looked at the guard, who pulled the lever down further. The prisoner was sent another foot off the ground.

"Jude Fawkes!" the prisoner finally shouted. "My name is Jude Fawkes!"

"Good," said Delacroix. The guard pushed the lever in, sending Jude downward. As soon as his shoes scraped the floor, he closed his eyes, breathing heavily.

"The only Jude Fawkes on record was born in Florence, Italy, about ninety years ago," said the guard, after looking up the computer file. "Prisoner's fingerprints and retina scans match. Fawkes disappeared at the age of twenty-four."

Delacroix smiled at the prisoner. "And you don't look a day over twenty-five." He held up the silver timepiece. "How does this little device work?"

"Please," said Jude, his eyes wide. "I can't tell you."

"And why is that?"

"It's broken."

"But you've used it. You used it to come here, all the way from Italy, all the way from another time. How is it there, anyway? I've never been to Florence."

He stared at the captain, breathing hard.

"I'm waiting."

Jude had regained his confidence. "Just kill me," he said. "I'm never going to tell you how to use that."

Delacroix walked over and pulled the lever. The rope pulled Jude into the air, leaving in dangling, crying out, thrashing. The captain watched him blankly.

"They say that someone has come after you, Jude Fawkes. A girl is running around the ship. All of my best soldiers have been dispatched to find her. You see, I don't need to get this information out of you. In a few minutes I can just ask her."

Jude glared at him. He took in a breath, closed his eyes, and stopped screaming.

"If Ariel is here," said Jude, his words punctuated by drawn-out breaths, "then you'd better run."

"Why?"

He started to snicker. "You don't even know, do you?" he whispered.

Delacroix heard a loud boom in the hallway outside. "Aren't those doors sound-proofed?"

The guards looked at him, worried, and he pulled out a radio. "Report."

"Captain," came the crackled response, "she's made it inside the cell block. She's taken someone hostage."

"I don't care. Why hasn't she been stunned?"

"She has—" The com went fuzzy for a moment. "—blaster that shoots lead—" After a loud crack, the transmission cut out.

Delacroix pushed the lever in, and the prisoner's feet touched the floor.

"Not doing so well?" Jude asked.

"If you can hear this message, do not open the door," the Captain radioed. "Do not, under any circumstance—" Another crack. He pulled out his blaster. "I'm going out there."

"Captain—" said the guard.

Delacroix turned, enraged. "Yes, cadet?"

The guard seemed to have changed his mind. "As you wish, sir."

4.

Ariel peered around a corner, observing a hallway that contained a row of several vault-like doors. The prisoners' cells. A few guards stood in the way, but that wasn't much of a problem.

"I get it now," said Ariel. "Jude's the prisoner I'm supposed to get out. He went back in time to stop them from tracking us. But they caught him, and realized we exist. Then they started tracking us."

"What?"

"You'll understand me some day. I think. But the question is, how do I get him out?"

"Isn't your teleporter working yet?"

She glanced down at the watch. "Time machine, and it hasn't recharged yet. About three more minutes should do it." A blast shot from behind came close to them, and she pulled him along. "All right, Agent Nineteen, how do I get in?"

"The guards have ID cards that open the door."

"Right. Okay. Can you just do me one favor? If a girl comes to you in the future, asking you to be her partner, then go! Even if you have to leave behind someone you love, it will save your life." She looked down. "But you probably won't remember that, so it doesn't matter."

Another blast. The Celestial guards were creeping closer.

"Watch out," he said. "The soldiers will shoot on sight."

Ariel pulled out a pistol. "Not if I shoot first." She darted into the hallway with the blaster in her right hand, the pistol in her left. The bullets smashing into the wall and floor frightened the guards long enough for her to hit them with the blaster.

Ariel grabbed a card from one of the unconscious guards' pockets. She slid it into the wall, but nothing happened.

"The guards from inside have to respond to unlock it," yelled Thomas. "Otherwise, you have to wait thirty seconds."

"Why didn't you tell me that before?" she screamed.

"Look out!"

The row of five prisoners' cells lay behind her, and Celestials approached from a hallway to her left and right. The whole area was shaped like a V, and she was trapped. She glanced down at the time piece. Still nothing.

"I give up," she said. "Shoot me."

"With pleasure," said Delacroix, from behind.

Ariel instinctively closed her eyes, but nothing happened. She opened them. The guards were firing at her, but they seemed to be in slow motion; when the sparks neared her, the air seemed to ripple. An invisible force field enveloped her.

She looked down at her faintly-glowing pocket watch, amazed. "It has self-preservation," she murmured. "Electricity can damage it, so it blocks it."

The agent in Pompeii hadn't been missing her. He just couldn't get a shot in.

There was, she saw with a bit of surprise, one trade-off to the protection. Apparently it required a large amount of energy to put up a shield, because her hologram failed. Her clothes blinked back to the style of the 21st century, instead of the all-black military garb she'd been displaying.

No matter. She pocketed the watch and pulled out her pistol, pointing it at Delacroix. "Open the cell. Now."

He didn't move. "How did that blast not affect you? It would take the fight out of anyone. How did your clothes—?"

She tightened her grip on the gun. Delacroix got the message. He put in his card and typed a security override, and the door opened.

"Thank you," said Ariel. She turned to Thomas, gave a quick nod, and slipped inside the room. The door slid closed behind her.

The lights had been turned off, and the room was dimly lit, with computer consoles glowing in one corner. *Looks like one of Di's video games*, she thought.

A guard appeared with a blaster, but she only turned, watching the blast flicker and fade away.

"What—how—" said the soldier.

"Time travel," she replied. She grabbed his arm and shot him with his own weapon; he hit the floor, stunned.

She stepped closer, and the lights flickered on. When they adjusted, her heart nearly hit her mouth.

A young man was standing with his arms pulled up, like a marionette. His head was down. Ariel slipped her pistol into its holster, her watch wrapped around her hand. It was glowing a bright gold, and started to tick.

The prisoner looked up, his eyes widening when he saw her.

"Jude Fawkes," she said. "Just the man I'm looking for."

When Delacroix forced the door open, Ariel and the prisoner were gone.

Chapter Nine
June 17, 2507

Ariel arrived back at the ship that evening, and found a twenty-five-year-old journalist pacing in the ship's lounge.

"Ariel! It's been awhile. Are you all right? Did you find your friend?"

She stared at him for a moment, realizing he had no memory of the incident. "Yes," she said. "Yep. He's fine now. He's at the base with Bailey."

"What's wrong?"

Her voice caught in her throat for a moment. "You don't remember anything about your time in the secret police?"

"Bits and pieces, why?"

"Thomas, I saw you. You were four years younger. You ... told me to call you Agent Nineteen."

He sat down. "You did see me. What did I do?"

"You helped me. Saved my life, really."

She was still stunned by what she was capable of. With Jamie, she had always been a carefree traveler. Now that she had to fight for her life, her strength frightened her. But she was also overwhelmed.

"I was off the planet!" she said, amazed. "*You* were off the planet. God, you don't even like cars! How'd you get into a spaceship?"

"I ... don't remember. Was it the *Lunitron*? They send soldiers up there all the time. Training ops, that sort of thing. Are you sure you're all right, kiddo?"

"I need a minute."

He considered. "Right," he said, grabbing his jacket. "I need to investigate Damien's case. We need to examine the facts, find out what we're facing. Maybe I can get an interview with someone involved with the Council."

"Thomas—"

"You talked to the forensic scientist, right? I'll look up the laws and see what the evidence will do."

"Thomas."

"I also can dig up documentation of other assassinations, and see what happened in—"

"Thomas!"

He turned to her. "What?"

Ariel sat down on the red sofa. "I saw you two minutes ago sounding and acting completely different. I just need a second." After a moment of thought, she added: "Also, I need my 'chill' playlist."

She pulled a little gadget out of her pocket. Based on the earbud headphones, Thomas guessed it was a music player. She turned it on and started listening.

"Is that from your time?" he asked. "I see you don't have wireless technology yet. Are you still on MP3s?"

She sighed. "What's your century on, O great music journalist?"

"Well, we tried a bunch of formats over the years—for some reason everyone really loves vinyl—but we're mostly back to digital. Sound technology hasn't changed too much, but the way we store files has, so the auditory quality's much better. How many songs can you fit on your device?"

"Oh, I don't know. A thousand?"

He shook his head. "You poor kid."

Ariel took off the MP3 player, wound the headphones around it, and tossed it to him. "Here, look it over. Maybe you'll find something interesting."

He poked through the controls. "This is … old." He sat down. "I still can't believe you saw me in the past. Could you go back in time and find out how I got shot?"

"No."

"Why not?"

"I really, really don't want to."

Neither of them really wanted to continue that line of conversation.

"Fine. Right." He paced. "What's our working assumption? That Damien is completely innocent, or that he did kill the king, but for someone else?"

She thought for a minute. "Let's go with completely innocent. His fingerprints weren't on the weapon, and he wasn't wearing gloves. So who killed the king?"

"It would have to be a male with dark hair," said Thomas. "I saw the shooter just for a second."

"How do you know that's what you saw? It was a stormy day, and it was getting dark."

"I saw it," he protested. "Dark hair."

"Anything else?"

"No."

"Then I'll have to go back," she said. "Scene of the crime. I can record video footage."

"Someone already did." He grabbed his laptop and put it on the table, and pressed a key to play a video.

It was a shaky recording from the crowd, and showed the king starting his speech. Then a shot rang out. The camera moved around and jerked up to where the shooter, standing on the balcony, turned away and darted out of sight, as screams sounded from the crowd. It was the first time Ariel had seen the assassination.

"I can't get a good look at him," she murmured. "But they're already pretty set on executing Damien, right? They just need the Council's final verdict."

"Pretty much."

"Ugh. I wish we were back in my time. They'd take years to do a trial, examine evidence, make appeals, everything. None of this summary-execution stuff."

"So what's the plan?"

"The plan is ... I don't have a plan. No, I'll go back in time to the scene, and stand on the balcony."

"You're not there," he said, playing the video again, then pointed. "There!" He paused it. "Just one figure. What kind of rifle is that, anyway?"

"M-16."

"Then I wouldn't barge in on the shooter if I were you."

Ariel sighed and trudged into the kitchen. Jack, the ship's repair-bot, stood by the sink. "I'm sorry, my processors are not acquainted with you. What is your name?"

"Ariel Midori."

A click. "Noted. How are things, Miss Midori?"

"Not good," she said, sitting at the table. "I've been here for, what, how many days? And I'm still no closer to anything than when I arrived."

"Perhaps you should rest," the robot said thoughtfully. "You seem tired."

"Maybe."

She wasn't supposed to be worrying about Damien, anyway. She should have found the lieutenant who was tracking time travelers...

Ariel sat upright. She'd forgotten to take Jude's watch back when she rescued him. Delacroix would still have it. And, going by a global timeline, the next time she appeared would have been to visit...

"Oh my God," said Ariel. "Jamie."

2.

Jamie Parsons hummed to himself as he put away his razor and shaving cream. It was almost seven p.m. on June 17, but the rock star lived by his own schedule.

He splashed his face with water, humming a tune. A new song? Maybe. His head had always held melodies, as far back as he could remember. He wiped his face with a towel, closed the mirror to the medicine cabinet, and then screamed.

Framed in the mirror was the reflection of a red-haired girl. Jamie turned around, gasping. "Don't do that to me," he said.

"Sorry," she said, sheepishly, and glanced down at her watch. "I just set it to find you." She looked up. "How've you been?"

He stumbled into the hallway, and became even more frightened when the girl followed him there. He had messy, jet-black hair, but his face still held the boyish good looks from his days as a rock star.

"You can't exist," he said.

"Jamie, it's me."

"You were in my bathroom. Ghost from the past, *in my bathroom.*"

"I didn't mean to startle you the other day. I got the date wrong, honestly. But, while I'm here, I thought I'd stop by. How long has it been? Six years? A few days for me."

"You're not real. I'm losing my mind."

Ariel put her hands on her hips. "It's *me*. Ariel."

That didn't coax him at all, and she felt a little deflated. Jamie, a great friend and one of the greatest rock musicians of his time, did not even concede to the fact that she existed? Perhaps he just needed a little convincing.

"Jamie, it's me! I'm a time traveler. We both were. Don't you remember?" She leaned down and whispered in his ear, "And yes, I missed you."

That did it. He collapsed into her arms, sobbing. "Ariel! I thought you'd forgotten about me. I couldn't say a word to anyone. I wondered if it all really happened."

Ariel let him weep without any reciprocating action on her part. She was actually quite confused. But it must have been a shock to see her, and Jamie always had a fragile state of mind. She looked down the hall to a case showing his various trophies, which included two Grammys. "You seem successful."

"Oh my God!" He sprung up. "Ariel, when I left, I was just thinking of starting the band. But it's been huge. Songs that topped the charts, legions of fans—"

"I know," she said. "I've always known."

He pondered. "Why are you here, then?"

She pulled a platinum pocket watch out from under her jacket, then held it out for him. "Your old watch."

He didn't move. "I don't want it."

She took his hand and put the watch in it, then closed his hand over it. "I need you to take it. I've got secret police on the lookout for me. If anything happens, you have to help Thomas and Zoe." She stepped back.

He seemed confused. "Why? What's going to happen?" He took a step closer. "You, uh, you know what's supposed to happen to *me*, right?"

"Jamie—"

"Forget it," he said, with a wave of his hand. "Why did it take you so long to come for me?"

"I tried to set the watch for 2501, but I must've messed up. And now people are tracking me, and if I can't figure out how to stop it, it'll be the end of the Saturnine Order."

"Well, maybe that's a good thing."

"What do you mean?"

"Stay in there too long, and Bailey's going to get you killed. How is that fearless leader, by the way? And Jude, is he still there?"

She turned away. "Fine. Anything else you want to warn me about? Watch out for falling meteors? Oh God, have sharks learned to live on land?!"

"Seriously, Airy. I worried about you. I thought you were dead."

"Well, you wanted it that way. Told me not to contact you."

"I nearly lost my mind thinking about you."

The TV flickered on in the next room, announcing the seven o'clock news. The distant murmurs of newscasters' voices wafted into the hall. Jamie stared at her.

"You lost your mind long before you met me," said Ariel.

"And you haven't changed a bit." He shook his head. "Six years of my life, and for you it's only been days? I can't even wrap my mind around that."

Ariel heard a familiar voice in the background, and she walked over to the living room. The flat TV screen showed a segment filmed the previous week. A familiar young reporter was speaking. He had dark hair, a standard British newscaster's accent, and bored eyes.

Brown eyes flecked with green.

They only needed to track her once, because they knew exactly who she'd go to.

"So, Thomas Huxley," Jamie remarked, strolling in. "Is he my replacement?"

"No. He's—" She turned, then took a step back. Jamie had put on a pair of gray sunglasses.

"What's wrong?"

She turned back to the screen. "Nothing. Thomas and I are going to leave before the Flyday's over. I need you to look after Zoë."

"You know I can't," he said, his jaw set.

Ariel glanced at him, tossing her red hair over her shoulder. "Then you're right, Jamie. I haven't changed at all. But neither have you."

"You're not going to try to stop me?"

"I tried a long time ago," she said. "Whatever you do now, it's up to you."

She turned and walked out the door. Jamie's eyes followed her as she went, but he made no move to make her stay.

3.

June 18, 2507

Thomas emptied out all of his suitcases, fearing he left the card back at his apartment in London. For years he had kept it under a false bottom of a drawer so any curious occasional visitors would not see it. Then he hid it in his bookshelf, until one day when it slipped out of sight.

Just when he nearly despaired of finding it, he opened up a wire-bound notebook and it slid out: A white card with the number 19 written in silver ink. (At a certain angle, the card looked blank.) He grabbed it and walked down the streets of Tenokte, then the side streets, until he found a small, dilapidated brick building on a deserted road. WHITTIER COMMUNICATIONS, INC., said the fading sign. He pushed open the creaky door and walked inside.

The next door was locked, but he spotted a staircase and, on a whim, went down it. When he pushed open the door, his surroundings looked vaguely familiar. The room seemed like a waiting area for a medical office. He walked up to the wood paneling on one wall, then put his ear to it. From the other side, he could hear a humming.

A computerized voice sounded: "Please show your identification."

He noticed a card slot in the wall, thanks to a little green light blinking by it. On a whim, he slid his white ID through it. He heard a click as something scanned the card, and the panel shifted. A security camera appeared, and he jumped back. The robotic parts seemed unperturbed, and it stretched two feet out of the wall until it reached his eye, flashed a blue light, and, satisfied, retreated back into the wall. Retina scan. A doorway appeared as some of the paneling swung inside, revealing a passageway.

The tunnel was dim, and had the sound of humming, louder now, but with no visible machinery to make the noise. Then he stepped into a wide, bright room with hundreds of flat computer panels covering the walls: security footage for every inch of the city. He looked up at the flickering images, amazed.

The square room had tables attached to the walls, and thirty swivel chairs. One man with light hair sat looking at the screens, then swung around, bored, until he recognized the journalist standing by the door. He jumped to his feet.

"Huxley! What are you doing here?"

Thomas still had his messenger bag slung over a shoulder, and probably looked as lost as he felt. "Uh—"

"Nevermind. I'm Agent Five, John Caxton. Do you remember me?"

"No."

"Ah, well, that's probably a given. You're in the headquarters of the Tenokte secret police squad."

Thomas nodded. "Right. Uh-huh. What's this for?" He held up the white card.

"That's your ID." Caxton returned to the computer screen, where he was inputting information.

"Right. But I'm not *in* the secret police."

Caxton looked up. "You were."

At Thomas's puzzled expression, the agent smiled. "You were Agent Nineteen. They told me you didn't remember anything. Bullet through the head ... partial amnesia ... old news. So, have you seen her?" Caxton asked eagerly. "The red-haired girl, I mean."

The journalist looked at him for a moment. With the squad looking for Ariel, he wasn't about to give her up. "Lt. Kira Watson asked me the same thing. Who is she?"

"Ah," said Caxton. "She's our anomaly. Jumps in and out of events. Usually shows up right before people die."

"Why are you looking for her?"

"Curiosity. Border protection. If there are people with advanced technology out there, or just people slipping through our surveillance, we want to find them."

Surveillance, indeed. They certainly had enough cameras. "What do you do here?"

"Everything and anything. The Celestial patrols do their own thing, but we run a lot of projects. Lately we've been trying to root out this rebel group called the Red Army. Ever hear of 'em?"

Thomas shook his head.

"Of course not. We killed most of them." He sat back in the swivel chair. "But we do other things, too."

"Uh-huh. So all the people who disappear ... this is where they go." Thomas took a step, looking out at all the screens. They flickered to show different locations. Some were out, fuzzy with digital snow, but seconds later they blinked and the screens were replaced by sharp, clear video footage. He could see a park, the inside of restaurants, views of residential streets. And he realized that each screen had a microphone; the secret police could turn it on and listen to conversations. Spooky.

"Does any of this look familiar?" Caxton asked.

"No." He looked up. "And I have to know. If I worked here, what did I do? I was a reporter. I had so many contacts …"

"I don't know. I think you were a detective. You just helped in any investigations your partner worked on."

"My partner?"

"Yeah, Agent Six. He's still around. Doesn't want to see you, though. That's why you got sent to Montréal for a few months, before your injury."

He looked at all the screens. His life was starting to make a bit more sense. "How many people know about me?"

"Everyone who worked here at the time. We were torn up over what happened to you."

"Would anyone be upset if I tried solving one more case?"

"Huxley? Last I saw, you're still a full agent. Knock yourself out."

4.

An hour later, Ariel saw Thomas walking down the street. Gray coat, upturned collar. Dark hair, messy but carefully casual. Messenger bag … could he get any geekier? Up above him were all silver skyscrapers and cars soaring through the slats of blue sky.

"You all right?" she asked.

"Better than that. Brilliant."

Ariel looked at him critically.

"I got a break in Damien's case, kiddo. I had to flip through about a thousand files before I found it. More video footage of the assassination."

"Better than the amateur one, I'm guessing?"

"Yes. You can see the shooter." He held up the flash drive. "I didn't tell them yet, because I want to make a copy of it. I have, in my hand, the proof of who shot the king. Do you really want to see it?"

"Of course! Why wouldn't I?"

He stared at her. "You probably won't believe it. And it doesn't exactly make the case against Damien any easier."

"Why not?"

He bit his lip.

Ariel considered, disheartened. "*Is* it Damien? If the secret police had proof of the real assassin, they wouldn't execute the wrong guy."

"Not quite. I'm guessing they just didn't see this. So many cameras ... one file could've slipped through the cracks."

"Okay, fine, tell me."

He told her, and she wished he hadn't.

5.

October, 2007

On a day long before she met an inquisitive journalist, seventeen-year-old Ariel Reynolds couldn't sleep. She tossed and turned, listening to the rain fall gently on her window, and ended up leaving for school about half an hour earlier than usual. She drove through the sloshing roads and before long she found herself sitting in the drenched parking lot, leaving her car running for the heat, listening to the radio.

There was nobody else there, but after about ten minutes, more cars came, and soon a light flickered on in the school. Ariel turned off the ignition and opened her door.

She trekked with her head down toward the stone steps, her jacket pulled tight to keep out the drizzle of rain, which seemed more cold mist than water. Another car pulled up to the entrance just as she reached the steps, and when a door cracked open, Ariel heard the audio lingo of her favorite radio station, and then the opening notes to a song. Then the door was slammed shut, and the car drove away.

She hurried along due to the rain, but still got soaked. When she finally reached the door, a young man stood in front of it.

"Hi," she said, and tried to walk past him, but he didn't move.

"That was your favorite song," he pointed out.

She stared at him, perplexed. He didn't go to her school; in fact, his clothes were cut in such a strange way, he didn't look like he was in the right country.

" 'Losing My Religion' is really popular," she said, trying to brush past him.

"If you had stayed in your car another minute, or left for school a minute later, you would have heard it. If you could go back in time, would you have changed what you did?"

"Maybe."

"But everything happens for a reason, doesn't it?"

She blinked, and realized that everything around her had frozen. No, not frozen; *stopped.* Rain droplets stood still in the air, defying gravity. Ariel reached out and touched one; it clung to her finger. She gasped and turned. A car that had pulled into the lot wasn't moving; its occupants, too, seemed immobile. The wind that had been gusting not a moment before was nonexistent.

"What did you do?" she asked.

"You're Ariel Reynolds, yes? I have something to ask you."

She turned and ran to the school, but the door was still locked. She pounded on it.

"They can't hear you," said the man. "I didn't mean to scare you, but I'm a time traveler."

"Sure," said Ariel, and she pulled away from the door to face him. The droplets were just standing there, like a three-dimensional photo. "It's a bit too early in the morning for me to be going insane."

"You see things no one else does. Another person who missed her favorite song might think of it as an unfortunate coincidence. You see something deeper. But you also have other skills. You've studied history, languages."

"So?"

"My name is Jude Fawkes. I want you to travel with me. Think about this for a few hours, and I'll come back to you. And ... here's a parting gift." He handed her a rolled-up newspaper in an orange plastic bag.

"Uh ... thanks," she said.

"Read it. I think you'll find it fascinating."

She blinked, and the rain pounded down again in a torrent, and the car zoomed away from the school, and the man was gone. Ariel stood there a moment, stunned. She pulled out the newspaper and skimmed the headlines. It was the paper her mother read every morning, she was sure of it, only it was dated for the next day.

Chapter Ten
June 18, 2507

Thomas, guided by a servant, walked into the enormous throne room of the palace. The roof was domed, the walls a creamy tan and ornately painted, the floors marble. This room served as a hall for entertaining guests, as well as a place for the monarch to call meetings or press conferences. At the end were two golden thrones, and beyond them were two wide staircases that curved inward and upward. Thomas moved up the left one, keeping one hand on the banister, and walked into a hallway.

"The princess will be here in a moment," said the servant, a pretty young woman wearing a pink dress.

"Thank you," he said, and the maid bowed and slipped away.

He would have to show the tape of the assassination to Kira. But how would he explain the identity of the shooter without giving Ariel away? At the moment, though, he had a different worry—his editor had asked him to interview the princess. And why not? Right now, everyone in the world wanted to know what was on her mind.

Thomas turned, then gazed at a long row of paintings on the wall: oils on canvas from the Renaissance. Some of them were astoundingly well-known and expensive: he saw the original of the *Mona Lisa* among them. Royalty, indeed. And in many of the pictures, he couldn't help but notice, the subjects were nude. He stopped at one, of a young man reclining on a sofa, when a voice made him turn.

"Ah, the gallery," said Princess Emily Montag, walking into the hallway. She wore a white gown with a saffron-red veil over her light hair. "They always make taking official photographs in this hallway difficult ... to say the least. My mom was always trying to sell them off, but my grandmother, more of a bohemian, always took a liking to them."

"I was just looking at the frame," Thomas said quickly. "It's, uh, a nice frame."

She smiled, charmed. "Who are you?"

"Thomas Huxley," he said, sticking out his hand. Then, thinking better of it (especially when the princess blinked, perplexed), he pulled it back. "I'm a journalist. Lt. Watson said I could—"

"The lieutenant! Man, I could've guessed. You do look familiar. You're on that news show, right? Your voice sounds different."

"Yeah ... happens when I'm in back home, I guess." He turned, looking at the paintings. "Your grandmother must have been something, your Highness."

"Mm," she said. "Reinette Deschaine, crowned queen at twenty-one. Her brother was Rémy, the great pianist ... and the musical talent has continued along in his family, I see." (Thomas, understanding none of this, nodded.) She turned, walking away from the historic paintings, toward the family portraits. "My grandfather died when I was a baby, and after that, Grandmama didn't have much drive to rule. She gave up the throne at sixty-five. My dad was forty-four; I was two. But she was always around, making sure we were presentable. And always at odds with my mother."

"And then..."

"She got sick," she said, her eyes misting up. "Wasn't long after that when my parents and uncle died, too. Car crash—isn't it always? Richard was nineteen, away at a university. I was at home, too young to be at royal balls. Only one to survive. Always the only one." She shook her head, then turned to him. "Are you taking notes?"

He did, in fact, have a notebook in his messenger bag, the strap of which he clutched, uncomfortable. "I didn't mean to—"

"But that's why you're here, isn't it? Capture the grief of the young princess. Historical record. Of course." She blinked back tears.

Thomas took her hand, guiding her to two chairs. Fortunately, there was a box of tissues nearby.

"Why would someone want to kill him?" she said, crying. "He was all I had in the entire world."

"I'm sorry. I've lost friends. It's not easy, and I couldn't imagine losing a sibling."

She nodded, dabbing her eyes with the tissues, ands she didn't even notice the notebook come out. She just kept talking, and Thomas, a faithful scribe, wrote.

Was there a reason why he always got the best interviews out of subjects no one else would touch? Why editors usually sent him to interview self-absorbed rock stars, until he was a guest host for a popular news show's music segment? Maybe. He didn't push questions. Didn't ask for the spelling of a name and title. (He usually called later to confirm it, which was a good segue into follow-up questions.) He didn't say, "Tell me more about that" or give a stiff "I see." He just shut up, and by doing so let people know he genuinely wanted to know what they thought. People were either quotable or they weren't.

And in the matter of being an accused assassin's sister's fiancé? It made no difference. The two were not subject and princess, but reporter and interviewee; except for the title "Her Royal Highness, Crown Princess" Thomas would stick in front of the girl's name in the article, he had completely forgotten she was the only heir to a vitally important throne. For a few moments, she was just a victim of a tragedy.

He stayed longer than he thought he would. When he walked out, he hoped he was in the clear, but another woman wasn't through with him. Lt. Kira Watson leaned against the glassy front doors of the palace.

"How'd it go?"

"Good."

The lieutenant pointed to an earpiece, winking. "So I heard."

Thomas shook his head. "Should've guessed."

"Just a matter of habit. I'm looking after her for now," said Kira, stepping toward him. Her heels clicked on the brick patio. "I need to find her a guardian, and I have one in mind. Emily does have relatives, you know. Just not ones descended from Dimitri Reynolds."

"I don't think I've heard of them."

"No? They're famous, just not in the way you think." She peered up at the sun, shielding her eyes against the glow with her hand. "All in good time, Thomas. Any visits from a red-haired girl?"

He thought of Ariel, and of the tape. "Nothing so far. I'll keep you posted."

Kira nodded, then strolled away. She'd scored him the interview, but not without a price: she'd want something. And when she did, he would know.

Thomas walked to the gates, pulling out his notebook. He looked at Emily's responses: direct, confident, royal. The perfect balance of emotion and reality. Her brother, though a compassionate monarch, had always locked himself in his room at the thought of a press conference, and left interviewing for his publicists. Emily didn't seem afraid of anything, except what she faced now: being alone.

2.

Ariel slipped into Dr. Taber's lab. "You rang?"

"Wow, you're fast. Well, it's the strangest thing," he said. "I ran the test, and the fingerprint seems new, made recently. It's a perfect match to only one person."

"So … ?"

"The man it belongs to went missing almost a century ago. He would've been twenty-four when he disappeared. I doubt he's still running from police and assassinating people."

"But … didn't you say it was a fragment? So maybe it was damaged somehow. Not a perfect match."

"No, it had a lot of points of similarity, and no differences. I'd say it was a perfect match."

Ariel sat down. "You don't say."

He sighed. "It's probably just an old print. Or maybe a computer-database error."

"What did you say the name was?"

"Jude Fawkes, from Florence, Italy. But like I said, the strangest thing. —Are you all right, kid? You look a bit pale."

"Fine," said Ariel, staring past him. So Thomas had been right after all. "You know what? I feel absolutely fine."

3.

When Thomas finished writing up the article, it was early afternoon. He sent it to his editor, then closed his laptop. And he realized that with Ariel's help, he could give the tape to Kira that night; all they needed was the real assassin in custody. Damien would be released, and Zoë would be happy again. They could go back to London. He left a message on Ariel's phone telling her what he needed (it was linked to her watch, and thus would reach her in the proper time delay, no matter where she was in history).

When Zoë returned to the ship just before dinnertime, after a visit to her brother, he realized she needed more cheering up than he alone could provide. She reluctantly agreed to attend a party thrown by some of his friends from college.

When they arrived, everyone toasted Thomas for his successful career, toasted a second time for his and Zoë's engagement, and as the night went on people started toasting for reasons that made no sense at all. But no one mentioned the looming execution of a young musician, which was a relief.

Thomas, always the wallflower, excused himself from the center of the party after a few glasses of champagne, and in the dim light watched the antics of the party unfold. Then he realized Zoë was not beside him.

"Hey," said a girl, sidling up to him. "Do I know you? You look familiar."

"Most likely. I'm a reporter."

"Yes! On the morning show. I wanted to ask you—"

"I really need to go," he said, and slipped away. He walked past the speakers, which were blasting rock music, went past the table of drinks, and went out to the balcony, which had been covered in patriotic white and sky-blue ribbons for the Flyday festivities.

Zoë was leaning over the edge, looking out at the crescent moon. Thomas realized that his necktie had been tied around his head like a bandana, and he slipped it off.

"Beautiful night," he remarked.

"Maybe."

"What's wrong?"

She turned around. "It's despicable, what they're doing. How can they have a party, after everything that's happened?

How can they play Pathways songs, when Damien could be killed?"

Thomas stared at her, realizing her point. "Zo, everything's going to be all right. I've got a plan—"

"The king died, Thomas. Damien's about to die, and they're—they're *celebrating*!"

"Then let's leave," he said quickly.

"Fine. You'd probably rather be with Ariel anyway."

He stared at her.

"What? You didn't think I knew? Staying out all night, and showing up with her? A girl can take a hint, Thomas."

"It's not like that."

"Then who is she?"

"An investigator on Damien's case."

"Then why is she always talking to you, and not to me?"

His voice caught in his throat. Her blue eyes sparkled in the decorative lights above the balcony, and she waited for an answer.

A few drinks ago, a few conversations ago, Thomas would have realized that something like this was a natural consequence of the assassination. But now he felt too shocked to comprehend it. The words that had once seemed clear and rational did not come together.

Music, filled with twanging notes and a mournful voice, faintly filled the air. Inside the house, they were playing "Dame de la Pluie." Lady of the Rain. Someone must have realized that this was a night for broken hearts.

"Zoë, whatever you think, it's not what's happening."

"Fine. If I'm just misunderstanding something, then by all means, explain."

"I love you. You know that."

"Tell me who she is. Please."

How many people had he loved before Zoë? Too many to count. And now it suddenly felt that he had never been alive until the moment he met her. She deserved the truth, no matter how unlikely it seemed.

"Ariel's a time traveler. I know it sounds crazy, but she has a time machine and everything. She needed help with something, and she came to me. That's all."

"You're drunk." She looked down at the skyline, her eyes watery. "I read your article. Very well-written. The princess, huh? No one gets an interview with her. And if it isn't enough that Damien killed the king, he made a girl cry."

"Zoë—"

"Your parents were right, Thomas. We really don't know each other. Go back to the hotel; talk to the press about what a horrible person Damien is. You're good at that." She slipped back into the party.

"Zoë!" he yelled. He tried to find her, but in the pulsing lights, couldn't see her. People tried to stop him and ask what was wrong, but he didn't pay attention to them; finally he made it out onto the street, breathless, but he was alone.

He could still hear the music and laughter from the party, and the last notes of Jamie's song. And suddenly he hated them all, every single one, especially himself, and knew that Zoë had been right. She'd been right about everything.

Thomas looked up at the sky, at the twinkling stars. Only when he went to wipe his eyes did he realize that he'd been crying.

Ariel flipped the page. She stood under a streetlight on a long, winding road on the edge of the city, and was reading the file Bailey had given her just a few days ago. She squinted to see the words in the dim light, and heard someone approaching from the end of the street. She slipped her watch in her pocket.

"You were right," she called.

Thomas Huxley stopped, then jogged over to her, still heartbroken from his argument with Zoë. "I'm always right. But now we need to catch that assassin and turn him in to the Celestials; lead him into a trap or something."

"Sure. Fine." She flipped the page.

"Ariel, a man's life depends on this. My relationship with *Zoë* depends on this."

"I know, I know. I'm just not used to turning in friends of mine."

"Homicidal friends," he pointed out.

"Yes, but—why on earth would Jude kill somebody? Why would he kill a world leader? It doesn't make any sense. He knows not to mess with history like that. Unless—"

"I don't know, kiddo. But as it stands now, an innocent man is going to die for that crime. And Zoë won't even talk to me."

"Right," she said. "So after we sort this out, you'll need to get away for awhile. Where should we go? I've always wanted to meet Napoleon."

"I'm not coming."

She blinked. "What do you mean?"

"I need to figure things out. I love Zoë, always have."

Ariel drew the folder closer to her, and he stared at it for a second. He remembered seeing that folder in her mind.

"What's that?" he asked, coming closer.

"Nothing."

"Let me read it."

"No!"

He grabbed for it, and one page fell out. Before Ariel could pick it up, he snatched it.

"You researched my life before you came to me," he said. "Found out everything I did, everything I liked. Didn't you?"

"Do *not* read that! I'm begging you."

His eyes fell to the bottom of the last page, and he froze. He looked up at her, then with a shaking voice he read it out loud:

Thomas Huxley was found dead on June 21, 2507, from two gunshot wounds. He left behind his parents, a sister, his fiancée, and a daughter, born eight months later.

Neither of them spoke for a moment.

"I see," he said. "You only visit people who are about to die."

She was nearly in tears. "I'm not even sure if it's true. But Thomas, you can come with me and travel for as long as you want. Years and years."

He looked down. "I won't see my daughter. I didn't even know I'd have one."

"I never knew my father."

"Don't. Don't even start. You have no idea what this is like!" He crumpled the paper and tossed it onto the ground.

"Fine. I'll turn Jude in. I'll do it before you can even blink. Just promise you'll come with me." She pulled out the copper watch.

"Ariel—" he said, but as soon as he spoke, he found himself alone.

Chapter Eleven

When Damien Martínez turned eighteen, he went looking for a singer.

He had been playing music with his best friend Kyle Jones since they were children, and during his long stays overseas with his diplomat father, he'd e-mail videos of his work to Kyle. Now that he'd graduated high school, he wanted to form a band. All they needed was a vocalist, but they had no idea who to ask.

One day on the street, Kyle was sitting in an idling car, waiting for his tardy companion. Then he heard a song—faintly, as if from another car radio. A dreamy, sad song, with great vocals. It wasn't quite *amazing*, just different. And it was exactly what he and Damien needed. Kyle stepped outside, but the car must have flown away, because he never found it.

A few days later, Damien stepped into a restaurant just as the song slipped out its closing lyrics, but no one there seemed to know who played it or even what the lyrics were. He called up radio stations, where people were equally confused.

"A song in French ... but the singer has an Australian accent?"

"Well," said Damien, "some of the lyrics are in French, but some are in English."

"Uh-huh. No idea. Want to hear 'Hey Jude' instead?"

At night they attended shows and critiqued the various singers, but they couldn't find one who matched their style. In the meantime, Damien worked as an EMT, and Kyle pretended to pack for college (he told his parents he'd been accepted to Harvard, where they had both graduated, but he hadn't even applied). As the weeks spun out, they thought they'd never find the song they were chasing.

When they recounted this to Zoë, she instantly named the track: "Dame de la Pluie" (or "Lady of the Rain"), by Jamie Parsons.

"He used to live in Sydney, but he moved to Tenokte when he was a teenager," she said. "The song's a big hit."

"Ah," said Damien, disappointed. He sounded famous. A famous vocalist wouldn't want to sing for a garage band.

"Tell you what," said Zoë. "Why don't you two stop by the café tomorrow? They have live music there. Maybe you'll find someone you like. It's good karma to support other musicians. After ten in the morning, the place is deserted."

The next day at 10:15, a steamy day in August, they walked into the café where Zoë worked. They were awestruck: in one corner, they saw a dark-haired young man performing the song with the French lyrics and the haunting melody.

Jamie was not famous: far from it. A local DJ had liked his song and played it nonstop all summer, but no one outside the area had heard it. And as he sang the song that had been everywhere for them, the pair knew they had found their vocalist.

They waited until they could speak to Zoë before they made their decision. When she reached their table, wearing a maroon apron and with her wavy hair pinned up, she still looked very much like a child, but already had the cool maturity and inner compass that would carry her far in life. She had arranged the encounter: Jamie stopped by the café once a week. The barista gave a bemused smile when she saw the looks of awe on the pair's faces.

"What do you think?" Damien asked.

Zoë put down two lattes and glanced over at Jamie, then moved her eyes back to the boys. "Ask him."

The next day the pair took him out for lunch, and when he recommended the name Biochemical Pathways, they knew they had a band. When they re-recorded his song and released it with a few new pieces Damien and Kyle had written, the album became a hit worldwide, and set records for downloads.

They still didn't have much money, as bands made most of their revenue from touring; Damien was still relying on his father's fortune to keep the band going. So Zoë, who had her pilot's license, signed the paperwork to leave high school, and went back her house to pack.

"So let me get this straight," said Milton Apollo, standing in her father's kitchen. "You were going to be salutatorian of your class, and you dropped out on a whim to be a rock band's chauffer?"

"Pretty much," she said.

"Word of advice? Run."

And run she did; but it wasn't hard to track down a groupie for a rock band. In Detroit, where Pathways were playing one of their first shows, the police briefly detained her. Her father had reported her as a runaway.

The three band members waited with her at the police station that night. When the diplomat arrived, there was a meltdown.

"Zo, what were you thinking? You can't run off like that. You need to finish school."

"I want to stay with the band."

"You're seventeen. This isn't even a matter of what you want."

"Dad, she's with me," said Damien. "She's fine."

"She's *not* fine. She needs to finish school. Unlike some people, she didn't eke by on straight D's."

"Mr. Martinez—"

"Kyle, this isn't about you. An underage girl can't hang out with a rock band."

"Mm," said Jamie, thinking of the diplomat's constant legal woes. "You'd know about those underage girls, huh? Though I heard your latest girlfriend was eighteen. Congrats!"

Police action was needed to restrain the diplomat, but in the end, Zoë stayed with Biochemical Pathways.

And the album took off. A few months after the first album's release, they were nominated for a Grammy. Kyle looked up the charts; "Dame de la Pluie" was #1 for six weeks straight.

"You were right, Zo," Kyle said. "My God, were you right."

One stormy day a few years later, Kyle and Zoë stood on a street in Paris, hoping to flag a taxi. The band was recording their fourth album, which was nearly finished.

"How can any of the drivers *see*?" said Zoë, staring at the torrent of rain.

"Come on," said Kyle. "We'll be fine."

Still, she decided to wait for her brother, and she saw Kyle off. In the end, she finally walked to her hotel in the rain.

Twenty minutes later, Damien called to tell her that there had been an accident. When she arrived at the hospital, paramedics told her that Kyle had not survived.

It hit her even harder than her mother's death, because she thought that if she had only talked him into waiting ... if only...

In the rainstorm, a driver did not see the signal change from green to red, and crashed into the taxi. The bassist had still been alive when paramedics arrived at the tangled mess of metal, where he was screaming his girlfriend's name; he still had a pulse when they put him onto the stretcher. But before a minute passed after the ambulance doors closed, he slipped away.

Thousands attended the funeral, but only Jamie, Damien, Zoë, and Kyle's parents, girlfriend Haleigh Melo, and young son were allowed at the grave. Zoë's heart went out to the toddler, who had his father's light gold hair.

The first question on everyone's mind was whether or not the band would continue. Jamie, normally the center of attention, withdrew from the cameras and did not want to make a statement. Damien, convinced he had caused his friend's death, was similarly mute. So they told Zoë what they wanted, and she went to the press.

Zoë arrived at the London morning show's studio at five in the morning, two hours before filming, just as she'd been scheduled. It was June 25, three days after the death. While backstage and waiting for the show to start, she couldn't help but smile when she saw an attendant fumbling to tie a reporter's necktie.

"Allow me," she said, stepping in. "I have an older brother." In a few quick twists, it was done.

"Thanks," said the journalist, a bit embarrassed. "I'm sorry for your loss."

She paused. "Thank you. I appreciate it."

When she later sat down on the set, she was surprised to see him sitting opposite her to conduct the interview. She answered the questions quietly, and said that no, the band would not continue. Biochemical Pathways had ended. Jamie would try a solo career, and Damien was taking time off to think about his future.

Later, in the break room, she watched the interview go on the air, and the journalist approached her.

"You did a good job with this tie," he said, glancing down. "It's perfect."

"You've never learned to tie one?"

"I did, but I can't function on mornings when I'm going on the air."

"Nerves?"

"Sometimes." He put his hands in his pockets. "I really am sorry. I always liked that band."

"Thank you," she said. "I've seen you on the show sometimes. You're ... Thomas Huxley?"

A nod. "It seems we already know each other."

Throughout their romance they felt something else moving them, making them feverish and dazed. The world went on with its smoke and drudgery, while they floated in a bubble, protected. They were deliriously happy and totally sure of themselves, when neither of them had ever been sure of anything before.

Zoë had put the brakes on the relationship at first, and turned Thomas down for two weeks, thinking it wasn't appropriate to date so soon after the tragedy. She would have gone on longer, but she realized she had thought of him at least once every day, and then finally called him. From then on they had only one life, each other.

In an era when paper was nearly obsolete, they sent each other handwritten letters, often coded with inventive lettering that the other always deciphered within seconds, as if they had the same mind. They realized that they were both quiet and private people, but Zoë compensated with a sunny personality and Thomas with his intellect and curiosity. He was born in the autumn, and she in the spring; he loved spicy foods, she preferred sweet; he always kept his feet firmly on the ground, and she loved to fly.

Both had their secrets, too: Zoë out of sadness and Thomas out of necessity. When Zoë was thirteen, after her mother had died suddenly, she packed a suitcase and boarded a plane to live with her diplomat father and the older brother she barely knew. Her father traveled as part of his job and vacationed often, so she seemed caught in a whirlwind and could never quite form a home, just long series of trips.

As far as she knew, Thomas's childhood and young life had been uneventful. Zoë knew he had a younger sister, and knew he studied journalism at the Tenokte Academy, a well-known college, but there was something else, something missing. She could feel it like a tear in a piece of cloth, but she could not identify it, so for a time she simply let it go.

During the summer's worst heat wave, when they had been dating about a month, they ran into a problem. Or, rather, Thomas did. He practically wilted in hot weather, and one day the temperature hit 102 degrees. The world seemed set on fire, and before long the city's electricity finally burned out. "Too many air conditioners," Zoë said, sighing.

He walked back from the studio at 4 p.m., heading for the cool subway, and saw the world bend and twist around him. He collapsed. Two kind souls dragged him under the shade of a tree, one of the few cures for the burning air, and poured cold water on him. When he awoke, they handed him a cup of an electrolyte drink.

"You don't look so good," said one of the strangers. "Must be heat stroke."

"No, worse than that," said Thomas, delirious. "I'm in love."

They gave him a ride home. He thanked them when they dropped him off and he tried to remember their names, but he barely made a phone call to Zoë before he blacked out again.

When he awoke, he felt chilled to the bone. He was lying on the floor with a wet cloth over his forehead, and a wet towel over his chest.

Zoë stood over him, and asked him questions: his name, the year. When he answered, she said, "Well, it's probably not the falling-sickness."

"Did I pass out?" he asked.

"I think so. How do you feel?"

"Dead," he replied. He sat up, and the towel slipped away, revealing a crisscross of thin scars on his chest. He pulled up the towel again, but Zoë acted as if she hadn't seen it. She handed him a cup of a flavored electrolyte drink.

He realized he had never seen ... well, he would have to wait. She was Catholic, and her modesty could not be surpassed: she thought doctors should perform open-heart surgery with the patient's clothes still on.

All around him in the city, people were cooling themselves with paper fans and still mourning a dead bass player. Zoë believed there was an afterlife for Kyle, one where the instruments were always tuned and the power never went out. What could heaven contain for Thomas Huxley? Ice cubes in the summertime. Memories printed out in pages, so he could tell what he'd imagined and what he had missed. Terrible, awful things he would enjoy.

Zoë reached out a hand and felt his forehead, then pulled it away, but he took it and put it back.

"One bullet, entering the prefrontal area," he said. He moved her hand. "Came out ... here."

She took in a sharp breath. "And you're still alive?"

"Barely." He explained his injuries, the coma, the miraculous recovery. "I don't think it was a random attack," he finished.

"No?"

158

"No. I can't explain it … and I can't even remember when it happened, I just … don't know."

Neither of them spoke for a minute, but a clap of thunder sounded outside. Zoë walked over to the window; rain had started to pour down.

"It's the first time it's rained since Kyle died," she murmured.

So he told her the story of when he interviewed the band, and she laughed as he recalled Jamie's drama-queen tendency, Damien's one-word responses, but how Kyle sat down and genially answered all the questions. "He seemed down-to-earth, like an old friend. Calm, normal. Showed me a picture of his son, just a little baby then."

"That's Kyle," she said, charmed.

The air conditioner clicked on with a whir, sending a stream of cool air at them. She knew Thomas would be all right now.

"If you want, we can talk about all this another time," she said.

He knew she didn't mean the discussion about her friend. "Another time," he agreed, and his smile put her at ease.

But they never talked about it. Zoë held off on piloting for weeks, still angry at the skies for letting Kyle fall, and instead threw herself into charity and diplomatic work, which she had dabbled in while her father had been alive.

She lobbied for better safety features for flying cars, and before long all new vehicles were manufactured with them. She raised money for hospitals and made visits. Critics accused her of trying to be a celebrity in spite of the band's disappearance, and one day when Jamie asked if that upset her, she shook her head.

"The only thing that upsets me is that I'll never hear Kyle play again," she said.

One of their songs had been playing on the stereo, and Jamie turned it up. "Can't you hear the bass line?" he asked.

Zoë bit her lip.

The next morning she decided to fly again. Thomas watched her, stunned, as she packed her things and left his London flat. He was no less anxious when he watched the golden ship take off at the airport, watched it grow as small as a firefly and then blink out of sight.

Over the next few days he wandered, dazed, and went to work but rarely slept, and when he dreamed, it was of her. He tacked a map of the world to his wall and traced her path with yellow string. She called daily, sending photos and video clips over e-mail from places all over the world.

One day he left a message on her phone: "Zoë, when you get back, I have to tell you something."

A week passed before he could see her again. When she saw him standing at the airport, she smiled, her blue eyes making twin mirrors of the sky.

He hugged her, and he told her everything right there: his dreams about the secret police, ending with his thoughts about his attack.

"I mean, a shot in the head, a broken leg, a broken wrist? It doesn't sound like a mugging. I didn't even have a watch or anything expensive. If they robbed me, what did they take?"

"Maybe that's why they shot you," she said quietly.

"No. Zoë, you have to believe me."

Anyone else would have told him he had lost his mind, but she leaned over and whispered, "You were there. Whatever you think happened, it probably did."

And that was it: he knew they could outlast anything.

May, 2507

One morning they sat together in a park, shaded by apple trees covered in blossoms. Pink-white petals drifted from the tree. It was the second of May, Zoë's twenty-third birthday.

Thomas held a video camera steady as she opened her presents. A bouquet of daffodils, her favorite flower, were already lying on the table. She opened a box containing a golden charm bracelet, and adored it instantly. The charms were a small spaceship, a clock, and a heart.

The next gift was an advance press copy of Biochemical Pathways' last album, which at the time had not yet been submitted to censorship review.

"How did you get this?" she asked, amazed. "Jamie didn't even give me a copy."

"We had a few extras kicking around the studio. Production company sent them. I thought you'd enjoy it."

She hugged him. "Thank you, Thomas."

He steadied the camera. "No problem. Oh, and there's one more thing." He reached into his messenger bag and took out a small box wrapped with a yellow ribbon.

She opened it, gasped, and put a hand to her mouth. Thomas moved the camera over to the inside of the box, which contained a diamond ring.

He sat back. "I was just thinking about my future, and the only thing I wanted to include was you. What do you say?" he asked.

"Yes, yes, of course." She kissed him. "I'll marry you."

Thomas put down the camera, then leaned over to kiss her.

June, 2507

Zoë thought she had avoided disaster when she chose to wait in the rain, but she only delayed it.

They were not Romeo and Juliet; they were the journalist and the pilot, the secret police and the music scene, the melancholy and the surprises. There are only two ways a story such as theirs can end, with bliss or with broken hearts. They hoped for a lot and gave everything they had. In the end, it didn't matter.

Alone in her ship, Zoë watched the clock tick away the minutes. Hours had passed since she left the man who had been her fiancé, and still she stayed awake, troubled by a pain she could not name. She turned over and tried to sleep, but as usual, she found herself thinking more of Thomas than of anyone else.

Chapter Twelve
June 18, 2507, 11:20 p.m.

Zoë knocked on the door. She waited a moment, then wrapped her arms around herself, shivering. She knocked again, but before she could pull back her fist, the door opened, and Jamie stood behind the screen, his dark hair messy.

"Are you okay, Zo?" he said. "It's almost midnight."

"I just need to talk. And I knew you'd be awake."

He unlatched the door and opened it. She stepped inside the dim living room. From one of the windows she could see the shadows of a lush garden in his backyard, filled with sunflowers and trellises.

Jamie disappeared into the kitchen, and she sat down on the couch, still trembling. She turned on the TV, saw a report about the king's funeral, and turned it off.

A moment later, Jamie re-appeared with a mug of coffee, and handed it to her.

"Thanks," she said.

He sat down. "So what's wrong?"

"It's me and Thomas. We got into a fight."

"What happened?"

Zoë's fingers traced the edge of the mug. "He's in love with someone else."

"What? He seemed to really like you. Maybe it's just a misunderstanding. I mean, what did he say?"

"Well, he's been seeing this girl. I asked him about it, and ... he just started mocking me. Called her a time traveler, or something."

"A ... a time traveler?"

"Oh, it all sounds so stupid now. I'm sorry to bother you. Maybe I should go."

"No, no. Uh, why don't I talk to him? Maybe in the morning."

"I can't ask that from you."

He took her hand. "Just wait here a minute," he said. He walked over and grabbed his guitar from its case. A platinum pocket watch—the one Ariel had given him—tumbled out.

"Stay as long as you need," he called over to her.

He turned over the watch. History was supposed to go one way, breaking Zoë's heart over and over again—but then, history could change.

2.

A year before Kyle died, Zoë Martínez was twenty-one and Biochemical Pathways was at the height of its fame.

It was 2505, and a national magazine decided to do a profile of the young woman. She sat for a full-page photo dressed in white and wearing a pearl necklace, her red lips a flat line, her eyes sparkling: the lovely and mysterious socialite.

Not by any action of her own, Zoë had become a high-profile member of the music scene. She had attended the Grammy ceremonies twice with the band, appearing on stage when they collected their awards. Though she recorded some vocals for the band's albums, and played synth live when the songs called for it, she did not consider herself a musician.

"I'm a pilot," she said to the article's reporter. "The open sky—that's my song."

She had thought the article would be a minor piece, but while on tour in London, Zoë stopped in the middle of the street and saw a rack of magazines with her face on them. She pursed her lips, and asked Jamie what he thought.

He didn't reply. He couldn't tear his gaze away from a billboard showing a slim brunette model. The advertisement was years old, and the model, disappointed by her fading looks, had long ago started a military career. But the image of eighteen-year-old Kira Watson still made Jamie's heart flip.

Zoë was many times more famous than the former model, but had never had someone fall in love with her, let alone as much as Jamie had with Kira. "How can you still love someone who never gave you the time of day?" she asked.

"There's a simple reason," Jamie had replied, "but I have no idea what it is..."

No one knew where they had met, and Jamie would never say, but when he was nineteen he fell deeply in love with young Kira Watson. They lived five streets apart in Tenokte, in different worlds: he was a penniless musician, and she could make thousands of credits in a single photo shoot.

The model politely declined all offers for a date. So Jamie composed a song for her: "Dame de la Pluie," the moody tune that would become one of his biggest hits. A local DJ, knowing and sympathizing with Jamie's plight, played it over and over again early in the summer of 2501 in the hopes that Kira would hear it. She did, and finally she said yes: she would give him a chance.

Jamie was elated. The summer of love, as he called it, saw him write nearly a song a day. But the relationship wore down, and though Kira couldn't think of a single thing she disliked about him, she also couldn't find anything she did. She left him.

A week later, at a friend's party, Jamie attempted suicide. Paramedics rushed him to a hospital, where he spent three days under evaluation and was then released. "I'll never be free," he lamented. "Cupid didn't hit me with an arrow. He shot me with a bullet."

He dropped out of sight for two days, not returning calls or answering his door. His friends, alarmed and fearing the worst, phoned the police. A dozen officers searched his apartment, but found nothing. Jamie Parsons had vanished.

Rumors sprang up immediately. Had he successfully committed suicide, and if so, where was the body? Had he run away to start a new life? A search went out for him for days, including monitoring his ID cards for any activity. Nothing showed up. The musician had dropped off the face of the earth.

Then, later that week, Jamie walked back to his apartment building, a guitar case on his back, and saw the yellow crime-scene tape. He spent an afternoon in an interrogation room, but only gave the following explanation: "Sorry for worrying you all. I lost track of time."

Kyle and Damien chased his song all summer, and finally caught up with him to start the band. As the songs rose on the charts and the three boys' bank accounts gained a string of zeros, a reporter asked Kira if she had made a mistake.

"No," she replied. "And my leaving him says more about my personality than his. I couldn't make the relationship work. I'd like to put the whole incident behind me."

By the time she'd left Jamie, she had already quit modeling and, against her mother's advice to become an actress, joined the military. There, the poster girl found an obsession of her own: the secret police. And in her years of pursuing time travelers, she never knew that she had missed them by just a few days.

3.

June 18, 2507, 10:35 p.m.

Kira sat in a taxi, headed for a party, when her cell phone rang. "Hello?"

"Lieutenant, I found something that I think will interest you greatly."

"Caxton? What's up?"

"Agent Nineteen returned to the base earlier today."

"What? Did he remember anything?"

"No. He asked a lot of questions, though."

"Anything about the girl?"

"No, but I found something rather interesting. Random cameras throughout the city have been only showing static for the past few days. We found the signal interfering with them, and someone was able to block it. I think you need to take a look. I'm sending a clip to your phone."

Kira looked at her phone, and saw that he'd transferred the clip. It was from that evening and was rather dark, but the image was unmistakable: a street in Tenokte, with Thomas Huxley speaking to a red-haired girl. Their time traveler.

She put the phone to her ear. "Has anyone seen it?"

"Someone e-mailed it to Delacroix."

That made things complicated. "Tell me you haven't sent out a team yet."

"They're waiting on your order. Huxley has been sighted near the canals. We've got a team following him."

"Right. I'll meet up with them. Thank you, Caxton. You've been incredibly helpful." She closed her phone and ordered her driver to change course. Then she sat back, perplexed. Thomas had lied to her. He didn't trust her.

And that's exactly the way I trained him, she thought.

4.

The night seemed unusually cold for summer, but the sky was clear and speckled with stars. Thomas wandered around, making his way to the canals. He knew that evening curfew had already started, but he didn't feel like going anywhere else. Finally he reached the bridge at the edge of the city, then leaned over the railing, looking out at the water.

Zoë would probably be in a better mood in the morning—maybe. But what if Ariel backed out of the deal, and he couldn't secure a release for Damien? What then?

Things were looking bleak.

His phone started ringing, and he opened it. "Hello?"

No answer.

He flipped it shut and turned around. Heading toward him were two Celestial patrols, their footsteps muffled by the sound of the water. Thomas took a step back, but they were already on the bridge.

"ID," said one of the Celestials.

He pulled it out and held it up. The helmeted officer walked over, pulled out a flashlight and read the card. Thomas put a hand over his eyes to block the light, and the Celestial turned it off.

"You're under arrest."

"What?" said Thomas. "It's after curfew, there's just a fine—"

A white car swooped down from the sky and slid down to hover a foot off the ground. Lt. Kira Watson stepped out, then slammed the door. The cruiser flew away. When she spoke, her breath let out a cloud of mist.

"Thomas," she said.

She looked otherworldly in her brilliantly white coat. Behind her was the distant sparkle of city lights.

"Out after curfew, and speaking with a wanted criminal," she said, grinning. "You're slipping, Thomas."

He looked at her, puzzled. "What's going on?"

"Ariel Midori," said Kira. "Does that name sound familiar?"

He moved his eyes to the guards, and he understood. So Ariel had been right: they were tracking her.

"We just want to talk to her. Our signal's gone dead, probably won't work again. Where is she?"

"I don't know."

Kira's eyes flashed. "Yes, you do."

"She left. She's not coming back."

The lieutenant considered. The wind whipped her hair and jacket, and she pressed her lips together. "Guards, leave us."

The Celestial soldiers walked off the bridge, leaving him alone with the lieutenant.

She smiled at him, but looked as if she would cry. "You were the best we had, did you know that? I personally oversaw the execution of the people who shot you."

He stared at her.

"Perhaps I owe you an explanation, Thomas. Ever since the Federation started, there have been classified projects. The Commander wanted me to investigate Project X, opened just a few years ago—after unknown individuals were seen aboard a Celestial ship. Time travelers, so it would seem."

"Right," he said. "Time travel. Sure. You've been lying to me for four years. Why should I start believing you now?"

"Trust your instincts," she said. "I always knew that she would come back for you. It was a mistake to let those two go. Imagine how their skills would benefit the secret police."

"Kira, even if I knew where she went, I wouldn't tell you."

"You wouldn't exchange that knowledge for the safety of others? Your family, perhaps? Or Zoë?"

The Celestials approached again, and he didn't bother to struggle as they pinned his arms back, handcuffing him. He was too heartbroken to fight.

Kira pulled out her blaster, checked the settings, and held it ready. She looked out at the street a moment, then back to Thomas.

"Look at you," she said, smiling. "They tried to kill you once, and here you are, alive as ever."

"I'm not going to help you."

"Oh, you will, Thomas. Trust me. I could always depend on you."

5.

When Ariel, a quiet shadow of her usual self, walked into the base, Bailey immediately noticed that something had happened. Ariel walked past without even a murmur of greeting and slumped into a chair.

"Bad night?" Bailey asked.

"The worst."

"Well, you saved Jude's life. He's fine now. When can I expect to see Thomas again?"

"I don't know. He doesn't want to join the Order."

Bailey knew this was a possibility, but had hoped against it. "You're sure?"

Ariel thought back. "Well, I don't know. He's not the traveling sort."

"Did you tell him that if he doesn't go, he'll die?"

"…that came up, yes."

"Go back and try again. Ask him one more time."

"I can't."

"Ariel, if he won't help you, then he could turn on you. He could be in contact with Celestials already. If he tells them what he knows—"

"He won't." Ariel strode past her and walked down the hall. She found Jude in the laboratory, studying something under a microscope. He looked up when he heard her come in, then smiled.

"Hey, kid. That was some rescue."

Ariel smiled faintly. "Don't mention it. How are you feeling?"

"Fine, thanks to you."

She nodded, but behind her tinted sunglasses, which were translucent in the room's light, her gaze was distant and careful. She tried to smile. "Jude, I need to show you something. It's in Thomas's time."

"No thanks, kiddo." He lifted up a slide, looking at it in the light. "I'd rather not go to that century again."

"It'll be great. Come on." She held a pair of handcuffs behind her back.

"Maybe later." He put the microscope under the slide.

She pulled her pistol out of her jacket. "I *insist.*"

He looked up, alarmed by the gun. "Ariel? What's wrong?"

"I don't know why you did it, but the king was practically my nephew."

Jude jumped up suddenly. "Ariel—"

"Why did you kill him?"

"They stopped tracking you after that, didn't they? Two bullets, and they stopped. No one's followed you since. They would've moved on to the other timepieces if I hadn't. Bailey's; Jamie's old one. How long do you think that would take?"

Ariel was stunned. He said he'd been out investigating why they were following her; apparently they had different understandings of the task. He had gone back in time to look at their files—their security systems were updated late in 2503, making that time his best chance—but he must've reached a dead end. And now…

"They tortured me," he said. "Those people don't deserve a king. And it was always going to happen, wasn't it? So why not me?"

"I saved your life," she said, taken aback.

"Yes, you did. And I saved yours. They took my timepiece, Ariel. It took them years to get it working, but they finally did. It's all they needed to track you."

So now it was her duty to turn him in: but oh, what a duty. The tape itself wasn't enough, nor were the fingerprints: without time travel, Jude Fawkes had no reason to be alive in 2507. As the forensic scientist had thought: computer error. Case closed. The Council would think so, too—at least, without the suspect in hand.

Thomas had asked her to turn Jude in, but she couldn't. It came between the Celestials having time travel and Damien dying … and the Celestials could never, ever have the power from those watches. But could she let an innocent man die?

What if she stole the watch back? Was it even possible? … but even if she took it, they would torture Jude for knowledge of time travel instead of punishing him for murder … and if, out of revenge, he gave any information about where to find a time-traveler-turned-singer, or any location for them to dig to find a base…

But she needed to turn him in; there was no question of it.

"They're going to kill an innocent man for this," she said. "You've meddled with history."

"So have you," came a voice.

Ariel turned: Bailey stood in the doorway, holding a revolver. Ariel didn't move.

"How did she know?" Bailey asked Jude, calmly.

"You *knew*?" said Ariel.

"She's going to turn you in," said Bailey, ignoring her.

"She won't."

"This is psychotic!" said Ariel.

"Even so ... if Huxley knows, he'll find you."

"He doesn't know," said Ariel, flustered.

"We're going to make this easy on you, kiddo," said Bailey. "If you agree to give up your watch and go back to your own time, you'll never hear from us again. If not..." She raised her revolver.

"Relax," said Jude, holding up a hand. He looked at Ariel, who was still pointing a gun at him. "That king was five centuries removed from your brother. You were about as close to that kid as you are to anyone else in the world."

Her eyes flashed. "You're right. I never knew him. But you're still a murderer. And I'm going to deliver you to the Council, so they can do what they like with you."

"Ariel," said Bailey, holding the revolver steady, "just hand over your watch."

"Try and take it." She rushed forward at Jude, who seemed hesitant to harm her. She tried to grab him, and Bailey fired, barely missing her.

Ariel tried to pull out her watch, but ducked; Bailey's bullets lodged into the wall. She had to take care of Bailey, too, or she'd come after Thomas...

Jude, however, knocked Ariel away. Ariel put the gun in her jacket and pulled out her sword—it felt much more natural in her hands.

"Ariel, I was your partner once!"

"Not anymore." Ariel swung it at him, missing.

Bailey was still shooting. A bullet cracked a tank of fireflies; a cloud of startled, luminescent insects took flight into the air. Ariel lunged, pinning Jude against the wall. She stopped her blade close to his throat, and he went still. The chain of her pocket watch was looped around her fingers, and she moved to touch the fob.

Bailey fired again, striking the wall just an inch away from Ariel, making her involuntarily jump. Jude grabbed the sword and wrenched it away from her, pulled away her copper watch, and she stumbled back, knocking into a shelf. A few test tubes fell off, tumbling and shattering as they hit the floor.

She was cornered. Bailey leveled the gun at her, Jude had her sword, but both of them were staring at the mess of broken glass on the floor, horrified. Ariel felt a sudden twinge of pain, and looked at the palm of her hand. She'd been cut by some of the shards of glass, and was bleeding.

"Bailey," said Jude, "when you said you were studying live falling-sickness viruses … you were joking, right?"

The scientist was standing back. "Now you don't have to worry about killing her. The disease will do it for you."

Ariel stumbled, wincing from the pain in her hand. And Jude did a quick set of mental calculations. First, this strain of the falling-sickness was spread by infected food or water—or by getting it into the bloodstream. There was no cure.

And second, now he only had to worry about a journalist who had too much knowledge of time travel.

"Jude—" said Ariel.

"I'm sorry," he replied.

Bailey loaded a tranquilizer dart into the pistol, and closed one eye. "I'm not," she said, and fired.

6.

Ariel Midori Reynolds turned over in bed and opened her eyes.

She sat up, confused.

She reached under her pillow to pull out her watch (for she always kept it there) but she did not feel the cold, ticking timepiece.

A scrap of paper lay on the nightstand. She picked it up and read the scribbled note:

Best wishes to your new life, short as it may be.
- Jude Fawkes

She looked around. Her window showed a sunny autumn morning. She wasn't in her room at the base, but in her bedroom back home. A cell phone still lay on her desk, charged, though she had not used it in a year; Bailey had given her one that worked across time. But she picked it up and looked at the date.

It was October. More specifically, the day she left.

Jude had her pocket watch, she had the falling-sickness, and Thomas Huxley was five hundred years away.

Chapter Thirteen
October, 2007

Ariel walked down the stairway, her hand on the banister, and took slow, plodding steps.

Jude had been careful: he'd returned her to the same day she'd left, just an hour later. When she woke up, she found her backpack, and everything she had with her while she traveled, lying by her desk. Well, almost everything: her pocket watch and pistol were gone.

Okay, she thought. *Think, Ariel. No one should miss me, and I haven't been gone too long.*

Just a year...

"Ariel, is that you?"

She winced. "Yeah, Mom." She stepped off the final stair, walked through the living room and peered into the kitchen. Her mother was reading a newspaper, and looked up. "I didn't hear you come in. When did you get home?"

"Oh, I don't know. A few minutes ago?"

"The car's not in the driveway."

Ariel thought back: she'd taken her mother's car to school. Why? Why not the Camaro? "Uh, someone gave me a ride home. I wasn't feeling well. I'll pick it up tonight."

Her mother nodded and looked down at the paper again.

Ariel walked over to a pot of coffee on the stove. She poured herself a cup, and without adding cream or milk, she took a sip.

She would be trapped here, in this century, for the rest of her (very short) life. Thomas would die in another century, and she could do nothing to stop it.

She poured her coffee into the sink and sat down at the table, looking absent-mindedly at her surroundings. Yellow walls, a table under the light of a window. Appliances from the 1970s, or so it seemed. Security and solitude. It was maddening.

On Monday she'd have to go to school, if she survived until then. She could barely remember what classes she'd been taking. It would take quite a bit of study before she was ready for any upcoming exams, to say the least.

A low rumble sounded outside—a noisy car engine—and her mother looked up. "Ah, there's our lieutenant."

Ariel, perplexed, walked into the living room to glance out the window.

A yellow '76 Camaro sat in the driveway. It had black racing stripes.

The license plate read TNOKTE.

The driver, back from a visit to his fiancée, had dark brown hair. In later years, he would be the founder of the Celestial Federation, the father of a long line of kings, and the maker of a new civilization. Now, he was just a soldier.

He opened the screen door and walked inside the house. "Hey, kiddo," said Army Lt. Dimitri Reynolds, to his sister.

Ariel's voice caught in her throat.

"Hey, Di," she replied.

2.

The morning's rain (which, for Ariel, had been a year ago) stayed all day. Under cloudy skies, the lights of old-fashioned lamp-posts blinked on early in the afternoon. The trees let their leaves drift to the ground, paving walkways with gold and orange.

Ariel and Dimitri strolled through the streets around their house, feeling drowsy from the damp air. They were far from the rusting heart of the city, a former mill town, where boarded-up buildings stood over empty blocks.

Dimitri looked up through the branches of a cherry tree as he walked, and could see shifting patches of sky. "I'll miss it here," he said. He looked down at his sister, who had her hands in the pockets of her windbreaker. "I go back tomorrow. It's strange ... freezing cold one day, hundred-degree desert the next."

She understood.

"So," he said, "where'd *you* go?"

Ariel stopped. "What do you mean?"

"Well, I don't know. You look like you went somewhere. You look different."

"Oh!" she said. "Di, I would need an entire year to explain it to you."

"Try me."

She took a sharp breath. "Have you ever given serious thought to the concept of time travel?"

"Not really, no. Why?"

"I had a clock that could stop time, and even send me to another place. I could go to ancient Rome, or the sinking of the Titanic, or even visit the colonies on Titan in the year 3000, and be back before anyone realized I was gone."

He paused. "That's pretty good. Like something Isaac Asimov would write. Or H. G. Wells."

"I'm serious," she said. "I've been to the future. You're a hero there. A legend."

"Let's go see, then. Where's this clock?"

"I ... don't have it with me anymore."

"Good one. You almost had me going there for a minute."

"You have to believe me. It's real. Why would I joke about this?"

She suddenly realized that if Jude had not abandoned her here, she might never come back. Why had she left on this particular day? Dimitri was officially on leave, but tomorrow he had to return to his tour of duty. That was the moment she was running from.

"You're just stressed out, kiddo," he said.

Everywhere she went, no matter what she did, people always called her a kid. And why should Dimitri not? He had finished college and graduated with distinction, fought in a war, come back a local hero. He still believed Ariel was seventeen, and had no knowledge of what she'd done. She couldn't explain it to him.

"Yeah," she said. "Sure, I was just kidding. It would be nice, though, if time travel existed, wouldn't it?"

He smiled and walked on.

She stopped. She had traveled with Jamie when the singer was nineteen, and then (at his request) dropped him back off without any promise of returning, without any proof of their travels. He had wanted it that way, but it must have been terrible for him to have seen so much and not be able to tell a soul.

History would spin out as it was supposed to: Dimitri Reynolds would achieve greatness, and Thomas Huxley would die, alone, because of her. Unless she lived for five hundred years, she could do nothing to stop it. Her life was winding down to days, hours, minutes.

"Di, if I could prove it to you," she said, "would you believe me?"

"Sure, whatever you want, kiddo. Race you back home!" He dashed away. Ariel glanced over her shoulder to make sure no white-suited Celestials were behind her, then flailed on after him, wondering in a casual way if history made mistakes once in awhile.

3.

A car's headlights cut through a downtown avenue.

The rain that streamed down in a drizzle all evening had now vanished; instead, it left the clear, inky skies of twilight. The streetlights winked on with a coppery glow, throwing shadows and a pinkish hue onto the asphalt.

On either side of the yellow Camaro were brick office buildings and restaurants, their windows shining with bright colors, like television sets.

A light up ahead turned red, and the driver eased the brake and stopped.

The '76 Camaro was the only car at the intersection. Someone must have pressed a walk button, or the light was timed: she couldn't remember which. And no wonder, since it had been over a year since she last drove through this road.

The light changed, and she drove on.

So she did think it was real? She tilted her head, watching the city pass by her windshield. Yes. It had been several hours and she had not once thought otherwise. But every minute, a little of it slipped away. *Could* she have dreamed it? It was certainly possible...

But then she thought of that journalist and his distraught fiancée, and knew otherwise. Occam's razor: The simplest explanation is usually the best one. Ariel's razor: If you think it happened, it did.

She tapped the steering wheel and turned up the radio. R.E.M.'s "Losing My Religion" was playing.

"Great song, don't you think?" she said.

She glanced at the passenger seat. Empty. All of this road, and no journalists to pass the time with. She sighed and pushed her pedal to the floor.

Six o'clock passed before she reached the house she wanted. She knocked on the door and put her hands in her pockets, waiting. After a moment the door opened, revealing a teenage girl with ringlets of curly brown hair.

"Ariel!" said Marissa. "What's up?"

"I need to talk to you." Ariel pushed past her, tossed her backpack by the couch, then flicked on the kitchen light. She leaned with against the kitchen sink and stared past her friend, who had never seen her in such a state. When Marissa asked what was wrong, Ariel just looked up at the clock above the stove.

Marissa tried again. "Ariel?"

Ariel looked at her friend, her eyes watery. "I haven't seen you in a year."

"What are you talking about? I saw you at school today. Where did you go, anyway? I thought you were coming to Sophia's party."

Ariel started talking, in a one-sided conversation that spanned about twenty minutes and three rooms. She tried to explain about time travel, Thomas Huxley, the betrayal of her comrades, everything.

"A dream," said Marissa, when she finished.

Ariel sat on the floor against her best friend's bed. She had one hand out, and Marissa was painting her nails. She glanced at the clock on the nightstand: 7:08 p.m.

"No," Ariel murmured. "It was real. Real as sitting here with you."

"Dreams can be realistic."

"Fine. Pull that notebook out of my bag."

Marissa grabbed Ariel's leather satchel, found a red school notebook, and flipped it open. On dozens of lined pages, she saw Ariel's neat handwriting in blue ink detailing notes, charts, dates and times. She saw a diagram of the Titanic, then turned the page and glanced at an account of watching parts of Rome burn to the ground.

"It's very imaginative," said Marissa, hesitantly.

"It's a few things that happened to me in the past year. I've checked some of the facts, and everything's true. It's pages and pages of work. Did I do that in one night?"

"You just put this together, didn't you?" said Marissa, grinning. "Is this a prank?"

One look at Ariel's face, however, assured her she was not. Ariel had never played practical jokes. She was the most serious person Marissa knew.

She turned to the next page of the journal. A sketch of Vincent van Gogh, with a note: *Crazy but pleasant. Remind him to draw that starry night scene.* "Some dreams, then, Airy. How could you travel in time, again?"

"I had a pocket watch that could take me to other places, other times."

"So what happened to it?"

She sat back, her gaze distant. "Someone took it."

Marissa sat back. Ariel had arrived in a black pilot's jacket that closed at the throat, dark pants, and matching Converse sneakers. But she also had several curious items, and their historical accuracy passed a quick Google check: a samurai sword made in fourteenth-century Japan; a bracelet made in seventeenth-century Italy; an amulet from ancient Egypt.

If she had made this up, she was doing one hell of a job.

"I don't know what to tell you," said Marissa. "I really don't. But that friend with the time machine, or whatever— can't you write him a letter? Ask him to come back for you?"

Ariel quickly pointed out all the flaws in the plan: any letter she wrote had five hundred years to get lost. Major overhauls to the Internet and postal service would occur. How could she get it through?

"Well, I don't know. Sometimes artifacts can get saved. Do you know anyone who becomes famous?"

4.

Soon after his sister got back, Dimitri packed his Army gear into a chest, locked it, and carried it out to the car. When he reached the driveway, he turned and saw Ariel standing on the front porch, her arms folded. It was dark, the stars twinkling in the sky. He had to be ready to leave for Iraq the following morning.

"I'll write to you," he called, from the driveway.

Ariel didn't reply.

"Come on, Ariel. I'll be fine."

She knew that. And even if he hadn't been called up to serve, he still would have volunteered for this mission. Most people couldn't handle a war, couldn't deal with the endless violence and mayhem, but he was born for it. All he ever talked about since he was young was being a soldier.

"One more year overseas," he said. "Maybe two, at the most. Then I'll come back, and I can conquer the world."

If he only knew.

"When you're done with high school, you can enlist," he said. "We need medics."

She looked away. "You don't believe that I'm a time traveler, do you?"

"Are you still going on about that?"

Ariel bit her lip.

"Here," he said, pulling out a vest. "Take this. We got new flak jackets last year; these are obsolete."

"A bulletproof vest?" she said, her eyes widening. She took the heavy jacket. "This would be great. I've got this friend who attracts bullets like crazy. They mostly go for his head, though..."

He crossed his arms, grinning.

"Thank you, Di." She threw her arms around him. "You are awesome."

"All right. I need to finish packing."

"Fine." She pushed a strand of hair back. "I can't go in the military, though. For ... lots of reasons."

He only smiled and turned his attention back to his equipment.

Ariel walked back to her room, still clutching the vest, and put it on her bed. She took out a piece of lined paper, thinking.

Letters lived on after people died, and a famous family could preserve an heirloom. If only she could find a way to convince Dimitri to take it.

On an envelope, she wrote, "Emily Montag: Please deliver. From October 17, 2007. To be opened June 19, 2507, by Jamie Parsons."

Inside, she wrote only two words:
Find me.

At nine o'clock, Ariel slipped downstairs for dinner. She filled a plate and walked to the table, not having thought of anything yet to persuade her brother, but when she saw her mother's newspaper lying to the side, she had an idea.

"I'll be right back," she said, and rushed to her room.

Jude had left her backpack with her. She pulled it out and found, tucked away toward the bottom, the next day's newspaper. She had never really done more than glance over it. When he asked her to join the Order, Jude had brought it to her to convince her of time travel. As if she needed convincing.

She took it to Dimitri just as he finished eating.

"Ha. They must have printed this early," he said. "Either that, or it's a good fake. Did you make it at your school's newspaper office?"

She snatched it back. "You know we don't have a newspaper. If you're not going to take this seriously—"

"Fine, I'm listening."

"If I can't get back, a lot of people are going to die. I need you to take a letter and promise to give it to your future children. They'll pass it down until one of your descendants lives in a certain time. Do you understand?"

"Vaguely," he said.

Ariel pulled the envelope out of her jacket, holding it at arm's length. "Promise me you'll give it to your kids."

"So if I do that, eventually a time traveler will come for you?" His eyes narrowed. "Are you feeling okay?"

"If you don't believe me, fine. Just promise me you'll do it."

Dimitri glanced at the newspaper.

"Don't play the lottery numbers," she warned.

He sighed. "Okay, pretending I believe you—what happens to me in the future?"

"It's hard to explain. You become a great leader. To many people, you're seen as a hero."

"Do you think so?"

She thought of the secret police, of a young king being shot, of cars that soar on air and crash and kill, or a journalist shot in the head for his work in the secret police—all under the banner of Dimitri Reynolds, the father of the new world.

"You're my brother," she said. "Nothing more."

He opened the paper with some curiosity, then dismissed it with the shake of his head. "Keep your letter, Ariel. This is all a bit too crazy for me." And he walked out of the room.

For a long time, Ariel sat in her room, thinking. She opened a music box that would, in a few centuries, belong to Princess Emily.

Finally she drifted off to sleep, and was awakened by someone's shouts. Dimitri appeared at her door, yelling. She couldn't quite gather what he was saying, but once sentence made its way into her brain:

"Ariel, just for fun, I bought a lottery ticket with the winning numbers in your paper—"

She froze. History told that Dimitri came across a large sum of money in his twenties; that he would invest it, and would eventually spend it on rebuilding the world after a devastating war...

He promised to take the letter. He promised to believe every word of what she said as true, and he would have his children pass it on if he had to mandate it in his will, because he had just won three million dollars.

Ariel had, more or less, directly caused the Celestial Federation.

She pulled out the letter and gave it to him, and long after he had gone, she sat down, confused. And she realized that even though Dimitri had taken the note, there was no guarantee it would ever reach Jamie.

5.

June 19, 2507

Morning dawned over central Tenokte, and in the living room of a musician's mansion, a woman with wavy blond hair lay asleep on a couch.

The room had a flat TV covering part of one wall, a couch and coffee table, a wide window, and a guitar case leaning against a closet door. A cell phone lay on the table.

The woman, normally an early riser, did not pay any attention to the world around her. Even as the sun flooded the room with light, Zoë Martínez did not stir.

The TV flickered on at eight o'clock for the morning reports, and a female anchor greeted the sleeping pilot, and the rest of the Celestial Federation. Zoë turned over at the low drone of chatter, only half-awake; and then she fell back asleep, catching only some of the words as her dreams slipped away like a mist.

"As the princess is not old enough to rule, Commander Edward Delacroix will serve as leader until her eighteenth birthday ... The king was buried in Tenokte's local cemetery yesterday afternoon..."

Jamie walked into the room and paused to watch the footage of the funeral procession while sipping a mug of coffee.

"...the World Council has decided to bypass a trial, and found Damien Peter Martínez guilty of assassinating King Richard II. Martínez will be executed in two days, just before dawn..."

Zoë sat upright, fully awake.

"Why do they always use three names for assassins?" Jamie pondered aloud. "First, middle, last. I've never understood it."

Without looking at him, Zoë said, "People only say your full name when you're in trouble. You know—when your parents are angry, they'll yell all three names. Well, when you're an assassin, you're always in trouble. People are always angry."

"Huh," he said. "I never heard my parents say my name. Not even once." He slipped into the kitchen.

Zoë grabbed her phone and followed him, then paused in the doorway and crossed her arms. "You've always been like this. Won't let anything upset you, even when it's your best friend who's about to die. You were making jokes when people were dying of the falling-sickness."

"Yep," he said. He was mixing a bowl of pancake batter, and poured some on the griddle. It sizzled, and the smell wafted throughout the kitchen. A rock star cooking breakfast: the thought struck Zoë as bizarre, and she sighed, frustrated.

"Doesn't it bother you that he's going to be killed?" she asked.

"I'll survive, Zo." He opened and closed various cabinets, shifting cups and plates around. She noticed with some surprise that he had already dressed; he usually didn't get up until well after noon.

"What's wrong?" she asked.

"What do you mean? I'm fine."

"*Exactly.* You've never been 'fine.' Not as long as I can remember."

Jamie turned. "Sorry if I'm not weeping, but he's not going to die."

She stared at him. "I'm leaving," she said, after a moment. "I can't stay here while they kill him."

"So where are you going?"

"Paris. I used to spend summers there." She turned her phone over in her hands. "Jamie, I may not come back for a long time."

"Still no word from Huxley?"

She shook her head. "No."

He flipped his pancakes, and Zoë's cell phone started to ring. She answered it. "Thomas?"

A pause. "I think we may have the same problem," came a voice.

Zoë shifted the phone to her other ear. "Who is this?"

"Audrey Huxley. Thomas isn't returning my calls. Is he with you?"

Zoë's mouth fell open. "No. I haven't seen him since last night."

"Oh. Let me know if you hear from him, okay?"

"I will. Bye." Zoë snapped her phone shut, then looked at Jamie. "He seems to have dropped off the face of the earth."

Before he could answer, Jamie's cell phone buzzed. He pulled it out of his pocket and answered it as he walked out of the room, his voice a low murmur.

Zoë sat down at the table and watched the clock tick. Each strike of the hand was a lost second, and before long minutes, hours, and days would slip away. It was 8:15 a.m. on a Sunday morning: right now people would be walking to stores or to church in the summer streets, mourning a beloved king, spreading news of an execution.

At a time like this, Zoë thought she should be feeling something besides numbness or shock. Some sadness, perhaps. She bit her lip and thought of Thomas.

Jamie walked back in and tossed the phone onto the coffee table. "That was Emily Montag," he said.

Zoë wiped her eyes. "The princess?"

Jamie grabbed a coat and slipped on a pair of sunglasses, then checked the time on a pocket watch. "Sorry, Zo. I'll have to explain later. Have some breakfast, and stay as long as you want. I'll be back soon."

"Wait, why do you have a jacket? It's going to be eighty degrees out today."

"I'll need it where I'm going." He opened the door. "You deserve better than this, and I'm going to fix things for you. I'm going to fix everything." He stepped outside and closed the door behind him.

Zoë walked over and pulled the door open again, then stepped out into the warm summer morning. She stared out into the street, with the tangle of Tenokte's skyscrapers and above-ground tunnels in the distance. Jamie was nowhere to be seen.

6.

Thomas sat in his cell, drifting off from lack of sleep. The lights were always on in his cell, and he couldn't tell if it was night or day. He wore the regulation white clothes of citizens being held by the secret police. There wasn't a cot in the room; just soft walls and floors. They'd let him keep Ariel's MP3 player, and it played strange (but soothing) music.

Suddenly he heard a murmur outside. He put his ear to the wall, and could hear snippets of conversation. They were discussing an upcoming death, but not the drummer's. He flipped through the gadget's functions, then set it on *record*. The screen went dark, but the device was still surreptitiously listening.

"—seem like an accident, if possible. Maybe a car crash."

Thomas's heart thudded.

"Commander—" Kira's voice.

"You're right; getting rid of her too soon would arouse suspicion. Maybe not right away, then. But at least before her coronation." A pause. "Will there be any problems?"

"No, sir."

"Good."

Just then, the door opened. Commander Delacroix walked in, his eyes meeting the prisoner's for a moment. Thomas's hair was tousled, and he was weary from lack of sleep.

Kira stood in one corner, her arms crossed.

"Hello, Mr. Huxley," said the Commander. "I take it you have information about the red-haired girl?"

"Information? Oh, not really. She talked to me once. That's it."

The Commander nodded, then to Kira: "Full interrogation."

She leaned over and whispered something in the man's ear. Thomas caught only the word "agent."

Delacroix reconsidered. "Partial interrogation, then. Let me know how it goes." He walked out the door. Kira stayed for a moment.

"What's a partial interrogation?" Thomas inquired.

"Just a few questions," she replied, her eyes distant. "Answer them all, and you just might get out of here in one piece." She frowned, then leaned to whisper in his ear: "I'm sorry. If I didn't arrest you, he would have. I'll get you out as soon as I can." And she straightened, then strode out, closing the door behind her. It clicked, locked.

And Thomas heard the voices outside his door again:

"Here's the deal. If he doesn't know anything, you can let him go. Just get rid of the princess. Is that understood?"

Thomas couldn't hear Kira's response. He only heard muffled footfalls, and stopped the recording. He slipped the music player in his pocket. *Would* he get out of here in one piece? He leaned his head against the wall, wondering.

7.

Late in the night, Ariel slipped out the back door, just as the day's rain turned into snow. Clouds swept in, covering the previously clear skies, and she had the impression that even the universe couldn't make up its mind. She walked into the woods behind her house, looking up from time to time at the falling snowflakes, which fluttered and swirled in the air, then crunched underneath her boots.

A little after midnight, the snow dissolved into mist and fog, and in the silvery glow she could not tell where the earth ended and the sky began. So she wandered around, lost somewhere along the invisible horizon.

She made her way to the streets, glossy and slick with slush. A car stopped for a red light as she passed. She glanced up at the sky; it would be centuries before flying cars roamed them. As she passed the car, she heard a snippet of a radio broadcast: two people so far had died from accidents, due to the unseasonable weather. Death seemed to follow her like her shadow, flat and empty.

The light changed, and the car zoomed away.

Travel had been her life, her escape. She had never asked for help before, never needed it. And now what? She was alone.

When she was nearly home, a soft wind started blowing in her direction. Any other person might not have noticed it, but she turned, and saw a path of footprints in the snow.

On the edge of the street, under the lamplight and across from her house, stood a dark-haired man wearing a leather pilot's jacket and jeans. He clasped a platinum pocket watch in his hand and wore a pair of gray sunglasses that blended in with the mist.

Ariel smiled. "Jamie Parsons, I've never been happier to see you."

He shrugged. "Received an urgent call from the heir to the throne herself. And Dimitri Reynolds isn't too hard to find. But what happened? Why do I have to find you?"

"You're the one who reads minds," she said.

He took off his glasses, then slipped him into his front coat pocket. "Fine. I'm listening."

"Jamie, it's a long story."

"I see. You broke up someone's engagement, you know. Zoë thinks you're in love with her fiancé."

"I'm not," she said, blinking.

"*I* know that, but that hardly matters, does it? He's missing, by the way."

"Missing?"

"Zoë can't find him. Come on." He held up his platinum watch. "Or you can stay out here in the snow. What do you say?"

Ariel would have to ditch her scarf and fingerless gloves, and go back for her notebook, but she was nonetheless pleased. "I suppose I'd better take you back, or you'll end up in the wrong century," she joked. "Where to? The Tenokte prison, circa 2507?"

"No. A ship called the *Halcyon*."

Ariel put out a hand to stop him, but before she could reach out, they had already arrived.

Chapter Fourteen
June 20, 2507

Princess Emily Montag glared at the dark-haired lieutenant watching her from the other side of a table. They sat in Kira's Tenokte office, a white room with a glass window making up an entire wall.

"I made your call yesterday," said Emily. "What is this all about?"

Kira was staring out the window. "Do you know that there's a red-haired girl who keeps showing up where she shouldn't?"

"Sure. The ghost of Dimitri Reynolds' sister. It's family legend."

"What if she isn't a ghost?"

Emily fell silent.

"She wrote a letter to a musician who didn't exist five hundred years ago. You don't find that strange?"

"It's not a real letter," said Emily. "It's fake, of course."

"Right." The lieutenant paused. "Well, I found a family for you to stay with. They'll take care of you."

"I can take care of myself."

"Your highness, right now you're not safe in Tenokte. There are people who might try to hurt you."

"But I'm the only one who can lead the Federation."

"The Council doesn't agree."

Emily crossed her arms.

"When you're eighteen, you can be coronated. But for now, we need you to be out of sight, and safe. I need you to trust me."

Emily was staring ahead. "Lieutenant, Damien Martínez didn't try to kill my brother. He wouldn't."

"Emily, I know you like their music, but…"

"I saw the killer. I looked up right before the shots and … it wasn't Damien."

Kira sat down. "Are you sure? Why didn't you tell anyone?"

"The Council didn't want to hear it. They all thought I must have been confused."

"Emily, you did see something awful. It happened so quickly, and to your brother—"

"That's just it," she snapped. "If you saw someone pick up a gun and kill someone you loved, wouldn't that be burned into your mind? Wouldn't you *always* remember that?"

Kira paused. "Would you recognize him if you saw him again?"

"Yes."

The lieutenant stood. "I will contact the Council and tell them what you've seen. And in the meantime, I'll arrange for transportation for you."

"No," said Emily, eyes wide. "You can't leave me."

"Princess, the person I'm leaving you with would not allow any harm to come to you. I would bet my life on it. Wait here. I'll come back for you in ten minutes."

Emily still was not consoled, but Lt. Kira Watson stood and walked out the door. When she closed it, Kira turned and saw Commander Delacroix standing in the hallway.

"How'd it go?"

"She's convinced," said Kira. "I'm having her taken to her guardian right away."

"Good work. Who did you choose?"

"John Caxton. He's my most trusted assistant."

The Commander nodded. Kira had been his protégé since she graduated military school, and hadn't ever disappointed him. "Very well. Carry on, Lieutenant," he said, and walked away.

Kira clutched a file to her chest, then turned and walked down the hall. She slid a card through a slot in the wall and two panels opened, revealing another passageway.

After a moment she walked toward an interrogation room, the windows of which were half-hidden by slatted blinds. Inside the room, a journalist was handcuffed to a chair, expressionless. A uniformed officer spoke to him in a low voice. When the officer saw her, he excused himself and walked out, carefully closing the door behind him.

"Anything?" Kira asked.

"He says he doesn't know where the girl is," John Caxton replied.

"Do you believe that?"

"No. But it's been a day and a half. Anyone else, I'd press on with, but him ... if he hasn't said anything by now, he never will."

"Will the Commander be convinced?"

"Yes. He left his release to your order."

Kira stared through the glass. "Do you really think time travel exists, Caxton?"

"Yes. But I don't think it matters."

Her gaze didn't leave the windows. "All these years, and he hasn't changed. Caxton, can you follow my instructions, even if they go against Delacroix's?"

"Captain? I'm in your squad. As long as no harm comes to the princess, I'll do anything you say."

Kira pondered that for a moment. She turned the knob and walked into the room, then sat down across from Thomas Huxley. Caxton stood at her side. The prisoner's hair was tousled, and his eyes were tired. He followed the two Celestials' movements but could not quite focus on them.

"Morning, Thomas," she said, flipping through a folder. "I heard you haven't been cooperating."

He looked up at her, and didn't reply.

"All we want is some information about this girl. Who is she? Where is she from?"

"I don't know."

Kira sat back and glanced at Caxton. "Well, if you won't tell us anything, you might as well make yourself useful." A white med kit sat on the table, and Kira opened it. "I suppose you know by now that you were a member of the secret police?"

"Yes," said Thomas, his eyes narrowing.

"There's only two ways a spy can leave the force," she said, snapping on a pair of nitrile gloves. "Death, no matter the cause, is a rather obvious reason. The second is a bit more tricky. The agent must ask for dismissal—because of illness or injury, for instance—and be granted it. Thomas, you have met neither of those conditions. Considering, therefore, your standing as an agent, you are being released. You won't be charged with any crime."

"Right," he said, glancing at the med-kit, but it was just a white blur to him. He hadn't brought his contact-lens solution to the party, and therefore didn't have it when he was arrested, so when he took his lenses out to sleep he had to have them thrown away. "What are you doing?"

"We could call upon you at any time to ask you to carry out a mission," Caxton explained. "And we have one in mind."

"Kira, Damien isn't your assassin," said Thomas. "It's a man named Jude Fawkes, born—"

Kira pulled a syringe out of the kit and held it level with the table. "I'm sorry," she said.

Caxton grabbed him and put a hand over his mouth, and she slid the needle into Thomas's arm. The prisoner tried to fight, but she pulled it out within seconds.

They let him go. He sat back, dazed.

"Just let me talk to Zoë," he murmured. "I just wanted ... to tell her..."

He saw Kira and Caxton peering at him, then the chemicals took over, plunging him into a dreamless sleep.

2.

Zoë knocked on the door, then put her hands in her pockets. She stood on the steps in front of a well-kept house in a middle-class neighborhood. After a moment she raised a hand to knock again, but the inner door pulled open, and a woman in her forties stepped in front of the screen.

"Can I help—" said Mrs. Huxley, and then, recognizing the girl, put a hand to her mouth. "Come in, come in." She held open the door, and Zoë stepped inside. "Make yourself at home. My husband's at work, and Audrey's at school—"

"I was hoping I could just talk to you," said Zoë.

Mrs. Huxley nodded. "I'm so sorry, Zoë. They're saying now that Damien might not have been the shooter."

"Thomas thinks that."

The woman nodded. "Sit down, please." She walked into the kitchen to pour a cup of tea, and returned a moment later as Zoë sat on the couch. She handed her the mug.

"So you're twenty-three? And a pilot," said Mrs. Huxley, sitting down. "This must be a hard time for you."

Zoë nodded. "I have to leave," she said. "Thomas and I sort of had a falling-out, and I can't find him. If you see him, could you tell him to call me?"

"Of course." She reached out a hand. "If there's anything else I can do, please, let me know."

"There is one thing—" Zoë shook her head. "But I need to talk to Thomas first. Thank you, Mrs. Huxley. I should go." She stood.

"Zoë, I don't know you very well, but your parents made quite a splash. Your father was well-liked in Tenokte, even if he stayed here only briefly during his diplomatic work. I attended his funeral."

She was taken aback. "I didn't know."

They sat down and talked for a few minutes, about their families, about everything they could think of. Zoë asked what Thomas was like as a child, and his mother showed her baby pictures. Zoë was amazed.

"Your mother was a prolific artist," said Mrs. Huxley, rising. "Come see." She led her into the hallway, where three framed paintings rested on the wall. The middle one, of a tugboat at sea, had a tiny signature at the bottom: *Valerie Deschaine.*

"I've never even seen this before," said Zoë, gazing at it. "It's beautiful."

"My husband bought it years ago. It's kind of like fate, don't you think? You can have it, if you like."

"I couldn't. Just keep it here, so I can see it when I visit."

Mrs. Huxley nodded. "You know, Thomas has always had the highest standards, and he thinks the world of you. You must really be something."

Zoë stared at the picture of a tugboat lost at sea, and gave a sad smile. She wondered if she would ever see him again.

Her phone buzzed: an incoming call. She apologized and excused herself to answer it. Milton Apollo's number. "Hello?"

"Zoë? It's Apollo. They ... they're about to make the decision."

3.

Milton Apollo walked with Zoë through the hallway of the courthouse.

"He wouldn't plead not guilty. The best I could do was ask for a life sentence."

"Did you get it?"

"Uh…"

Zoë sighed. "What about the forced confession? The lack of evidence?"

"It was a kangaroo court, Zo. Unanimous vote, 6-0, in favor of the death penalty. There was nothing I could do."

"That's it? All this, and you're going to give up? The tape—?"

"They didn't even look at the tape, and won't permit an appeal. It's over." He stopped, standing at the doors of the courthouse. Outside were dozens of reporters and photographers.

"There's got to be something you can do," she said.

He looked up at her. "I'm sorry." A pause. "Where's that cute boyfriend of yours?"

"We got in a fight."

Apollo seemed taken aback. "Because of what I said?"

"No. Because of a lot of things."

"I see." He looked down, shaking his head. "You should reconsider that, my dear. I mean … the way things are going. No one else is going to stick with you like he did." He looked at the doors. "You're not going to get a bill. And they're going to, uh, cremate the body, so you don't have to worry about anything."

Zoë was silently crying. "I see."

"He's headed back to his cell now. They'll let him talk to the press, and to family. My advice? Visit him now, and don't leave until you have to." He picked up his briefcase, then walked through the doors, to a barrage of questions; the door closed, and everything was quiet.

Zoë stood there a moment, then finally asked a guard to escort her out a back door. She took a cab to the prison, leaning her head against the window. It was raining, just like her first day back in Tenokte. She sobbed, overcome with grief.

By the time she reached the prison and walked the long dark path that led to her brother, her makeup was ruined but she still kept her head high.

"Hey, you," said Damien, from inside his cell.

She looked at him and started to cry.

"Don't," said Damien. "Listen, Zo, I'll be fine. No Huxley?"

She just leaned her head on the bars. "I can't lose you, not now. Thomas and I …"

"Yes?"

"Me … Thomas … we're going to have a baby."

"Really? That's great! Congrats."

She wiped her eyes.

"Zo, it's fine. Really. You're going to get through this."

"Tell me you didn't shoot him," she said.

"Zoë …"

"I can't stay for the exe—for what's going to happen. I just can't. The whole city's going to be a mess. *I'm* going to be a mess."

"I know. But try not to be."

"So I guess this is goodbye."

"Maybe."

"Damien, tell me you didn't shoot him. Please."

"You won't believe me."

"Have I ever?"

"They won't believe me."

"They never did."

"I didn't shoot him," he replied.

Zoë cried even more.

That morning, she flew out of the airport, headed for Paris.

She stepped out of the pilot's cabin for a moment and walked into a hallway of her ship, then heard a noise in the kitchen; pots and pans falling over. Startled, she walked toward the doorway, and saw two people standing inside: Jamie Parsons, and the girl she remembered as Ariel.

"What are you doing here?" she asked, stepping in the room.

Jamie looked at Ariel, then brushed the snow off his jacket. His sunglasses had a thin coating of ice on them. "Um," he said, "hey, Zo."

Zoë stared at both of them.

"You'd better explain," Ariel said to Jamie.

"I can't explain. Jude was always the one who explained." He turned to Zoë. "We kind of slipped into your ship."

"What? When?"

Ariel checked Jamie's platinum watch. "About ten seconds ago."

"That's ... not possible."

"We kind of let ourselves in."

"Uh ... how? We're flying over the Atlantic."

Ariel turned and looked out the window. She could see a sparkling sea beneath them. "Whoa," she said.

"Zoë," said Jamie, "this is my friend Ariel. And ... there's something we need to tell you."

4.

When Thomas awoke, he felt disoriented, as if the world would not stop moving.

"Ah, welcome back," said Kira.

He squinted, then he grabbed for something, anything, when he realized where he was. He turned to the window, and saw buildings and cars pass them in a sea of blue sky. They were in a flying car.

He sat back, his heart beating madly.

"Relax," said Kira, from the front-passenger seat. "We sedated you, or we'd never have gotten you inside. We're just moving over Tenokte, in my personal car. It's about the only place in the city that isn't bugged. You already know John Caxton, my faithful assistant."

"You've been out all morning," said the Celestial agent, who was driving.

"What am I doing here?"

"Well, why don't you ask her?" said Kira.

Thomas turned and realized someone was sitting next to him. He couldn't make out the face, but the girl had a pink scarf over her hair.

"Hi, Mr. Huxley," said the girl, in a sweet voice. "I'm Emily."

He turned to Kira, his eyes wide.

"The princess was hoping you could transport her to her guardian."

"What? No, you can't do this to me. I'm sorry, but you can't give me this kid who could get assassinated any minute—no offense, your Highness, but—" He paused. "Wait, what? I thought you wanted Ariel."

"Delacroix does," said Caxton, "but we're pulling a *coup d'etat*."

"If the Commander finds time travelers, he will have no need for the traditional secret police," said Kira.

"You made me wait two nights to tell me that?"

"We had to make a show for Delacroix and wait until we could get Emily out. Delacroix knows that someone has her, but not whom."

"And who's that going to be?"

Kira only smiled. "We have your things." She tossed him his cell phone, and pulled out a pair of black plastic-frame glasses. "I don't know if these will help, but you wore these in college and left them at my apartment one day."

He took them hesitantly and put them on. The prescription was close enough, at least until he could get his contact lenses. He opened his phone and listened to his messages, oldest to newest.

"Hey, Thomas, it's Zoë. If you get a chance, please call me back."

Beep.

"Zo again ... look, I'm sorry for what I said. But I really need to tell you something. Give me a call."

Beep.

"Thomas, please pick up. We need to talk..."

"It must be really important," Kira murmured, glancing at Caxton.

Thomas ignored her and listened to the rest of the messages: from Zoë, from his sister, from work. Finally came to his only saved message: *"Bonjour, mon ami..."*

He snapped his phone shut, as if it had given him an electrical shock. He had re-saved that message roughly every ninety days for four years. Within the next week he would have to save it again ... or if Ariel was right, and he would die, it would disappear.

"That was Madison, right?" said Kira. "It's been so long."

He didn't hear her. Ariel. Where was Ariel? He had told her to leave, but she always came to people when they died. He saw that in her mind. And if anything, he needed her now. And he wanted Zoë, too ... he had a feeling he knew what she wanted to tell him.

"I need to find my fiancée," he told Kira, as the car twisted and turned. "Where is she?"

"Probably in her ship. She's flying out of the country."

"What? I need to see her now. You have no idea how important this is."

"Then call her," said Kira.

He turned his phone over in his hands. "I can't involve her in this. Where do you want me to take Emily, anyway? My job is to report news, not conduct secret operations, espionage—"

"It's only one trip. I gave you a full pardon to get you out of that facility. And if you do this for me, I'll tell you what happened on the morning when you were shot."

He glanced over at Emily, then back to the lieutenant. "This is going to get me killed. Why are you going against Delacroix? You're his protégé. He's guided you your entire career."

"Yes," said Kira, "but I feel he might try to harm the princess. There has been some cover-up involved in Damien's case. In my opinion, the Commander is no longer fit to rule."

"So why me? Why not any other agent?"

"No one will suspect you," said Caxton, glancing at him from the rear-view mirror. "It's been four years since your last assignment. And you already know Emily's selected guardian."

"You kept me in the dark for four years for this? To call me up when no one else will do?"

"No. I wanted to protect you," said Kira.

"Then let me see Zoë."

"Call her," said Kira. "She'll only come for you."

Thomas looked from her to Caxton. "Right. And you need her ... why?"

Kira adjusted the rearview mirror. "It turns out that the princess does have relatives, though not descended from Dimitri Reynolds. Related by marriage, through her grandmother, Reinette. The late queen had one brother, Remy Deschaine, who had a daughter, Valerie. Valerie's two children are still alive. By tomorrow morning, one won't be."

Thomas turned to Emily. "Zoë's your *cousin*? Wait, *Damien's* your cousin. How come—how come no one knew that?"

"They're not descended from Dimitri Reynolds, so they're not considered to be part of the royal family." Emily shrugged. "They brought it up in the hearings. It's been mentioned a lot in the news. I take it you haven't been watching much?"

Thomas sat back. No, he hadn't. Not with his fiancée controlling the remote. But still...

"This is treason," he mused, to Kira. "If you're caught, you'll be executed."

"Only if you fail," Kira said smoothly, "and I would bet my life on you. Come to think of it, I have..."

Thomas dialed the number. "I don't owe you anything, you know. And you won't get at Ariel through me. I'm just going to call Zoë. No promises."

"Agreed," said Kira.

He put the phone to his ear, then waited for her to pick up.

5.

Zoë thought she knew a lot about the world, but that changed when two time travelers showed up in her ship's kitchen.

"How did you get here?" she asked. "Did you sneak on before I took off?"

Jack, the ship's robot, rolled in. "They were not here at liftoff," he said.

"Then what?" She seemed totally bewildered.

"She's a time traveler," said Jamie, gesturing to Ariel.

"Oh, don't even start. Really, this isn't funny."

"It's true," said Ariel. "I didn't want to tell you unless I had to."

Jamie took off his sunglasses and handed them to Zoë. "It was really cold, and it was snowing."

She looked down at the ice coating the plastic and then handed them back, shaking her head. "You could've just put them in the freezer. Please, I don't need this right now."

Ariel looked at the kitchen's clock: 12:30. "*Doce y media.* Wow. What day is it?"

"A better question is, what are you doing here? You stole my fiancé away, and then—"

"Uh, no. I'm sorry if you thought that, but what day is it?"

"June twentieth," said Zoë.

Ariel cast a critical eye on Jamie.

"What?"

"I wanted to be here on the nineteenth."

"I set it for the nineteenth. It's going wonky."

"All right. I'm a bit behind, but while I'm here, I might as well stay. Where's Thomas?"

"You tell me," Zoë said, surly. "He hasn't been returning my calls. And will you *please* tell me what's going on?"

"I can travel in time, all right? I can reach any day, in any place, in any year. Sort of. That pocket watch Jamie has? It isn't just for measuring time—it's for controlling where I am in it. The Celestial Federation found out, and started tracking my device."

"Then why come here?"

"Because I found someone who I thought could help me. Now Thomas is in serious danger because of it. And— why are you flying over the ocean?"

"I'm going to Paris," she said. "I'm not staying to watch Damien die."

"Right. Good. But go back to Tenokte instead, because he won't die. Trust me." She slipped on her green sunglasses. "If something happens and I don't come back, tell Thomas you love him. Just once. That was always your only regret." She opened the pocket watch, and was gone.

Zoë stepped back, alarmed.

"Class A teleport," remarked the 'bot. "My programming did not anticipate this. A bit flashy, but effective."

Zoë turned to Jamie, confused and nearly in tears. Her brother's execution was a tragedy, but an alteration in the laws of physics was world-breaking. She was starting to doubt her own sanity. "I suppose it's too late to ask if this is a joke," she said.

Jamie shook his head. "Impossible. She has no sense of humor."

Zoë landed the ship in an airport field in Tenokte, only an hour after she had lifted off. She left the pilot's cabin to her robot, and walked out.

"You still don't believe it, do you?" Jamie called, trying to take off his seat belt. It clicked, and he sprang up, chasing after her.

"No, I don't." She crossed her arms.

"She vanished. That doesn't mean anything to you?"

"Just because I can't think of anything else to explain it, doesn't mean it's true."

Jamie walked through the kitchen, and saw Thomas's laptop still sitting on the table. He checked his own phone, and saw with some dismay that Damien's death had been set for the following morning. He slipped the device into his pocket and didn't mention it.

"So who is she, really?"

"Ariel? Oh ... I can't even begin to describe her." He thought of all the times he'd spent with Ariel—ancient memories now. She reminded him of a melody heard long ago, where the words are forgotten but the tune remains.

"A long time ago I traveled with her," Jamie said finally. "And she was brilliant."

Zoë poured a mug of coffee, then sipped it. "You make terrible pancakes," she said.

"Oh, man, that was yesterday morning, wasn't it?" he said. "I'm out of it. I've been on Dimitri Reynolds' street today."

She looked at him critically. "Are you all right?"

"I'm fine."

"There you go again," she said. "All right. If you've traveled in time, do you know the future?"

"Yes," he said. "In a way."

"Does Damien die, then?" She hinged the question with more than a bit of importance, and closely watched for his response.

"I don't know." To her disappointed glance, he added: "Time can change."

A faint ringing sounded, and Zoë pulled out her phone. Who'd be calling now? She looked at the number, and her eyes widened.

Thomas.

Chapter Fifteen
June 20, 2507, 5 P.M.

The candle-lit cathedral in southern Tenokte contained only a few people. Some sat in the pews or walked up to the front, genuflected, and settled into their seats. The evening Mass wouldn't be for an hour, but some people needed prayer more than others.

Zoë sat in the third pew from the back, thinking and gazing at the ornate designs. The cathedral's walls and ceilings were painted in swirls of white and gold, and its windows showed stained-glass depictions of Biblical scenes. Her mother had taken her to this church once, many years ago, during a visit to the city.

The pilot was dressed all in white, from a barrette in her honey-colored hair to her blouse, tiered skirt and boots, except for a gold charm bracelet on her wrist. Dressed for prayer. Tomorrow she would be dressed for a funeral.

One lone figure strode in, giving everything a quick glance, then took off his glasses and slipped them into a pocket. He slid into the pew, then sat beside her.

"I haven't seen you in awhile," she murmured.

Thomas gave a shy smile. "It's been worse. Remember when you went on a trip for three weeks?"

"You knew where I was."

"Not the whole time. What did you want to tell me?"

She moved her eyes to him. "All week long, I was sick. I thought it might have been stress, you know? So I went to a clinic ..." She looked down, shaking her head. "I don't know how it happened. I was taking the medication, never missed a single dose. It's supposed to work; it's *always* supposed to work."

"Zoë?"

A tear slid down her cheek. "I'm pregnant."

He had that thought in his mind, dancing like the shadows cast by a flame, and with a sinking feeling he realized Ariel's prophecy was coming true. But he brightened. "Zoë, that's wonderful."

"No, it's not," she said. "I'm not ready. I want to travel. I want to go to college. And I don't want you to stay with me just because of this."

"A baby," he said, daydreaming, then he snapped back. "Wait—what? You're still mad at me?"

"Thomas ... it might be better if we took some time apart. Just until I can think things through."

He sat back, a bit wounded. "Fair enough. But Zo, if something happens to me, give the baby to my parents."

"What?"

"They've always wanted another kid, but you know the law: two per couple. They've been bugging me since I turned about thirteen, wanting grandkids. They'd help take care of her."

"Her?"

"... or him. We don't know yet, do we? But listen. I want to stay with you forever, and I want to be a father, but if something happens to me..." He took her hand. "Then do what you think is best."

"You'll be fine. But Thomas, I'm not sure I want your parents to take care of her."

"Audrey and I turned out all right. Well, maybe Audrey..."

"Thomas, old-fashioned conceptions can cause a lot of problems. No one ever does it that way. It's too risky. What if there's a problem with the baby, and it's all my fault?"

"I never told you, did I? I was a surprise for my parents, too."

Zoë looked at him, and started to laugh. "That's what I'm afraid of!"

"Oh, you're awful," he said, grinning. "Listen, if it were a girl—what would be your favorite name for it?"

"I haven't even thought about it."

"I'd really like if you named her Madison. No reason; it's ... just a beautiful name."

"You really think something will happen to you?"

"Oh ... I don't know. This week has been insane. I wasn't avoiding you, Zoë. I got arrested."

Her eyes widened. "Why?"

"It's a long, long story. But the point is ... I don't even know if I can convince you of the point. But I love you. I always have."

She glanced down.

"Don't you feel the same way?"

"I don't know. With Damien about to die, I don't even know what to feel anymore."

"I don't know about that, but ..." Thomas moved his eyes toward the rear of the church. "I found someone who could use our help."

Zoë looked confused for a moment, then followed his gaze to where a teenage girl stood admiring a statue.

"I have a favor to ask," said Thomas.

They walked back to Zoë's golden ship, the *Halcyon*. Emily shivered as she boarded it.

"No guards," Emily murmured, glancing back at the takeoff fields, which were lit by a blazing sunset.

"Just us," said Thomas. "One trip to Paris. Dimitri Reynolds built up the Federation from that city. When you're eighteen, you can return."

She grasped the handle of the metal door, then stopped. "I can't leave. How can I?"

"Your brother was just killed," he said. "Any of us would do the same."

Emily looked up at him, then to Zoë. Finally she walked inside, her head high. The couple followed her.

"Good evening, Miss Martínez," said Jack, the ship's repair-bot. "Good evening, Mr. Huxley. Good evening ..." A click. "I'm sorry, what is your name?"

"Emily," said the girl.

Click. "Good evening, Miss Emily."

Thomas walked into the ship's tiny lounge, and heard slow, plodding footsteps on the grated floor. Pacing.

He motioned for Zoë and the princess to stay back, then stepped inside. He pulled out a blaster.

"Jamie?" he called. No response, and the footsteps stopped. He stepped into a hallway, pushed open the door to the kitchen. It creaked open; and he sighed, relieved. Ariel was standing by the stove, illuminated by the light streaming from the kitchen window.

"He's gone," she said. "Went back home. I was looking for you. Seems you got out of jail yourself." She blinked. "This toaster, like, *butters* toast for you. Can you believe that?"

"Crazy, huh?" He stepped closer. "You okay, kiddo?"

Ariel waved her hand, disinterested. She pulled off her sheathed sword, let it fall to the floor with a thud, and leaned against the counter. "Tenokte, huh? Just another turn of the earth." And she collapsed.

Thomas rushed to her side. "Ariel! Talk to me. What happened?"

Her eyelids fluttered. "Inevitability."

Zoë and Emily walked in, and when the pilot saw the girl, her eyes widened. "Thomas?"

Ariel's skin was pale a moment before, but now it looked flushed, glowing like coals. Thomas picked her up, moving her to the red sofa.

Zoë moved her eyes to her fiancé. "Has she been vaccinated against the falling-sickness?"

"It can't be that."

"If she's from another time, she'd have no immunity to diseases here."

Thomas sat next to Ariel. "Kiddo, are you okay?" No answer. He smiled bitterly. "I thought I told you not to come back."

She still didn't respond. He checked her breathing and pulse: both were there, but her breaths came faintly.

"Kiddo, talk to me. Please."

"She can't answer you," Zoë whispered.

"Ariel! What year is it?" He was nearly shaking with grief.

"It's 1995, Di," Ariel murmured.

He sat back and looked up at Zoë for help. She leaned over and put a hand to the girl's forehead.

"She's burning with a fever," Zoë murmured. "Oh, anything but that. There's no cure."

"No. I'll take her to a hospital," said Thomas. "I'll—" He glanced down. "They're looking for her. If one of the Commander's soldiers recognize her, they'll lock her up, they'll…"

Zoë looked down at the sleeping girl for a moment. "That virus is a mutation of an old influenza strain. They had that in Dimitri Reynolds' time, didn't they?"

"So you finally believe me?"

"Well … yeah. Maybe her body is so used to being battered by germs, it won't even affect her."

"It's affecting her now."

She looked down at Ariel. "She's really Dimitri's sister?"

Emily stepped into the room, staying away from the scene. "She's come because of Richard, hasn't she?"

Thomas stood and walked over to her. "What do you mean?"

The princess looked down. "Well ... she only comes when somebody dies."

His mind was whirling. Ariel Midori Reynolds, the great explorer, dying in a starship in the twenty-sixth century? It didn't seem right.

"It's not the falling-sickness," he said. "It can't be. It—"

A sharp knock made both of them jump. Thomas turned, wary.

Jack wheeled into the room. "A Celestial patrol is at the door."

"Right." Thomas walked over, lifted Ariel, and moved her over to the couch in the next room. He turned to Zoë. "I'll go out and see. Seal the door behind me and prepare for a launch. If it's Celestials, take off."

"No. Not without you."

Another knock, faint against the ship's armor. He glanced over at Emily, who looked frightened. He turned to Zoë:

"I'll call when I want you to let me in."

Zoë followed him into the hallway, opened the door to the pilot's cabin, and pulled him inside. She closed the door.

"Thomas, if I've got this straight, you want me to take Princess Emily Montag to Paris because the government might be planning to assassinate her, and we've got a possibly-dying, time-traveling fugitive asleep on our couch."

"That's ... pretty much it."

"Right." She bit her lip. "So you I take it you really were in the secret police."

"Yeah, I was."

She glanced down. "You used to have nightmares. Scream in your sleep, everything. Did you know?"

He thought of his dream of the gunshot, now nearly a week ago. "Yes."

"I don't want to see you get killed for this."

"I won't."

"Thomas, everything I said the other night ... I meant it. I don't know if I want to marry you. But that doesn't mean I want to see you get hurt."

"I know. But just trust me." He pulled her close, kissed her, then dashed out the door while she was still entranced, before she could open her eyes.

"Rascal," she murmured.

He entered the chamber that would be air-locked when the ship launched, then pressed a code on the panel. Another door closed behind him, then locked.

After a moment, he stepped outside and closed the ship's main hatch behind him.

The sun had already slipped under the world, making a swirled pattern of dark cerulean clouds. In less than an hour, it would be totally dark. A meteorite cut through the afterglow, burning a pale line into the sky.

Thomas looked down, and saw only Lt. Kira Watson.

"Hey," she said. "I phoned in a request at the airport. Gave the week's code word, everything. They won't search the ship before you go."

"Right." He smiled, relieved. "We were worried when we heard the knocks."

"Sorry, I just wanted to check up on you. Take off a soon as you can. Delacroix noticed Emily's missing, and he's ... well, guards will be sent to every ship, and soon they'll stop even launches I authorize. Hopefully the girl can be in Paris before that happens."

He stared at her. "How can you protect Zoë and the girl from here?"

"The police there have my instructions. Trust me. I've already sent agents—they'll know how to keep the girl in hiding."

"And what about Damien?"

"Still slated for death in the morning. Not sure if you want to try to change that."

"What do you mean?"

"Shift change is such a hectic time at the jail," she sighed. "If an escape were to happen, it would be then. But if someone could teleport, it wouldn't be much of a problem anyway, now would it?"

She wore the uniform of a police lieutenant, and had a captain's authority to control an underground network of agents, but in her eyes, between her long lashes, he saw the girl he had grown up with.

"Damien didn't really kill the king," said Thomas.

"The princess thinks he didn't. I'm not so sure." She stared at the golden ship as a breeze whipped at her hair and coat. "They need to leave. And I should go. So long, Thomas." She turned and trudged back through the fields.

Thomas stood there for a minute, pondering, then turned back toward the ship.

2.

"You have to fly out of here," said Thomas. "Now."

Zoë sat on the couch, not moving. Emily stood in the kitchen doorway, her arms crossed. She wore a pink T-shirt and jeans, and had red barrettes in her golden hair: not the classic image of a princess, but he would accept it.

Ariel still had not awoken.

Zoë paced. "Are you coming with me?"

"I can't."

"Then where will you go? Where can you take her?"

"Back to her home."

"She belongs so far away," Emily murmured. "So long ago."

Ariel started to stir. "It's dark," she whispered, her eyes closed. "No, no, get me out!" She sat up, awake, then glanced around the room.

A pilot, a journalist, a royal teenager, and now a robot were watching her with hesitation.

"Are you all right?" Zoë ventured.

Ariel stood, wobbled, and stretched. "Perfectly."

"That happens," Zoë whispered, glancing at Thomas. "When they wake up, they seem fine for a few hours. Then ... "

"He's coming after you!" said Ariel, pacing. "I need to stop him. How do you stop an assassin?"

"With deadly force," piped up the 'bot, his eyes lighting as he spoke.

Thomas blinked, then looked at Zoë. "Who programmed Jack?"

"My dad ... I think some of his personality might have rubbed off on him."

"I see," said Thomas, quietly.

Ariel wasn't listening."I need to save Damien. Only ..." She pulled out the platinum watch. The antique looked a bit tarnished, and its face was cracked. "It's Jamie's. And not as reliable as mine. Often goes to the wrong hour ... the wrong day. The lieutenant is going to be tracking it, and maybe Bailey too ..."

"Forgive me if you've already covered this," Zoë interrupted, "but if you're a time traveler, why are you here? Of all the places in history, why stop in this particular place and save one person?"

"It's complicated," said Ariel. "Damien's in trouble because of Jude, my former partner. If I didn't meddle with time, Damien would be okay."

"Did this Jude kill Richard?" Emily asked quietly.

Ariel pressed her lips together. Emily deserved the truth. "Yes," she replied.

Everyone was silent for a moment.

"Then why not go back in time and save the king?" Zoë asked.

"Well ... predestination paradox. I have memories of the king's death; therefore it already happened, and always *will* happen. Plus it's a huge, major event, one that would affect too much if it never happened. On the other hand, I still have a chance to change things for Damien."

"But you want to break him out of prison?" said Zoë. "A *high-security* prison? What if that doesn't work, like you said, and the guards suspect something? They're armed. They will kill you."

"To be honest, Miss Martínez, I don't need your approval," said Ariel.

The woman turned to Thomas. "You're not going, are you?"

"I have to."

A pause. "Would you excuse us for a moment?" said Zoë. She pulled Thomas out of the room and closed the door. She whirled to face him. "Two minutes ago she was unconscious. Now she's got some wild idea, and you're going along?"

"That's exactly why I'm going along. She can't do this herself. And this could save your brother's life."

"But you could die trying to do this. What would I tell our child, when she asks what happened to her father?"

He stared at her. "Tell her that her father died doing what's right."

"*This* isn't right. It isn't legal, it isn't safe."

"It's not legal or safe, but it's right. You're the one who said all along that Damien was innocent."

"Yes, I said that. I still think they're going to pardon him. Just come with me. That way I know you'll be all right. I might lose Damien, but I don't want to lose both of you."

"You have to get Emily to safety."

"No. I can't leave without you."

He smiled. "I've got a time machine. If I see danger, I can run away."

"That's not like you. And what if it breaks, like she said?"

"Zoë, I'll come back to you. Nothing's going to stand in my way."

He opened the door, but Zoë pulled him back. It creaked open, giving a full view of the ship's lounge.

"If they find you," she said, stepping into the lounge, "and you can't get out—well, you can break through locks, get past security codes, but the guards answer to the Commander, and to him alone. How could you escape? They have blaster-proof helmets, shields, vests—"

Ariel picked up her sheath, and with one swift motion she pulled out her sword. Thomas simply looked at his fiancée and grinned.

It was Emily who decided the matter. "Yep," she said. "That'd do it."

Chapter Sixteen
June 20, 2507, 11:55 p.m.

The prison security personnel questioned the reporter's need for a midnight appointment, but they considered his reasons and relented. Thomas Huxley was the only journalist the prisoner would speak to, and as the execution grew closer, it was better for him to do an interview as soon as possible.

A protest had formed outside the prison, calling for the convicted assassin's early execution, and it quieted as Thomas passed. He walked into the building, and they resumed their shouts.

The journalist flashed his ID, picked up a pass, and walked with a guard to the maximum-security section. The arrangement had changed since he last visited: Damien Martínez was on death row, and was under full guard.

The prisoner sat locked in Cell 19.

"You're looking better than last time," said Damien, from behind the bars.

"So are you." Thomas grinned, pulled up a chair, and started the interview.

Damien talked candidly about his time with the rock band, and his memories of his family, but he skipped aside questions about the crime. Thomas wrote quick but detailed notes in a paper notebook, a habit he picked up in high school and never shook off.

"Is Zoë in Paris?" the prisoner asked finally.

Thomas faltered. "Leaving for Paris. She wanted to come, but ... the whole week's been hard for her. People have been hard on her. She had to leave the city."

Damien sat back. "Will you tell her I didn't kill the king? Just that."

"Whoa, is that on the record?"

"Yeah. Put it your notes."

The guard shifted uncomfortably.

Thomas adjusted his black-framed specs. "Last week, you confessed to this crime."

"Yeah, but ..." Damien shrugged. He was wearing regulation sea-green prison garb, and his cell was drab, and the dim light cast odd shadows. "They said it would just be easier to confess. They made pretty direct threats against me ... and Zoë."

Thomas pulled off his specs. "Who did?"

"I would like to remind you that the prisoner would be willing to tell any lies to delay his fate," said the guard.

"Excuse me?" said Thomas. "Oh, for a second I thought I was interviewing Damien. But I see that you know everything! Who's in charge of interrogations here?"

"That information is classified."

"It was the secret police," said Damien.

Thomas had stopped taking notes. A memory flashed in his head: dim lights, a scream ... and he remembered where how had seen this jail, years before.

The secret police had no accountability. If they saw fit to torture or execute someone, they could do it.

"Damien ... they didn't suspect that you killed the king," he said. "They knew you were innocent the whole time. They just couldn't catch the real shooter."

"A brilliant deduction, Huxley," came a voice. Commander Edward Delacroix strode toward him, flanked by two guards. He raised his flashlight and shined it at the reporter.

Thomas moved a hand up to shield his eyes.

"Take him."

He barely had time to open his mouth before the guards shoved him against a wall and clicked handcuffs onto him. He thrashed and fought, but they held him tight. "You can't do this!" he yelled, before the soldiers pulled him away.

"Sorry for the disturbance," Commander Delacroix said to the guard. He turned to the prisoner. "Nothing personal. You're going to die for your country. Not many people have that honor."

Damien didn't say a word, just moved his eyes as the Commander walked away, then the guard. Then he screamed and kicked at the bars, again and again, but the sound only echoed off the walls.

So the plan had failed brilliantly, just minutes into it. Commander Delacroix hadn't been away; Kira had led him into a trap.

The Commander walked behind the guards, who pulled Thomas along, but stopped when he heard a faint ringing.

"It's his phone," said the Commander.

They searched Thomas and found his cell phone, and one of the guards handed it to Delacroix, who pulled it open. "Hello?"

A pause, then a stern female voice: "Where's Thomas?"

"He can't answer his phone right now," said Delacroix, watching Thomas try to pull away. "He's a bit tied up at the moment. Can I take a message?"

No reply.

"Which one are you? Zoë, the intrepid pilot ... no, this must be the time traveler. Ariel Midori, isn't it?"

"Let him go."

"In four minutes he'll be in Cell 45," said Delacroix. "I hear you have a time machine. Meet us there." He closed the phone, then pressed a button for the elevator. The doors slid open.

"At this point I don't even see the benefit in keeping you alive," said Delacroix, as the men shoved him in. "Tomorrow the public will wake up to find that Thomas Huxley, beloved journalist, is dead. Brain aneurysm. How sad, but not so unlikely after that accident a few years ago. And after all the stress he and his fiancée went through..."

Thomas's eyes flashed. The guards shoved him into the elevator.

"Aren't you a bit overqualified to be murdering reporters?" Thomas snapped. "Go on then, shoot me. Wouldn't be the first time someone did. Ariel knows what you're up to, and she'll stop you."

Delacroix raised his gun.

Thomas's heart thudded. He was backed up against the wall.

"Stop!" A brunette in full officer's dress stood in the hallway. Lt. Kira Watson. "Don't kill him," she said, her eyes wide.

The Commander turned, enraged. "Do you make the decisions here, lieutenant?" And as Kira gasped, he aimed the pistol at Thomas, and fired.

A single gunshot lit up the elevator car; a sudden pain ripped through Thomas's shoulder and radiated down his arm. Caught off balance, especially with his hands cuffed behind him, he toppled over, on the floor, bleeding, gasping. But he couldn't die. Not when he'd survived a bullet through his head.

Delacroix strode over, looking down at him. "If I were you," he said, "I would start being a lot more cooperative right now."

2.

Ariel lifted the map. They were actually blueprints, but they were a map to her. The architect (who had designed the prison hundreds of years ago) had either been very absentminded, or several secret parts had been built into the prison.

Probably the latter.

Dimitri had once drawn her the plans of a jail that made it easy for secret agents to get in and out if they knew the way. These looked strikingly similar.

"Put an office building across the street," he had said. "In the cellar of that, there could be a door to an underground passageway to the jail. Put a fingerprint reader on the door; only secret police can get in and out."

Ariel stared at the door. She stood in a dusty basement, with piles of boxes stacked everywhere.

A fingerprint reader stood between her and the tunnel.

She looked down at Jamie's pocket watch. It ticked softly, but she knew it could be tracked whenever she moved in time. She had to save it for when she really needed it.

The plan was that Thomas would get inside, find out Damien's location, and text her. The shift change occurred from 11:00 to 11:30, and it would not be extraordinarily difficult to sneak Damien out through the secret police's tunnels, if they had to.

Yet here she was, blocked by the first barrier.

She heard a creak behind her; someone had opened the door to the cellar. Ariel turned off her flashlight, but the intruder pulled out his own.

"It's okay," he said. "Lt. Watson sent me to help you."

Ariel put a hand over her eyes and stood blinking in the dusty light.

"I'm John Caxton," said the sandy-haired man. "An agent of the covert ops." He stepped off the stairs, edging closer.

She didn't reply.

"Or, rather, kind of a liaison between the covert ops and the uniformed—"

"All right, I get it. What are you doing here?"

He strode over to the door, put his hand on the fingerprint reader, and the steel door slid open, revealing a dark tunnel.

Ariel stared at him.

"This passageway has been abandoned for awhile," he said. "We've got newer facilities for holding our suspects."

"Uh-huh. Why are you helping me?"

He strode forward, and she followed him.

The door clicked shut. Locked. No matter. She would have a different, more trustworthy agent to help her get out.

Caxton's flashlight lit their path. Pipes dripped above in the stone passageway. "This was all built at Dimitri Reynolds' request," he said. "You should be very proud."

"You know who I am?"

"I'm the lieutenant's assistant now. I know all her projects." He shined the light. "The ghost. That's what they call you. They're still looking for you."

Ariel pulled out the map. "Then I'll need to be careful."

The flashlight shined for a moment on the inner walls' graffiti. Beside numerous curse words in various languages, someone had scrawled *Kilroy was here*.

Ariel saw the metal ladder and rushed up to it. She took out her phone, dialed, then waited. A pause, and she looked up, wide-eyed. "Where's Thomas?" she asked the voice on the other end of the line.

She stared at Caxton as she listened. "Let him go." After a moment she snapped her phone shut, then put a hand to her mouth and turned away.

"Were you expecting that?" Caxton asked.

She climbed up the ladder. "They're arresting him to try to get me to give myself up."

Caxton didn't reply.

"Why are you helping me?" Ariel asked. "Kira must have ordered you to arrest me."

"I have my doubts about Damien's guilt," he replied. "Kira will keep Huxley safe."

"Right." Ariel climbed off the ladder and onto the next level—a hidden part of the first floor of the prison. "And why not release him yourself? You're in the secret police."

"Delacroix is tightly supervising the prison. But I informed the guards to let a red-haired intruder through," he called.

"And if they don't?"

He shrugged. "Do what you have to. You'll need that watch to get out, in any case."

She nodded and sprinted down the hall.

Caxton took out a radio, and flicked it on, hearing a buzz of static. He could just arrest her now ... but she would use that pocket watch to escape. He lifted the radio to his lips.

"Kira," he said, "she's headed your way."

3.

The *Halcyon* drifted through the sky, making its way across the cities below, where lights flashed like jewels among the darkened streets.

"It's beautiful," Emily murmured. She sat in the co-pilot's seat, and Jack stood off to the side.

"You'll like France. I spent some time there as a teenager. My dad was a diplomat."

"Yes. I knew him."

Zoë smiled faintly. "You would've been about twelve when he died."

"I still remember him. I've been meeting public officials since I was baby."

"Ah." The pilot's smile widened. "Always on top of everything, huh? You'd make a good queen."

Emily stared out at the sky.

The ship's radio sputtered. "Pilot, what is your direction?"

"East, to Paris." Zoë read the navigation directions on the screen for him.

A pause. "You need authorization to fly out of North American airspace. How many passengers are you carrying?"

"None." Zoë gestured for Emily to get out of the pilot's cabin. Emily clicked off her seat belt and scrambled out.

"What is the purpose of the flight?"

"A vacation."

"Pilot, reduce speed. Prepare to be boarded and searched."

Zoë saw a Celestial ship approaching on one of the main screens.

"Oh no, not again," she groaned. She grabbed the thruster. "Jack, has anyone resisted a Celestial ship and won?"

Jack's eyes flashed. "You are piloting a Celestial ship, Miss Martínez."

Her eyes turned toward the screen, and she pushed in the thruster.

The ship blasted off into the sky.

4.

Ariel rushed up a stairwell and pushed the door open. Five minutes remained until the end of the shift change.

She managed to skirt past guards' blasts until now, but when she turned a corner and skidded to a stop, she stood face-to-face with a dozen guards.

"I—" she started.

They fired.

Ariel's hologram blinked out, revealing, instead of dark clothing: her actual attire: a white jacket over a flak vest, jeans, and Converse shoes. She didn't flinch. "Anything else?" she said.

None of them moved.

"Right. Here goes."

She went into a rage. A flashlight clicked on from the other end of the room, and the guards only saw the girl spinning and whipping her sword in the air, a silhouette that danced and struck. She only had to strike two or three to send the rest running. When she had cleared them, she leaned against one wall, catching her breath.

Caxton stood on the other end of the wall. "Nice work. How'd you survive those blasts? No one should be conscious after that..."

"Long story," she replied. She darted up a stairwell.

He followed. "You can't expect to make it, kid. Let it go. Kira won't let them hurt Huxley."

Ariel ignored him, and emerged from the stairs in a hallway. It was completely deserted. She took a breath and walked through, taking hesitant steps.

"Do you—"

"Shh!" She held up a hand. "Do you hear that?"

She could hear heavy breathing—no, gasps. She started to run, and saw someone sitting in the hall up ahead, against the wall. Thomas.

"Don't," he said, but she came closer and dropped to her knees.

"Oh my God."

Thomas's right hand was cuffed to a pipe, and he'd been shot in the left shoulder; he was bleeding profusely. All thoughts of Damien evaporated from her mind.

"Ariel, get out of here, they're going to surround you—"

She blinked, and everything froze around her. The pipe had been leaking, but a drop of water hung suspended in the air. She turned, and saw guards who had been in the shadows now half in step toward her, still as statues. The only thing she could hear was Thomas's ragged breathing.

"Huh," she said. "My grip's slipping." She stumbled, leaning against the wall for support; she dropped her sword, and it clattered onto the linoleum.

"Ariel, *go.* Just leave me and get Damien." Thomas was wide-eyed. "Are you okay?"

"No. I'm getting worse." She swallowed and looked at his wound. Not fatal, but it had damaged the bone. It had to be extremely painful, and required immediate medical attention. "I'll get you to a doctor."

"Ariel, the soldiers, they're moving—!"

Before she could react, someone grabbed her from behind, slipping a gloved hand over her mouth.

"Well, well," said Commander Delacroix. Several guards appeared around her; the watch had apparently slipped back to the normal timestream. "You're going to be very helpful to us, Miss Midori," said Commander Delacroix.

"Let her go," said Thomas. "She's sick, for God's sake—
"

Ariel, dazed, couldn't form any resistance. They injected her with a sedative, but their efforts were unnecessary. She had the falling-sickness, and was lapsing into the *falling* stage: complete unconsciousness.

The last thing she heard was Thomas yelling her name.

Chapter Seventeen
June 21, 2507, 4:14 A.M.

"We're not very good at this," said Ariel.

"No. We're not."

They sat in a windowless cell in the prison. It was cushy, at least, with the walls painted white, like a hospital. A sort of secure waiting room, she realized. She sat on a cot, and had just woken to find Thomas pensive. His hair was messy, his arm in a sling.

"How long was I out?" she asked.

"All night."

"Well ... it's pretty normal to sleep at night, isn't it?"

He stared at her. "You just sort of ... froze. Even before they grabbed you. So no, I'd guess that's not normal."

"You were screaming," she pointed out.

He didn't reply.

The idea to break into a prison, which seemed totally logical the night before, baffled her now. Maybe a sense of fate had been tugging them back, some inescapable destiny that defied reason—after all, Thomas couldn't die in Tenokte if he were flying to Paris—but Ariel realized they had made a mistake.

She had put both of them in danger, and had to set it right. How? What could possibly save them now?

Her thoughts were muddled. "Did you sleep at all?" she asked.

Thomas shook his head. "It was Kira," he murmured. "She knew I'd come for Damien, and she knew you'd come for me."

"And they shot you."

He heard the blast in his head, the blast that recurred in nightmares every few weeks, the echo of the shot that should have killed him years ago. "Yes. Why didn't you run?"

"I couldn't leave you," she said. "And like you said, I just froze." She bit her lip, looking at his shoulder. "That must hurt."

"Only when I move." He tried to lift his arm, and winced. "They pulled out the bullet, though. I just have to wait for it to heal."

"So what happens now?"

"They'll want what you know about time travel. Listen, kiddo, no matter what they threaten to do, don't tell them anything. Even if they…" He bit his lip.

Ariel stared ahead. "They'll torture us."

"No. Maybe. How are you feeling? You're looking better."

"Do I have to answer? We're both locked up, with imminent death approaching."

"That's redundant. Imminent *and* approaching?"

She blinked. Neither of them spoke for a moment.

"I'm just saying, maybe you got over that illness. You're from another time, one with more germs. Your immune system might be stronger."

"You think so? Then we still have time. I'll stop Damien's execution, get us out of here, and get you back to Zoë."

"Uh-huh. Didn't you say that the assassin is coming after me?"

"Jude's figured out that you know he's the shooter, but there's no way I can turn him over to the Celestials without killing him first. And how are they going to release that on the news? 'Time traveler shoots king.' No way that'll fly. They'll still want Damien as their scapegoat."

"Uh-huh." He closed his eyes. "That is hard to explain, come to think of it."

She looked at him for a moment, then smiled. "Those glasses look good on you."

"You're a bit late. I'm already engaged. Or at least ... I thought I was."

"I'm just saying." She leaned her head back. "There's got to be more than a chance we can get out of this alive. Let me think. I've got a good immune system. And Jamie had some theory—said he had a plan to change things."

"Oh, great. My life's in the hands of a rock star. But for what it's worth, I'm starting to remember more." He opened his eyes. "No wonder Kira didn't want to tell me. Do you know?"

"I have a vague idea," she said.

His eyes widened. "Those glasses! I could read minds with them, figure out a plan to get us out of here. You have to let me wear them."

"No," she said.

"Why not?"

"Because *I* can read minds with them."

It had happened slowly, but once she recognized that the whispers she heard were really thoughts, she had focused on them more.

She could tune in to anything: hear a person's breathing and heartbeat, sense the movement of a fly in the next room, and see shadowy outlines of people passing through the hall, even though an opaque door separated them. She knew when the guards would try to strike almost before they could move, and she could see every fragment of memory that Thomas saw.

It didn't always work, though. If she focused on something else and stopped listening, well...

"You can't read my mind," he snapped.

She knew that he meant that she *shouldn't*, not that she couldn't. "Why not?" she said. "You wanted to do it to everyone else."

"But—" He sighed, put a hand to his eyes. "You're not doing it to save your life. You're just doing it out of innate curiosity. And sooner or later you're going to see things—"

"What the ..."

"That maybe someone your age—"

"Oh, wow."

"—shouldn't see."

She put a hand to her mouth, grinning. "Okay, now you read my mind."

"What?"

Ariel took off her sunglasses, then handed them to him. He switched them with his own, and in a moment saw her swimming in a lime-green filter.

"Looks like a video game," he said.

"Do you see anything?"

"Uh, no." The last time he had tried these, the images rushed into his head like a wave. Now he didn't even feel a trickle.

"Give it a second. Do you think there's any chance of Kira going to the Council?"

"Over what?"

"Over anything. Damien. Emily."

"I guess. But who knows? Why do you care about Damien's life, anyway? People die every day, people who don't deserve it, and you're not breaking down doors to save them." He tapped the sunglasses, then looked at Ariel and realized the glasses *were* doing something. He could see her clearly, as if the glasses fit his prescription. Nothing else came.

"Because time travelers messed up here, and I need to set things right."

"Hm. So by that logic, you'd have to let me die." He sighed, took off the glasses and rubbed his eyes. "Do you believe in an afterlife, kiddo? That we go somewhere nice when we die?"

"No."

"Dimitri did."

"Well, I'm not him." She looked away.

"Huh," he said. "I'll never even see my daughter. What's she like? Have you looked that far?"

"No. Didn't think to." She looked at the glasses in his hand. "They didn't work?"

He shook his head.

"Hm. Maybe you need some curiosity to read thoughts. Maybe they show what you want to see, whatever you need to see. The first time you used them, you wanted to see everything they could do, right?"

"Maybe."

Ariel pondered a moment. "How do they plan to execute Damien?"

"I don't know. Maybe lethal injection? The Council will be there to witness it, in any case."

Ariel leaned back. "I see. Have you ever watched anyone die?"

"I don't know. I'm sure I must have."

"It's horrific. It's about the worst thing anyone can see."

"Then why do you always go looking for it?"

"I don't," she said, perplexed. "I don't go around watching people die—why, is that what you think?"

He shrugged.

"I can't be remembered. Time travelers need to be at least partially anonymous. People who are about to die, not necessarily dying, never have much time to talk about someone they met."

He considered that. "Explains why you like me so much."

She snapped her fingers. "Anesthetic. That would explain the telepathic field of the lenses not working. Did they knock you out when they took out the bullet?"

"I don't think so."

"No? They didn't, uh, give you *anything*?"

"Well, maybe. I was screaming a lot. Mostly over them taking you away. They might have given me something to relax me."

"You don't say."

He sighed. "Kiddo, this isn't about Damien anymore. They want *you*, they want what you know. They're hoping you can teach them how to use the pocket watch. And you can't."

"I wouldn't."

"At first they'll say this was all a misunderstanding. They'll promise you your freedom, a great job maybe, and the safety of people you care about. Maybe they'll drug you so you don't even realize you're giving them information. But if that doesn't work, they have another option. Most people tend to give up information very quickly if they see a friend being tortured."

She sat back. "I won't let that happen."

"Doesn't matter. I'll be dead tomorrow. Today." He leaned his head against the wall. "I guess it's them who kill me, huh?"

"I don't know," said Ariel, quietly.

"What happens to Zoë? And the baby?"

"I don't know." She was quiet for a moment. "Is that how the secret police recruits?"

"What?"

"They promise you things, say your loved ones will be safe; heck, they say you're doing it for the good of humanity … sound about right?"

"No. The secret police are a force for good. They're supposed to prevent these sorts of things."

"Well," said Ariel, "they're certainly doing a wonderful job."

2.

12:01 A.M.

A missile exploded into the *Halcyon*, sending it veering off course.

"Not again!" Zoë yelled. She increased the speed, trying to dodge the missiles. "Just once I want one normal, uneventful flight."

One of the control panels blinked. "Pilot, prepare your ship for docking. You are in violation of international law—"

Zoë shut off the radio com. "I can't do this," she said. "In a war, I'd have about five other ships helping me. And all the ship's weapons were removed after the war. There's nothing to do but run."

"We should have left sooner," said the robot, sadly.

Zoë considered. No matter what speed she pulled off, they kept right after her. How long could she let them chase her? Her job usually involved keeping track of navigation, altitude, weather—not an enemy.

Beneath them was the wide Atlantic ocean. If she crashed, the ship wouldn't burn. It would sink.

On the controls, she saw the narrow Celestial fighter move in place beside the *Halcyon*.

"Oh, no you don't," said Zoë, jerking the controls to the left. The ship followed, then latched onto the *Halcyon*.

238

"Celestials boarding," said the pleasant voice of the ship's computer. "They are executing a search warrant, and looking for a missing person. Name: Emily Montag. Hatch will automatically open in—fifteen—seconds."

Zoë slowed the ship, then sat back. "We're done for." She swung toward her robot. "Jack, if a Celestial asks you a question, any question, you have to respond with a truthful answer, don't you?"

"Yes, Miss Martínez," he replied.

"Then, Jack ... can you keep a secret? If they ask you something, don't say a w—"

The door to the ship burst open, and guards rushed into the pilot's cabin and pointed blasters at them.

"Hands in the air! Don't move!" one yelled.

Zoë's hands went up. Jack's wiry arms raised an inch.

"Jeez," said a guard. "One's an assassin, the other's a smuggler. What the hell is wrong with the Martínez family?"

"We weren't loved as children," Zoë replied.

3.

5 A.M., Tenokte

The guards led Thomas and Ariel to the lieutenant's office.

Glass formed one side of the room, and showed the glittering lights of the evening skyline, which seemed like a golden necklace on a dark cloth.

The office itself had sparse furnishings. A gray desk, with two chairs on the opposite side. A bookshelf. A tiny cactus on the desk. This could be the stylish office of a magazine editor, not the lieutenant of a small city and the assistant to the most important man in the world.

Lt. Kira Watson stood by the glass wall. She turned as the visitors entered.

"Don't restrain them," she murmured.

"It's Delacroix's orders," a guard replied.

She didn't reply. The guards handcuffed Thomas's right wrist to the chair, but didn't even glance at Ariel, who stood by the door when it closed.

Kira turned, then smiled at the time traveler. "I don't think we've met, Ariel."

"Don't you *dare* speak to her," said Thomas. "After what you've done—"

"I'm sorry if you feel that way, Thomas," said Kira, "but I wasn't addressing you." She turned to Ariel, who crossed her arms.

"Long night, huh?" said Ariel. "I hear you've been tracking me."

"Hm." Kira stared out the glass. We've wanted to get that project started for years, but the clock would only light up intermittently. We tried a few times, and it didn't work. Finally we got the funding, got a daring volunteer, and it lit up. A perfect Venn diagram of conditions. It took four years and happened only once."

"I see. But the king died that day. You didn't match up the events at all? Even I knew there had to be a connection."

Kira turned. "What do you mean?"

"I know who killed the king. It's a man named Jude Fawkes, a time traveler. I can find him."

"How?"

"He took my copper time piece, and you've tracked it once. Do it again, and you'll have your assassin."

Kira shook her head. "That project has been shut down. It was a failure."

"You knew I'd come," said Thomas, glaring at the lieutenant. "You *knew.*"

"Yes, I knew. And it was my duty to report you. Ariel, Commander Delacroix is quite interested to see you again. Anything you ask for, we will try to grant to the best of our ability. He knows you have some incredible talents. You could teach us a lot."

Ariel gave a sad half-smile. "A few years ago, you were against a secret police who could use time travel."

"Ah, yes, but I realized it wouldn't eliminate our police force. It would make us stronger."

"All right. So if I worked for you, what would you give me?"

"Citizenship, an identity. A fair amount of money. Huxley would be pardoned, of course, and his life would be spared. He'd be free to return to his fiancée."

Ariel nodded at all of the provisions. Just as Thomas predicted.

"Did Zoë make it?" Thomas asked Kira, desperately.

Kira stared at him.

"I'm sorry?"

"Emily and Zoë! Flying off to France? No? Not ringing a bell? Or did you set them up, too?"

Kira looked at him blankly. "Emily's missing, yes, but we're searching for her. You had a pretty bad injury, Huxley. Are you sure you're all right?"

Ariel put a hand over her mouth, but Thomas could see she was smiling. She glanced at him: "You're not seeing it, are you?"

He looked at her lime-colored glasses, then at Kira.

The entire building had microphones and cameras hidden everywhere. Certainly every meeting or prisoner interrogation would be monitored. Kira hadn't turned toward Delacroix's side, and she wasn't just playing coy to keep her job (or her life). She was trying to help them.

"Okay," said Ariel. "I can have anything I want, right? Within reason?"

"Yes."

"I want to watch Damien Martínez's execution. And Thomas has to come with me."

Both Kira and Thomas stared at her, surprised.

"I'm sorry, but for security reasons—"

"Put as many guards around us as you want. With no time machine, neither of us are going to escape. I just want to see it. You can grant me that, can't you?"

Kira was taken aback.

"It's just a thing she has," Thomas said, trying to suppress a smile. "She likes to visit famous deaths in history ... I don't really get it either."

"Uh, very well. You can attend the execution. Commander Delacroix wants to meet with you later, Ariel. I'll have a guard escort you to your room; I need to talk to Thomas for a moment."

"No," said Thomas. "Whatever you have to say, she can hear it."

"It involves the events leading up to your injury four years ago. Most of the information is classified. I can't say it in front of a civilian."

"Then don't say it," he said. He glanced at Ariel, who had gone pale. She turned to him: she already knew.

Thomas closed his eyes. "Don't say it," he repeated. "Tell me some other time."

Kira glanced down. "Very well. I'll have the guards escort you to your room." She walked over to the window, her heels clicking on the floor.

A moment later, they walked in the hallway outside, flanked by guards. Thomas whispered, "You read her mind?"

"Yes," said Ariel.

"So what do we do now?"

"I have a plan. Leave it to me."

"What happened to me?" he asked, his jaw set.

She glanced down as they walked, accompanied by the guards. "I don't quite know how to explain."

"Ariel, please."

"It's in *your* head, too. You just don't want to know."

He sighed and walked on. "Damien is going to die today," he sighed. "And there's nothing we can do."

Chapter Eighteen

Zoë waited with her arms crossed as the white-uniformed soldiers searched her ship. Jack stood by her side, his eyes flashing from time to time, his internal gears clicking, but he did not speak.

The captain of the Celestial cruiser asked her a long string of questions in a tone that reminded her of the frantic buzzing of an insect.

Or a kazoo.

"This search was mandated by the Commander himself. No vehicle coming out of Tenokte is exempt, and resisting a search is a criminal offense. What makes you think you're outside the law?"

"I'm sorry," she said, shrugging. "My brother's going to die today. I must've been a bit absent-minded. You know how things go."

"Your worthless brother killed my king."

"Yeah, keep thinking that."

"Show some respect for a Celestial officer, you insolent—"

Jack rolled forward, his eyes flashing faster. "You will not speak that way to Miss Martínez."

"Worthless 'bot," said the captain. "I'll—"

A guard approached. "Sir, there's no sign of anyone on board."

"Keep searching." He squatted down to look at Jack. "Okay, robot, answer this question carefully, or I'll take you apart with a wrench and pair of pliers. Are there any passengers on this ship?"

Zoë's heart nearly hit her throat.

"No," said the repair-bot.

"There is no one beside the pilot?"

"There is no human on this ship who is not a pilot, correct," said Jack.

The captain stood, gritting his teeth, and glared at Zoë. "Then why the hell did you run?"

"I like to mess with you guys."

He raised a hand against her, but she didn't flinch.

"What are you going to do?" she said. "Execute me?"

"This is your second attempt at refusing a search, Miss Martínez. Most people don't run unless they have something to hide."

"So arrest me," she said. "I'm sure it will make a lovely news story. Put it right in my brother's obituary."

The captain turned away. "I've got other ships to search. Let's go," he said to his men. "Nothing to report." They walked off the ship and sealed off the hatch.

In moments, the *Halcyon* was drifting off by itself.

Zoë walked over to the storage room, then tapped the ceiling. A trap-door opened, and Emily slid out, jumped down to the floor, and brushed the dust off her clothes.

"How'd you find that hiding spot?" Zoë asked.

"I'd have to be pretty daft to miss it. These fighters always have a spare compartment for storage of extra supplies. Thanks for the help, by the way."

"No problem." She turned to Jack. "Nice work. I get it. The ship has no passengers, but there's a co-pilot."

"I try," said Jack, his eyes flashing in pattern meant to simulate cuteness.

It worked: Zoë smiled. "Now, to Paris. Oh, you'll love the city, princess. It's beautiful."

"I want to go back," said Emily.

The pilot turned. "What?"

"There are secret police everywhere, even past the Federation's borders. I can't hide, Miss Martínez. Especially when my people need me."

"After what just happened? No. We need to keep going."

"The risks involved are exactly why we *should* turn back. Besides, I heard you talking with your fiancé. You're with child. I can't ask you to put your life on the line for me."

Zoë didn't reply at first. She pulled out her cell phone, checked for any messages from Thomas, then snapped it shut. He had promised to call when he got out with Damien. There wasn't a call.

"Well, it's your choice. I was asked to take you to Paris, and I'm not afraid of what happens."

"This is what I want."

The pilot nodded. "All right. And Emily?"

"Yes?"

"You really would make a good queen."

Emily beamed, and they headed back to the pilot's cabin.

2.

Jude Fawkes looked up at the white skyscraper from his place on the street.

People shuffled past him, all wearing clothing of a different style than he had grown up with. The twenty-sixth century always baffled him, so he rarely came here and never stayed very long.

His long gray coat billowed in the wind.

One shot. Maybe two. That's all it would take, and this century's government would never learn anything more about time travel. And history agreed with Jude's choice.

Only, his target had vanished, swept into the doors of that prison. So what next? When was the best time for a journalist to go missing?

He saw a car idling outside, remembered something minor about June 21, 2507, and had an idea.

3.

7:23 A.M.

"*Hanging?*" said Ariel.

They stood in a field outside in a small crowd of Celestials and officers, in front of the gallows. One guard stood by her and Thomas.

In front of the gallows were empty chairs for the six members of the World Council, as well as other officials. *Front-row seats to an execution,* Ariel thought gloomily.

"So, that plan," said Thomas. "Uh, it's better than the last one, right?"

"Trust me, it'll work."

"You know, if you still had your time machine, you could bring Dimitri Reynolds here to pardon Damien himself."

"That would break all sorts of time travel code."

"I'm just saying."

The guard shushed them.

Commander Delacroix walked into the field with Kira, and they sat down. Kira gave one nod at Ariel before moving her eyes to the front.

"Thomas, are we in front of the firing squad wall?" Ariel whispered.

Thomas glanced at the brick wall behind them. It was riddled with bullets. "Yeah."

"This is rather disconcerting."

"Shh," said the guard.

The six members of the World Council walked out of the prison and into the field, taking their seats in the front.

Through another door, two guards led in Damien Martínez, who was blindfolded, his hands bound behind his back.

Thomas's eyes widened when he saw him, and he turned to Ariel. "What on earth is your plan? You've got about thirty seconds to start it."

"Hold on," Ariel whispered. "If I can get to Kira, I can get the watch, and get him out of here."

"*That's* your plan?"

"Shh!" said the guard.

Both of them turned to him, but let it go.

Damien now stood on the platform. He looked serious, and not at all intimidated by the guards, who were about to put the noose around his neck.

"Ready?" Ariel whispered.

"Ready."

"Lieutenant!" came a scream.

Ariel turned to the messenger, surprised.

A guard had left the prison and was running toward the front. "Urgent message for you, lieutenant." He handed her a phone.

Kira took it, listened a moment, and turned up the volume.

"Uh, hi," came a voice. "If this works, Kira, you should be receiving it well before the execution. Don't try to shut it off: it'll show up on every radio in the Celestial Federation."

Not many people recognized the voice, even though the speaker was on the radio constantly. But on all those occasions, he'd been singing.

"Jamie," Thomas whispered.

Everyone in the field stood riveted, listening to the message.

"This is Jamie Parsons, by the way, if you haven't guessed. I used a journalist's computer to hack into the radio broadcast. They'll trace it, so let me apologize. He didn't tell me the security code. I'm just pretty good at hacking. I couldn't be much better if I could, I dunno, read minds ...

"In any case, yeah, I was pretty upset about those censorship laws. My last album couldn't be released because it displayed ideas that are considered anti-Federational. One of my best friends died last summer, and the world can't hear his music. So here's a pretty bold political statement for you: I killed the king. Damien Martínez did not. He was trying to stop me."

People gasped, and Damien looked surprised. The recording continued:

"I did not intend for Damien to be found and blamed for this. In my room you can find the schematics and plans for the assassination.

"You don't have to hunt me down and kill me. I've taken care of that last bit for you. Good luck, Federation. Today the sun is going to rise, the sun is going to set, and everything will be right."

The message went to static, then silence. No one could speak.

Kira pulled out her own cell phone and dispatched police to Jamie's residence, but they were already on their way.

The Council deliberated, then unanimously agreed to suspend Damien's execution. The workers took the blindfold off Damien, and he stepped down from the platform that was he not meant to emerge from alive.

No one seemed to remember that Ariel and Thomas were still there. They stood against the wall, dazed.

"Were you expecting that?" said Thomas.

"No. Were you?"

Kira was speaking to the Council, and the two time travelers could only catch a few words.

"I'm sorry," said the Councilwoman, "but without speaking to the princess, we can't make any decision—"

Another phone started ringing. Kira pulled it out of her pocket, checked it. "It's yours," she called to Thomas, tossing it to him.

He caught it with one hand and opened it. "Hello?" he said. "You're back already? Is Zoë all right?" He listened. "Okay. I'll pass it on." He held up the phone. "Message from Emily Montag. She wants to speak to a member of the Council."

"The princess?" said the Councilwoman. She took the phone and listened. "You're sure?" She looked up, then spoke to Kira for a moment, then turned to the guards.

"Arrest the Commander immediately for conspiracy against Damien Martínez and the princess," she said. "We need to conduct a full investigation."

"No—wait—you can't—" said Delacroix, as guards handcuffed him. "Kira! Tell them I didn't do this."

Kira stared at him for a moment. "You don't make the decisions around here anymore," she said. She nodded to the Council. "Take him away."

"No," he protested, as guards pulled him back into the prison. "Kira! *Kira!*"

A member of the council was speaking to another. "But do we have any proof of a plot, besides the girl's word?"

Thomas strode up to them, clearing his throat, and handed them Ariel's music player. "Here," he said. "Listen to the first recording." Before the woman could ask questions, he slipped back into the crowd.

When he found Ariel, she looked perplexed and flushed.

"…Kiddo?" said Thomas.

She swayed, and Thomas caught her. He signaled to Kira that he needed help, and she came over. (Between the Council making calls to the press to do damage control and discussing the Commander's possible plot against Emily, no one noticed them.)

"She's sick," said Thomas. "It's the falling-sickness, I think—"

"You should get out of here anyway," said Kira, not quite listening. "I'm in charge of the investigation now, so consider yourselves released."

By the time they reached the parking lot, Caxton was waiting for them in a car. Thomas and Kira helped Ariel inside. Her eyelids fluttered and closed.

"He can take you to the hospital. If there are any problems, call me."

"Thanks," said Thomas. He climbed in next to Ariel.

"Wait!" A blond teenager flailed after them. Emily. She rushed up to them, out of breath. "Miss Martínez and I just came. Let me come with you. Please. She's not a citizen, but with my authorization, they'll treat her."

Kira hesitated, then relented. "Go."

"Where's Zoë?" Thomas asked the princess.

"Headed to see Damien."

"I need to see her."

"No," said Kira. "Go with your friend."

"Right. Uh, Kira, can you tell her just one thing for me? Tell her I love her."

"Sure," said the lieutenant, but she seemed baffled. "Okay."

Emily climbed into the front passenger seat, and Thomas closed his door. Kira stepped back, walking toward the building, and Caxton started the car. It lifted off the ground and flew into the sky.

Thomas was seized by a sudden panic when he saw the world moving beneath them. He sat back, unnerved.

"You'll be fine, kiddo," he said, even though his heart was still thudding. He took a breath, and realized they had left behind Jamie's watch. Kira still had it. Ariel had no way of getting back.

"Oh my God, listen to this," said Caxton.

Thomas faintly listened to the report on the radio, then froze. Celestials had burst into Jamie Parson's Tenokte home, ready to arrest the singer, and found they couldn't.

"Offed himself, huh?" said Caxton. "That's epic."

"It's *awful*," said Emily. She was in tears.

Thomas turned to Ariel. She was drifting off, and if she heard the news of Jamie's suicide, she didn't give any indication. But, then again, she already knew, didn't she? And so did Jamie...

He sat back, his head hurting. Damien had survived, but he and Ariel wouldn't. He was probably never going to see Zoë again.

"How long now until I die?" he asked out loud, to no one in particular.

"Oh, Thomas," Ariel murmured, "you were never supposed to know."

Chapter Nineteen

At the age of nineteen, Jamie Parsons climbed as high as he could go.

He reached the roof of a friend's apartment complex and looked over the edge. Cars flew above him, like fish in a great sea of sky and clouds, but no one who saw the figure below thought it was a possible jumper. There could be a lot of reasons why a young man would climb to the top of a building. Photography, maybe. Only, he didn't have a camera in his hand.

The most beautiful girl in the world, or so he believed, had dumped him. From here, there was nowhere to go but down. He reached out his foot, looked below to the distant street, and stayed a moment in the breeze. His mind said *Let go*, but he just wanted to stay there for a second, thinking.

Then felt someone grab him from behind. Paramedics.

Jamie spent the night recovering in a hospital bed, sick and slowly detoxing. They put him on suicide watch for three days, and he felt absolutely miserable. He turned away all visitors, even his parents, and spent his time staring at a poster on the wall: a flowchart of the human body's biochemical pathways.

The next afternoon, he turned and saw a young woman standing by his bed. He hadn't heard her walk in.

"Go away," he said.

"You're Jamie Parsons, yes?" she asked.

"What do you want?"

"Unrequited love, huh?" The girl sat down on his bed. "You'll need something to cheer you up. How do you feel about traveling?"

"I hate traveling."

"But you owe me something," she said, smiling. "Who do you think noticed you left the party? Who called the ambulance?"

He froze. She'd been there; he remembered now. A red-haired girl, watching him.

"I wanted to die," he said. "Why did you stop me?"

"Because history says you should live. You need to get used to traveling, too. You only hate it because you left Sydney. Was it nice there?"

He nodded slowly.

"Sydney, Australia. And that would be, oh, five years ago, right? Want to go visit?"

He didn't quite understand what she meant. But a few days later Ariel took him there, and she explained everything bit by bit. He had a good run, exploring different cities, ancient and future, for a few months—until he tripped over a memorial emblazoned with his name and the date of his death.

His request was simple: he wanted to forget her. Go back to his own time and think it was all a dream. The last night they were together, he and Ariel sat in a diner with wide windows that opened out to the street. The occasional car passed outside, its headlights flashing. Aside from a waitress who came every ten minutes to refill Jamie's coffee, they were alone.

Ariel tapped her fingers on the table. "So Bailey knows?"

"Yep. It's all set. You just have to train a replacement." He leaned back, smiling faintly. "I peeked. The band gets huge, doesn't it?"

"Quite."

"And it'll just form on its own?"

"History says so."

"So you're fine now, do you think?"

"Sure. Why wouldn't I be?"

A waitress came by, picked up their plates.

"I mean," he said, "won't you miss me?"

She was taken aback by the question. How could she not? This was their way of life: late nights blending into early morning, thriving when all connections were cut, when tomorrow was long as they wanted to make it. And it was all about to end. They had been perfect partners, laughing their way through history: Jamie with his curiosity, Ariel with her clairvoyant way of looking at the world.

"Of course I'll miss you," she said. "But I'll know where to find you if I need you, won't I?"

He accepted that answer. She left him in Tenokte, said a quick goodbye, and walked out of his life. He took one pill, an amnesia drug, hoping to wake up in the morning and forget everything.

But he didn't. Six months of constant traveling is harder to erase than a night of partying. So was alone with all the knowledge of time travel and no way back to it, all the details of his short but explosive future, and nothing to do but wait and watch it pass by.

And only after Ariel was gone did Jamie fully realize he could read minds with the sunglasses. Sometimes he stood on crowded streets, the thoughts of passerbys drowning out all the music in his head, and he waited for one brief unspoken mention of her. But it never came. If she were real, wouldn't she come visit him at least once? Of course she would. So it couldn't be real, he thought, and he couldn't die just yet.

Six years for Jamie; a handful of days for Ariel.

All that time he wished he could contact her, just once, to know that he wasn't losing his mind. And when she did come back, not even a week before the date he'd seen carved in stone, he lost control of everything.

And he knew that dying wasn't easy, so he tried to do it right.

After he heard his false confession on the radio and received news that Damien's execution was stalled, he took an overdose of pills to stop his heart. But when that didn't work fast enough, he slashed his wrists and plunged them into the warm water of his bathtub.

Everything seemed unreal, and the room looked bright and hazy. He wanted to die, and he especially wanted to die before the Celestials reached his house. Would anyone weep for him, after what he admitted to doing? No, and he didn't want them to.

When the police arrived, the rock star's eyes lay open, as if he were staring at someone who was longer there. The paramedics pulled him out of the tub and attempted resuscitation. Then they brought out an AED.

"Clear."

Jamie's body jerked.

"Clear."

Another thud. No response.

"Call the lieutenant," said Commissioner Huxley. "He's gone."

3.

Dawn burst over the sparkling silver city, and a car zoomed toward the hospital.

"We'll be there soon," Thomas said to Ariel, even though by now she could not reply.

He sat back in the seat.

So Kira had been helping them, or at least been sending suggestions toward Ariel. The lieutenant turned the kaleidoscope of the world, and seemed to get whatever she wanted—no matter what stood in the way. Thomas and Ariel had not saved Zoë's brother, or at least not yet, but Jamie had gained valuable time for them.

"You really care about her," said Emily, peering back at them from the front seat.

Thomas looked down at Ariel, but didn't respond.

"How'd you get hurt?"

He looked down at the sling. "Long story," he said. "I—" He stared ahead, eyes wide.

The driver tried to swerve, but too late: another flying car slammed into the front of their vehicle, spraying shards of glass everywhere.

Thomas grabbed for something, anything, but the car was spinning out of control, and falling. He could hear Emily screaming, but he had no time to be terrified, and remembered the indisputable fact of flying cars' crashes: it wasn't the first impact that caused death.

It was the second.

Only when Thomas opened his eyes did he realize he'd survived. The first rays of sunlight teased his eyes, and he felt pain, but could not quite identify it.

Ariel sat with her eyes closed, her reddish-auburn hair swept over her face. The driver was unconscious. Emily was turned away, and he could not get a good look at her. In the distance, he could hear sirens.

He unbuckled his seatbelt and looked around: they were surrounded by blue skies. Skies? When he pushed his door open, he understood why they were all alive. They'd landed on the roof of a skyscraper.

Suddenly he felt someone grab him. He screamed and tried to fight, but the man slipped a gloved hand over Thomas's mouth and slammed his head into the door frame, knocking off his specs. His head burst with pain, and, dazed, he stopped protesting. The man dragged Thomas away from the car.

Emily stirred when she heard the noise, and, realizing what happened, pushed open her door and ran out. "Stop!" she screamed. "Don't hurt him."

The assassin paused: he did not expect her to be there. He suddenly started to laugh. "Who are you, then? No one important, I hope."

Thomas closed his eyes. *Don't say your name, Emily.*

"What did you *do*?" she said. "Did you—?"

The man peered over the edge of the building, where ambulances and fire trucks sat around a crumpled car. "Teen drivers," he sighed. "I didn't do a thing. Such a dangerous way to travel, though."

Thomas tried to stir, but he heard the click of a gun and went still.

A golden glow bathed the horizon, then reflected off the skyline of towers and covered tunnels.

Emily suddenly recognized the man. "You killed Richard," she said.

"I did," said Jude Fawkes. "Have to protect my own. So, Huxley, any last words? Something I should tell Zoë?" He slid his hand off Thomas's mouth.

"Don't hurt the girl," said Thomas. "She's just a kid. She won't remember you."

"How sanctimonious of you," said Jude Fawkes. "Hear that, doll? Last words were to save you. I guess I'll have to grant them. Nothing personal, Huxley, but you're a liability. If you live, I'll have to run. And I'm not going to run anymore."

A soft voice made both of them turn: "Hey, Jude."

The assassin whirled around; Ariel was standing ten paces behind him, pointing a gun at him.

"Ariel—" said Jude.

"Drop it. Drop the gun and walk away."

"Ariel, just run! Mmmph—"

Jude slipped a hand over Thomas's mouth. "How did you get back?"

She smiled. "Jamie."

"Ah. Should've figured. But he's already dead, so that's taken care of. You shoot, Huxley dies. That is, unless you can take me out in one shot, without missing, before my finger moves. How's someone's aim in the last stage of the falling-sickness? Don't you start to see double?"

"Put it down."

"I have to kill him, Ariel, but I don't want to hurt you."

"Jude—"

"I have to."

"You don't—"

Two gunshots sounded.

At first, Thomas thought Ariel shot the assassin. Her expression hadn't changed. In fact, she didn't move at all for a few seconds, but then she blinked and put a hand to her chest, where two holes had appeared in the dark cloth. She looked down, as if perplexed, and collapsed.

The world seemed to slow down. Thomas fought, he tried to get away, but Jude twisted his left arm and he screamed and went still.

"Easy, now," said Jude. "Don't make this harder than it has to be."

"She saved your life," said Thomas, through gritted teeth.

"It doesn't really matter now."

Thomas closed his eyes. He was going to die. Nothing could prepare him for this. Everything flashed before him: Zoë. His daughter, whom he would never see.

Ariel—

A gunshot rang out. Thomas opened his eyes, but when he drew another breath, he realized he hadn't been hurt.

The assassin let him go, and Thomas turned. Jude crumpled to the ground, his eyes wide and lifeless. A bullet had gone through his skull.

Thomas heard a soft sobbing behind him. He turned.

The princess stood about twenty feet away, holding a pistol, her face pale with shock.

"Emily," he murmured.

She looked up at him, her eyes glistening with tears.

Thomas kicked the Jude's weapon away from the body, and a glint of copper caught his eye. He took the timepiece from the assassin's hand, then, as an afterthought, he checked the man's pulse. Nothing. He walked over to Emily.

"He—" she stammered. "He killed—"

"It's all right." He gently took away the pistol, put it to the ground, then held her for a moment.

"I wouldn't have done it," she said, tears streaming down her face, "but he was going to kill you. I didn't know what else to do."

"It's all right." Then he jumped. "Ariel!" He turned and dropped down to the girl's side. "Ariel, can you hear me?"

No response. He checked her injuries. Two holes were in her jacket, right over her heart. "No, no! Ariel, listen to me. You have to be okay." He listened to her chest. Faint breathing. "Ariel..."

Emily crouched down beside him. "I'm sorry."

"No, no, no." Thomas lifted Ariel's head, cradled her body in his arms. "Ariel, you have to wake up. Please."

Emily put a hand to Ariel's jacket, then pulled it back, looking at her fingers. "There's no blood."

Thomas stared at her, eyes filled with tears, and realized she was right.

Ariel took a breath, and her eyelids fluttered open. "Hey," she whispered, then winced. "Ow ... flak jacket. Pain. Not cool."

"Kiddo!" His eyes widened. "Oh my God, where did you get a bulletproof vest?"

Ariel closed her eyes. "Di."

"Di?" said Emily.

"Her brother," Thomas said quickly. "He's a soldier."

Ariel was already unconscious again; he could feel in it her soft breaths. The sirens grew louder, and an ambulance and police cruiser landed on the building, attracted by the gunshots. They checked and covered the assassin's body, and walked toward the group. A paramedic asked Emily what had happened.

The princess pointed to Jude's body. "That man killed my brother, and he was trying to kill me and this reporter." She looked down at Ariel. "She saved our lives."

That simplified matters greatly. The sun burst over the horizon, turning the sky a reddish-orange. The workers asked Thomas questions, but he couldn't reply. He was crying silently, holding Ariel in his arms, not daring to believe his luck, not wanting to move. It was June 21, 2507, and he was found above a street in Tenokte, very much alive.

Chapter Twenty

Over the course of half an hour, a team of doctors poked and prodded Thomas several times, but they found nothing wrong with him—nothing new, anyway. They looked at his X-rays, whistled at the one of his skull, winced at the one of his shoulder, and moved along.

He slid off the table and went in search of Kira, and in the process passed Emily Montag, who breathed in and out as a physician's assistant listened to her chest with a stethoscope. Beyond minor shock, she seemed to be doing fine.

Lt. Kira Watson was arguing with the staff over Ariel's treatment.

"She has no identification," said the nurse.

"This is an emergency. I authorize it. And the princess is here, for crying out loud. If *she* can't authorize it—"

"I'm sorry. The retina scan can't identify her, and with no personal ID card, they can't manually enter her into the computer as a patient. Her treatment's going to be delayed while they work it out."

Kira walked back, scowling. "Commander of the globe!" she said. "And I can't even get a check-up for her."

Thomas stared ahead. "Doesn't matter. There's no cure."

"So what are you going to do?"

"I'll—take her back to the ship," he said, distracted. "I'll take her back to her own time if I have to."

"Do you even know where lives?"

"Yes. At least, I know who her brother is." He looked at the clock. "I'm not supposed to be alive right now. I should've died up there."

"She really stole Caxton's gun and shot the assassin with it?"

"Borrowed," he said. "She borrowed his gun."

Kira smiled. "The assassin's body was taken to the crime lab, and they analyzed the prints. The one partial print matched Jude's, and Emily's testimony and the video evidence stacks up. You found the king's killer."

"Good," said Thomas. "That's good."

"The Council released Damien, too. He's under police protection, obviously."

"What about Jamie?"

"We found that someone called his house phone and talked to him right before the assassination. He couldn't have killed the king. Chalk it up to his mental state."

He watched the medical staff pass by. "Right," he said. "You're the one who caused his mental state, you know. He was always infatuated with you."

"Please. I can't take credit for all that myself."

He sighed. That was true.

"Delacroix has been imprisoned, and the Council's looking at his case. They also discovered the full extent of his plans against Emily ... no chance of him getting out anytime soon." She reached into her pocket and took out a cracked platinum pocket watch. "The other watch seems to be broken, but this one was on Ariel when we took her in. Take it."

"You won't want to use it to find time travelers?"

"Please. I have enough trouble keeping track of people without adding *that* into the mix."

He pocketed the device, and glanced over at Emily. "Is she safe now?"

"Yes. Well, reasonably. She's going to need a lot of security, but the people love her. They're even trying to modify the laws so she can be coronated early."

"How early?"

"This summer."

Thomas smiled. He glanced over at one of the other beds, where a doctor was treating John Caxton, Kira's assistant, for a broken rib.

"Seems everyone survived," he said.

Kira nodded. "If you want ... I can tell you what happened."

He looked at Ariel, lying asleep on a stretcher. No, not asleep, in limbo between life and death. He remembered most of the incident, but needed someone to fill in the blanks.

"Tell me," he said.

"You had some trouble with your partner, Agent Six, and I thought a change would do you some good. We sent you to Montréal and I gave you a new partner, Agent 27, Madison Delgado. She was very beautiful, and they warned me there was a risk that anyone would get too close to her. But you must understand, I was working under the impression that you were, well…"

"Gay," Thomas supplied, distracted.

"Yes. Not to put too fine a point on it, but you had never dated a woman before. Apparently you two hit it off well. She had an infant son, the father out of the picture, and you loved the kid. You took three classes at a university up there, and spent the spring studying and writing articles.

"When you came back to graduate, you asked Madison to come with you. She did. But she was working as a double agent, and knew too much about you. Do you know anything about the Red Army?"

"Uh—someone at the base mentioned it. I take it it's a rebel group?"

"Yes. It's been around for quite awhile, and they were responsible for a revolt in Italy the year before your capture. Madison was working for them, but apparently she didn't know enough about the secret police to satisfy them. In August of that year, around the time the epidemic started, her group gave her a choice: give up your identity, or they would harm her son.

"She chose to give up you. Five of them ambushed and kidnapped you. According to their reports, you thought it was some sort of prank at first. Then they broke your leg and your wrist, and cut your chest almost to ribbons, and you realized they weren't joking."

Thomas flexed his wrist. "What did they want?"

"Names, information. Anything they could get about the secret police. You knew my name and several others', and you were always pretty clever, so you probably knew more than you let on."

"And?"

"You didn't tell them anything, and we found you. You disappeared around Friday afternoon, and early Monday morning we received a call with your whereabouts. It was from a female operative in the Red Army. And …"

"And?" said Thomas.

She sighed. "We didn't get there fast enough. There were shots …" A pause. "We found you lying on the floor, not moving, not breathing. We had to revive you."

He tried to remember what they'd told him after he woke from his coma. The bullet had gone through the front of his skull, passing straight through the side, hitting very little brain tissue. After undergoing surgery to close up his skull, he didn't wake up, and started showing signs of infection.

"They wanted to take you off life support," Kira continued, "but you were *talking*. In your sleep you were saying things, asking questions of people who weren't there. So they kept you on it. Suffice to say, you recovered."

"What happened to Madison?"

She was quiet for a moment. "Thomas, do you really want to know? Even if it's not the answer you were hoping for?"

He nodded.

"Thomas, the rebels who kidnapped you, they … shot her. In front of you."

He closed his eyes. No wonder she didn't want to tell him.

"I'm sorry," she whispered.

"You should have told me."

"I know. But I couldn't. Not when you didn't even remember her. I just wanted you to start over, Thomas. How would knowing that have helped you?"

"But I never knew. All these years, I've been wondering…"

"Does it make you any happier to know?" she asked. "I didn't think it would."

"No," he replied, finally. "But now I know." He paused. "What about her little son? Her baby?"

"He's fine. Growing up with his father in Montreal." She paused. "We arrested five people responsible for your kidnapping, and they were executed by lethal injection. But according to all of their statements, there's one more kidnapper at large. They all pointed the blame at him for killing Madison. He wasn't in the building when we rescued you."

"He's still out there?"

Kira nodded slowly. "The suspect's name is Peter Masaccio. He's rumored to still be running the Red Army, although they're quite underground now." She paused. "Thomas, if you want to leave the secret police, I'd understand. You went through a lot. But if not ... we still have a place for you."

Thomas thought of Madison. He had no memory of her murder ... but he was remembering more and more every day, so that could change. "Kira," he said, "does the secret police have an office in London?"

She smiled. "I'll let them know you're coming."

He took Ariel back to Zoë's ship. Jack had cut the wires to the TV, at the pilot's request, and so they went on with their activities in blissful silence. When Thomas arrived, he lay Ariel down on the couch.

Zoë kissed him, then sat down, recounting all the details of Damien's release. When she finished, she looked down at the time traveler, suddenly subdued. "Will you take her home?" she asked.

"I don't know where she belongs."

"With Dimitri Reynolds."

"But when?" he said. "I can't look up the date she went missing. Not now."

"Then don't," said Zoë.

A pause.

"I hear you did some good piloting," said Thomas.

"Not good enough. My father could've done better." Zoë said it almost without realizing it, then looked surprised. She grabbed her jacket, then opened the hatch of the ship with a creak.

"Where are you going?"

"I don't know, but I can't stay here. When I look at her, I think about Jamie." She wiped her eyes. "I'm sorry, Thomas. My mother died of the falling-sickness." She walked out the door, and in a moment Thomas heard the metallic slam of the hatch.

He stood there for a moment, anguished, wondering if he should rush after her. Finally he walked back to Ariel's side and sat down.

For an hour or two he put cold cloths on her head, waiting for her to sweat out a fever while the world outside was celebrating the summer solstice.

He couldn't do it. He walked over to his room in the ship, screamed and pounded and cried, and turned and saw a robot staring at him with wide, bicycle-reflector eyes.

"Is something the matter, Mr. Huxley?" said Jack.

Thomas slumped to the floor. "Jamie's dead. Ariel's sick and I don't know what to do. I just found out that the person who killed my old girlfriend is still alive. And Zoë's out there, and she won't even speak to me."

"I am sorry," said the repair-bot, his eyes flashing. "Those problems are beyond my repairing capacities. I can only offer my deepest consolations."

"Thanks anyway," said Thomas.

"Death is a part of life. It must always happen."

"Right. Next time, tell me something I don't know." He walked back to see Ariel.

What had changed to make him live? She could tell him if she woke up. He tried to think, tried to trace the path through time, and realized it was like trying to visualize a storm by looking at the debris. He was alive. Did it even matter?

"You can't die, kiddo," said Thomas. "That'd mess me up. Just open your eyes. I've got your time machine. What day do I take you back? When's the first moment your brother misses you?"

His phone rang, and he scrambled to pick it up. "Hello?" A pause. "Yes, I know I've been reactivated as an agent, but I can't right now, I—" Another pause. "Fine. Just give me a minute. I'll be there."

That afternoon, Thomas found himself sitting at the head of a long table. The Council had called him up to present his findings on the assassination.

His heart was grieving for a dying friend. But life, as they say, goes on; and he needed to present a case for Damien's innocence, so he let them ask questions: with one disclaimer.

"With all due respect, I don't really have any new information for you," he said. "I'm just a journalist."

"You were a homicide detective," said Marietta Jones, chairwoman of the council, sliding a file toward him. "Solved every case you started. And you used CPA resources to investigate this case, didn't you?"

"CPA?"

"Celestial Protection Agency," said a council member. "The secret police."

He hadn't heard that euphemism in years. So his secret was out, and he was pinned up against the wall.

"Don't worry; we've met thousands of agents, many of them testifying on cases like this. The lieutenant gave her recommendation to you. Please, just tell us what you know."

Thomas stood. He thought of Ariel, of a fever taking away that perfect mind...

"I suspect that Commander Delacroix wanted to kill Emily before she could be crowned. He was the highest-ranking person outside the royal family, and he was in your favor. By default, the throne would go to him."

"I see. We've reviewed your recording. It's very informative about the matter." The woman slid the music player over to him. "Lt. Kira Watson has also testified about this case. Do you think Delacroix hired the assassin who attacked King Richard?"

"Not quite. I think he simply took advantage of the situation." He pulled out a laptop and opened a file. "This is the profile for a man arrested on the *Lunitron* four years ago. Name: Jude Fawkes. No one knew how he got on the ship, and he disappeared from his cell without a trace. Deleted from the main files, naturally, but Project X kept a copy."

"Project X?"

"A mission dedicated to investigating time travel," said Thomas. "As you can see, the prisoner they found had fingerprints and a retina scan that matched that of a man who, according to your files, went missing nearly a century earlier."

One of the Council members looked at the date of birth. "So the cross-referencing was a mistake?"

"Either that, or Fawkes hacked into the file to corrupt it. The facts are these: a man, acting alone and probably with rebel sympathies, assassinated your king. The Commander threw a new plan into motion, planning to harm the princess. And the assassin found out I was investigating the case, and came after me."

"And your friend shot the assassin, correct?"

"Yes," he said, his eyes distant. "But she doesn't have any information for you."

"The CPA are seriously investigating time travel?" said a Councilman. "Have they found any evidence it exists?"

Thomas smiled. "No clue. I deal with facts. You'd have better luck asking a conspiracist. But think about it: is it more likely that people are popping in and out of time randomly killing people, or that one rebel managed to get a clear shot?"

The Councilman realized the silliness of his question. "Thank you, Agent Nineteen. That is all."

Thomas reached for the laptop, then paused. He had written about their news, all their laws and decisions, commenting on the world they controlled. But today he was a clandestine agent, telling them what to do. He gave a businesslike smile and left the board room. Damien would go free; the real assassin was dead, his body in Celestial custody. But he still felt troubled and sad when he thought of Ariel.

He stepped outside. The day was sunny with patchy clouds, and not even a whisper of chance for rain.

2.

Zoë, dressed in a loose tan jacket and jeans, walked into Apollo's office—then stopped. The lawyer had pulled his leather-bound books from the shelves, and his knickknacks were scattered on his desk. He lowered an iron scale into a cardboard box.

"You're leaving?" she said.

Apollo nodded. "Retiring. I'm finally moving to San Francisco."

"Northampton's closer, you know."

"True." He dusted off a statue of Lady Liberty (besides Zoë, the only woman he allowed in his life) and put it in the box. "Still, I could use a change of scenery. Heard the news about your friend. I'm very sorry."

Zoë glanced down. "I should've paid more attention to Jamie. All the signs were there."

"Perhaps. Or, perhaps it's just destiny. Maybe there's a reason things happen, and it's not just random." He sighed. "Don't blame yourself, my dear. Life's too short for that."

She nodded, her eyes watering. "It's just … Kyle, and now Jamie … I can't go on like this. I just can't."

"I know it's hard for you, with your parents gone, but trust me, things get better. You have a lot to look forward to. Motherhood, for one." He winked.

She put a hand to her abdomen, jolted. "How did you—?"

He shrugged. "I just know these things. Also, Damien *might* have mentioned it." He put his briefcase on his desk, rolled the dials on the brass combination locks, and popped it open. "I don't do murders anymore, like you said. I mostly handle financial matters. And I'm very good at prenups." He took out a piece of paper, then put it on the desk. "Standard form. You can look it over, then make any necessary additions."

She blinked. "I'm not getting married."

"Of course. I'll just leave this right … here." He edged over, then snapped up his briefcase, then grabbed the box. He gave her one last smile, then walked out the door.

Zoë sighed. Her phone buzzed, and she answered it. "Hello? —Yes, I'm Jamie's health-care proxy." A pause. She listened to the message, stunned, and the phone dropped out of her hand.

3.

Thomas stayed with Ariel for the rest of the afternoon, and Zoë didn't return. He realized it was almost exactly a year since she lost one friend, and now another had died.

Perhaps he had been too concerned with his own problems, or Ariel's. Maybe he was out of touch with his fiancée, and she was giving a subtle hint for him to get out of her life.

He listened to the time traveler's breathing. Air in, out.

In, out.

"You saved Damien," he said. "And me, and Emily. She's going to be queen, too, and sooner than I thought. You probably knew that already."

In, out.

"I decided not to take that newscaster job," he said. "Sure, it pays about ten times what I make now, but I found a job that's even better. And I'm still taking Audrey to London for the summer. Can you imagine? She's got a boyfriend. Did you have a boyfriend when you were that age?"

No reply.

He ran a hand through his hair, and got up to walk over to the kitchen. But a voice from the next room over stopped him:

"Thomas, *you* had a boyfriend when you were that age."

"Ariel!" he said, delighted. He rushed over to the lounge and saw her sitting up on the couch. Her skin looked less flushed.

"What day is it?" she asked, her voice still drowsy from sleep.

"Tuesday the twenty-first, and nearly evening. The Flyday. Are you okay, for real?"

"Yeah. I think so." She slid off the couch. "I feel better. I guess I've got a strong immune system. What about you? Are you all right?"

"Perfectly." He was standing in the doorway, and felt as if his heart had simultaneously stopped and started beating faster than he'd ever thought possible. "Zoë said that in your time, people got sick a lot, and your body should be used to a battering. Have you ever had influenza, or the rhinovirus?"

She blinked. "The flu? The common cold? Are you *kidding* me?"

"Uh ... you've never had them?"

"We get them all the time! The flu swings around every winter, and kids get a cold just about every month. Don't you ever get sick?"

He thought back. "I got an infection after my injury four years ago."

"Man, you must not be able to keep a contact lens in for two days straight without your immune system shutting down."

"Yeah," he said. "Crazy..."

She stretched. "What happened while I was out?"

"Uh..."

"Did I kill Jude?"

"No. Emily did."

"And Jamie..."

He didn't reply for a moment, and she understood.

"Oh!" He pulled out the copper watch. "I took this from Jude."

Ariel's eyes lit up. "Brilliant," she said, taking it by the chain. "Want to pay Jamie a visit before he goes?"

He clapped a hand to his mouth. "Watch him *die*?"

"I'm feeling lucky," she said. "Maybe it's my brain cells overheating. Let's go!"

The ship around them melted away, and in a second, they stood in a hallway.

A rock star's hallway.

A door lay ajar, and they heard music blasting from the room inside.

"I don't think this is a good—" Thomas started.

Ariel pushed the door open, then walked inside the bathroom. She turned off the stereo. *Who has a stereo in their bathroom?* Thomas thought, then he realized: This was Jamie.

Jamie sat in the tub with his eyes closed. His clothes were soaked. He had two gashes on his wrists, which he held under the flowing water. Thomas saw bottles of pills strewn all over the sink.

"Ariel," Jamie said, his eyes flying open. "What are you—?"

Ariel shoved him against the wall. With one hand she untied her shoelaces.

Very affectionate, Thomas thought.

"I heard that," said Ariel. She had pulled off one lace and tied it around Jamie's arm, above the artery.

"You can't do this!" Jamie yelled, but he was too weak to do much more than complain. "I'm supposed to die today. June 21, 2507! I saw that on the monument."

"Maybe they etched it wrong," said Thomas. "They could've meant 2570 or something. Typo, misprint. I mean, this is hundreds of years in the future, right? You shouldn't bet your life on these things."

Jamie gave no response. Ariel pulled out a bobby pin from her hair and stuck it in the makeshift tourniquet, then twisted it until Jamie screamed. She shut off the water, pulled out another shoelace and went for the next arm.

"You're not supposed to use tourniquets," Thomas corrected. "Just apply pressure to his arms."

"I can't be applying pressure to his arms when the paramedics come in, okay? They'll find him before he needs his arms amputated."

"What?" said Jamie, his eyes wide.

"Fine. Allow me." Thomas reached in and didn't stop twisting the pin no matter how much Jamie protested. "That's for hacking my account," he said, clipping it in place. "I'm probably going to get in trouble over that."

"Did it work?" said Jamie. "Did it save Damien, I mean?"

"Yeah," said Ariel. "No reason to off yourself, though."

"You don't understand. The police are coming. They'll—"

"Stick you in a hospital," said Ariel. "For 72 hours, then you're out."

"Why are you doing this? I want to die."

"Jamie," said Thomas, "people are crazy about your music. And for some strange reason, Zoë is fond of you. She was upset, crying—well, will be. Would have been—?"

"She was?" Jamie asked.

He decided to stick with past tense. "Yes."

They heard a banging on the downstairs door.

Jamie's eyelids fluttered, and he looked pale. He had lost a lot of blood, and still had toxins in his body that would shut down his system without immediate medical attention.

"Jamie, stay with me," Ariel urged. "Remember all the fun we had? Tossing barrels at the Boston Tea Party? All those crazy parties in Versailles? Or the sinking of the *Titanic*? *Remember*?"

The singer didn't reply. They were losing him.

"Jamie!"

Jamie took a breath, exhaled—and did not take another. He stared at both of them, unblinking.

"No. I thought I could stop it," Ariel whispered.

They heard the door burst open downstairs.

Thomas turned. "We need to go. We're already in Tenokte once right now."

Ariel risked one more glance at musician, covered her mouth, and looked away. Thomas took her hand, pressed the button on the watch, and they vanished.

Commissioner Huxley walked inside. Even as EMTs rushed in and checked for a pulse, he knew what had happened: Jamie's eyes were wide open, staring at someone who was not there.

They pulled him out of the water and attempted CPR, then dried him with a towel and set up a defibrillator.

"Clear."

Jamie twitched.

They tried again. "Clear!"

His body jerked, but his eyes remained wide open.

"Call the lieutenant," said the police commissioner. "He's gone."

They made the call, but the paramedic tried one more time.

"Clear."

Jamie's body jerked again, and the rock star sucked in a breath. He closed his eyes, coughing and sputtering.

"Ariel!" he moaned, and started to cry.

4.

Thomas and Ariel stood in the next room.

"Is this going to break the time-space continuum?" Thomas whispered. "You know, unravel time, create a black hole or something?"

"I don't think it should." Ariel pressed an ear against the wall, listening. "I think we were always meant to come here and save him."

"But what about *me?* I don't know if you realize, but I'm supposed to be dead right now too. I'm not going to get hit by a falling meteorite, am I? Or die in a hotel fire?"

"I don't know. Maybe the note about your death in my file was a mistake? Historians make errors all the time. In any case, right now you have a blank future. So make it good, okay?"

"Sure. I'll try." He paused. "You knew Jamie for awhile, right? What's wrong with him?"

"Well, it's kind of self-explanatory. When he's up, he thinks he's the greatest thing ever, doesn't sleep and has the drive to make award-winning albums. And then he doesn't take any medication, because if he was sick, why would he feel so great? Then he gets really sad and something happens to throw him off and ..."

"He tries to kill himself."

"Pretty much. He must've had it rough as a kid. He's a musician and an only child, and both his parents are deaf. They were always very supportive of him, but it must have been hard, with all that noise in his head, to live in a house that was so quiet."

Thomas could understand that. He paused. "Were you really on the *Titanic*?"

Ariel smiled but didn't answer. She looked again at the etching on her watch's cover: a sun, either rising or setting. She thought of Jude's silver watch, which had a picture of a crescent moon ... the gold one, which showed a sun high in the sky ... and Jamie's; what else? Stars.

She pressed the fob, and the two angels of death reappeared on the *Halcyon*.

Chapter Twenty-One
June 21, 2507

Clouds fluttered by in the skies above a blue and green planet. Cars flew over invisible highways, driven by people with one route on their mind and a million in their hearts. Sunset had started, and the world seemed more dazzling than it ever could be again.

Ariel slipped through the streets, which were all familiar to her but by different names, and passed a group of teenagers lighting candles at a vigil for a musician. At midnight, it would be one year since Kyle Jones's death. She met some of their eyes as they passed, and knew their grief; but after a moment, she turned the corner, and they were alone with it again.

She passed shops with hologram displays blinking and twirling in the windows, she looked up and saw a streetlight turning magenta, and watched cars stop and go. She passed a Celestial police officer, with his white uniform and blue helmet, and after a quick moment of apprehension, she realized it was okay: after all, this was the year 2507.

When she reached a white palace, she looked up, then pulled out her copper watch and pressed the tab.

Meanwhile, a girl of sixteen stood in her bedroom, looking out the window into the royal courtyard.

Princess Emily Montag, heir apparent of the Celestial Federation, wore a pink dress, her golden hair pulled up under a silver tiara. She glanced back when she heard footsteps, then relaxed.

"You really are a ghost," said Emily.

Ariel Midori, standing a few feet away, stared back at her, perplexed.

"When I was a child, my grandmother told me a story. On the eve of her coronation, a girl appeared to her, wished her good luck in her reign, and then departed. No one knew how she had entered the palace, and my grandmother never saw the girl again."

"I see."

"I didn't think much of it until a few days after her death, when I heard my father asking the servants if they'd seen a young woman walking through the palace. Much later, when Richard was crowned, he mentioned a visit from her. I thought he was joking. But then I found my great-grandfather's diary, which included an entry about this mysterious visitor. He also painted a portrait." She moved her eyes to the wall above the fireplace.

Ariel looked up at the painting. It detailed a girl with reddish-brown hair, wearing green-tinted sunglasses, standing in front of a burning building.

"I love it," said Ariel.

"The girl is always the same. She never changes, not in all the years." Emily frowned. "Every time there is death or destruction, you appear. Ariel Reynolds, sister of our first leader, you should have died a long time ago."

"I'm a time traveler. Sorry if I didn't stop for an explanation. Things were a bit hectic."

Emily sat down. "I've sat in on a few of Richard's meetings. There have always been whispers of you. I take it a young lieutenant was looking for you?"

Ariel smiled, impressed. "You're good."

"Traveler, tell me this. If you can move through time like the years are windows and the centuries are open doors, then why couldn't you save my brother?"

"I couldn't."

"You saved the journalist. He seemed convinced he would die; now he's alive."

"Technically, *you* saved Thomas. If you hadn't come along and distracted the assassin for a minute, he would have died. It's a crazy loop—I try not to think about it too much."

"I see."

"Saving the king would create a paradox, as I arrived in a time when he was already gone. No matter what, I was never meant to save him. It was too vital to history that he die."

Emily turned away.

The princess had inherited her mother's beauty and heart, and the brilliant political mind of her father, but for a flashing instant Ariel realized how young this girl was. Sixteen, and already she'd lost her entire family, and not easily. The entire world looked up to her ... but they wouldn't be disappointed. Ariel saw a mature young woman who, with a little experience, could stand with the wisest of adults.

The people loved Richard, but they feared change, and they feared a government riddled with secret agents even more. Emily, a blooming rose of a girl, would light a path for the future.

"You did the right thing, stopping that killer," said Ariel. "Don't let yourself think otherwise, not for a moment."

Emily's eyes watered. "My parents loved Richard. They left their throne to him. They wanted me to wave at the cameras and appear at charity events. Now everyone expects me to know what to do."

"But you will. The world is about to enter a golden age. In the thirtieth century, you'll be considered one of the greatest rulers of all time. Right up there with Dimitri Reynolds."

"You've been to the thirtieth century?"

"Oh ... once or twice."

The princess looked down. "I'm the last of my family."

"No. Not for long. You'll get married, have a few children. Don't worry about it now, though."

"Then how long will my family survive?"

"For as long as they're needed."

She looked up at her. "Right," she said, not especially convinced. "In the past week I saw my brother killed, I had to flee for my life, and I had to shoot an assassin. This doesn't sound like a golden age to me."

"No. Maybe not yet. But you're the only one the people trust to lead them. Are you sure you're all right?"

"Yes. I'm a lot stronger than people think."

"Then good luck." Ariel strolled to the door of the girl's bedroom, past the ornately carved tan walls, the many oval mirrors, a fireplace and a portrait, and she vanished.

The future queen walked back to the window, staring out at the gardens.

Tomorrow would be the first day of her preparation for ruling, for planning for a coronation, for choosing advisors. The summer solstice, longest day of the year, waned. An end and a beginning. But she felt happier now, wiser, as if the heaviest part of her burden had been lifted up and carried away by the breeze.

2.

June 15, 2507

As for what had happened to the drummer: When it came to bad luck, Damien Martínez had enough to last a lifetime.

The musician was running late, and rushed through the covered tunnels of Tenokte. The subway had been delayed by twenty minutes, but if he timed it right, he would make it into the field just before the king's speech started. If he came any later, he wouldn't be able to get up to the front with the press, and would have to meet up with his sister afterwards.

He dodged a small crowd of people, running at full speed through the narrow hallway.

"Damien Martínez!" gasped a teenaged girl, star-struck. "Can I get your autograph?"

"Write me a letter and I'll send it to you! Gotta go!" he said, darting around a corner.

The girl sighed. "Rock stars."

Damien checked his watch. Three minutes left. He could hear the distant booms of fireworks, which made the city seem like a war zone. Okay, he had to turn left—no, wait, was it right? He skidded to a stop.

Left?

He rushed down the hall, only to find himself on the street. People were still arriving for the speech. Not this way. He ducked inside the building and ran in the other direction.

He had two minutes. He turned another corner. One minute. When he realized the speech had already begun, he stopped. Okay, he'd just slide in the back and meet up with Zoë later. Easy enough. He waited a minute to catch his breath, then walked toward the exit.

Soon he heard another loud crack, then another. More fireworks? No idea. He rushed down the corner.

"Hey! Don't go that way!" someone called. "It's, uh, not a good idea."

He skidded to a stop, and saw a red-haired girl. He stood by an elevator and flight of stairs which, though he did not know it, led to a balcony a few floors up. The elevator car was coming down, but no one was inside.

"I've got to find someone," he said.

"Da—"

He turned another corner, to an exit, and saw a group of Celestials rushing down the hallway. "You, stop there! Hands up!"

They all pointed blasters in his direction. Damien put his hands up almost instinctively, but doubted he had anything to do with whatever had happened. And he wondered if Richard was still giving his speech.

"Did I miss the king?" he asked a patrol.

A Celestial officer appeared behind him, and addressed the police commissioner. "Sir, someone took two shots and ran out. We—" He suddenly noticed Damien.

The police officers threw him against the wall, handcuffed him, and pulled him outside. The bewildered drummer had no idea the king had been shot until someone told him, and had no idea his question would be considered a confession. He expected the matter to be cleared up immediately. The last thing he expected was several days of confinement on death row, a rescue attempt by a journalist and a time traveler, and a release engineered by a depressed singer.

But, to be fair, everyone else had been as surprised as him.

3.

June 21, 2507

Zoë dreamily wandered back onto the ship. "Jamie's alive!" she said. "I just stopped by the hospital."

"I know," said Thomas. He'd plugged the TV back in to watch the early-evening news. Zoë tossed her jacket on the sofa, looking at the screen.

"Jamie Parsons was successfully revived early this morning. The singer is staying in a hospital for treatment and

a three-day mental-health evaluation. Police attributed his confession to temporary insanity."

"Temporary?" Thomas asked, and Zoë hushed him.

"In an astonishing ruling, the Council has overturned their previous decision and declared Damien Martínez not guilty for the crime of regicide. He is staying at an undisclosed location.

"The suspected assassin, Jude Fawkes, has been wanted by the government for several years. He apparently died following a car accident yesterday morning."

Thomas turned off the TV, walked over to his room and started to pack his clothes.

"Going somewhere?" Zoë asked, standing in the doorway.

"Well, I was hoping you could take me and Audrey back to London. But if not …"

"I'll take you."

He stared at her. "Right. I'll be with you for the baby, but just so we're on the right page, do you still want to get married?"

"I don't know."

Thomas felt as if she'd slapped him. "What?"

"You're right. We have had a lot thrown at us. Maybe we should stay apart for a bit, just to see how we feel. Then we can decide."

"Zoë, just consider this. We'll take this one day at a time. Whenever you've got something on your mind, you tell me. Whenever I've got something on my mind, I tell you. And we just go, day by day, and see where it takes us."

"Thomas, I don't know if I can do that."

"But we're going to have a baby."

"It's not that simple."

"If it helps," came a voice, "I'm leaving."

Thomas turned, and saw Ariel standing in the doorway. Her reddish hair had been pulled up in a ponytail, her sword slung over one shoulder.

"I'm just—" Thomas said to Zoë, motioning toward the girl.

"Go, go on," said Zoë, her eyes watering.

He stepped outside the ship with the time traveler. The summer solstice, the longest day of the year, now faded into memory, and the sky unfolded with light.

"Thank you for staying with me," said Ariel.

"It's nothing, kiddo."

"How's your shoulder?"

"Better." He looked at her for a moment. "You broke that assassin out of prison. He must have meant something to you."

"He showed me time travel."

"Nothing more?"

"I was fond of him. I'm glad you survived, and not him. That's all."

He understood.

"I went to the base, and couldn't find any trace of Bailey. My guess is that she went back to her time."

He suddenly remembered the platinum watch, then pulled it out. "Oh, kiddo. Kira gave this to me. I don't need it."

"Keep it. You're an anomaly, and the universe might try to get rid of you. You never know when you might need a time machine."

Thomas pressed the fob at the top, opening the watch. He looked up at her. "Are you going to keep traveling?"

"I really don't know. I've got some unfinished business at home. Graduating high school, for one. I've got to …" Ariel's eyes widened, and she clapped a hand over her mouth. "Oh no. I've destroyed history."

"What?"

"Listen. This is vitally important. If Zoë wants to run for public office, do *not* discourage that, okay?"

"All right," he said cautiously.

"Public office. You have to be all for it."

"What are we talking about? Governor, or—can't be president, we haven't had one in…"

Ariel's smile grew.

"Oh my God," said Thomas.

"Anyway, whatever happens is a long time away, but do *not* mess this up, okay?"

"Uh … I won't, kiddo."

"Good." She turned to go.

"Wait, you haven't asked me if I want to be your partner. You wanted my answer on the Flyday, right?"

"I already know your answer. You want to stay with Zoë. Besides, there's no Saturnine Order anymore, no silly pairs."

"So that's it? It's just you?"

"Yes. Just me."

"And you're not going to infect anyone back in the 21st century, right?"

She stared at him, nonplussed, then shook her head. "Not enough germs in me to spread it. My body fought it off. And people are still alive now, so I'm pretty sure I don't wipe out humanity."

"Ah … right. And how is that different from you saving me?"

She shrugged. "People can't be wiped out and still be alive now. That would be a paradox."

"Oh. Time travel logic." He pulled out the music player. "Here. Thanks for letting me borrow it. And—kiddo, has anyone ever told you how amazing you are?"

She pocketed the device. "Daily. But it doesn't mean nearly as much as when it comes from you."

He smiled. "Anyway, what I want to say is, this week has been crazy and mind-numbing and wonderful. And I'm really, really glad I met you. I mean, you don't even make fun of my accent."

"What accent?" she asked, smiling mischievously.

He sighed. "Yeah, that. Am I ever going to see you again?"

"Are you kidding? Count on it."

"Then have a fantastic life, Miss Reynolds."

"And you, Mr. Huxley."

Thomas watched her walk away, a figure silhouetted against the twilight glow. He shielded his eyes for a moment, blinked, and she was gone.

The pocket watch was still in his hand: he could go back for her. He lingered a moment, tempted by the idea, then thought better of it. He walked back into the ship.

Zoë sat at the table, and looked up when she saw him. "I just received a call. Damien's on a plane, headed to safety."

"So you can't see him?"

"No. But I know he's all right." She glanced down at the day's news on her e-reader. A plate of toast and bowl of cut strawberries lay beside it. "I like your articles today," she said.

"You always did."

She put the e-reader down. "You were the first person I ever loved. Did you know that?"

He knew.

They stepped outside the ship to watch the sunset. Zoë looked up at the sky, mesmerized. Dusty lilac clouds floated across a backdrop of faded blue, and the lower sky glowed a soft pink as the last golden bursts of sun slipped under the horizon.

"Do you still want to get married?" Thomas asked.

She smiled and turned to tell him, but he already knew the answer.

About the author

Laura E. Bradford is working on the rest of the Flyday series. Follow her progress at:

http://lauraebradford.blogspot.com

Printed in the USA
CPSIA information can be obtained
at www.ICGtesting.com
LVHW011731251123
764904LV00048B/1566